P9-CAY-266

JE - - '15
√5 8/16

MYSTERY OF THE
DINNER PLAYHOUSE

WITHDRAWN

This Large Print Book carries the
Seal of Approval of N.A.V.H.

PROPERTY OF CLPL

MYSTERY OF THE DINNER PLAYHOUSE

MIKE BEFELER

WHEELER PUBLISHING
A part of Gale, Cengage Learning

GALE
CENGAGE Learning

Farmington Hills, Mich • San Francisco • New York • Waterville, Maine
Meriden, Conn • Mason, Ohio • Chicago

Copyright © 2015 by Mike Befeler.
Wheeler Publishing, a part of Gale, Cengage Learning.

ALL RIGHTS RESERVED
This novel is a work of fiction. Names, characters, places and incidents are either the product of the author's imagination, or, if real, used fictitiously.
The publisher bears no responsibility for the quality of information provided through author or third-party Web sites and does not have any control over, nor assume any responsibility for, information contained in these sites. Providing these sites should not be construed as an endorsement or approval by the publisher of these organizations or of the positions they may take on various issues.

Wheeler Publishing Large Print Cozy Mystery.
The text of this Large Print edition is unabridged.
Other aspects of the book may vary from the original edition.
Set in 16 pt. Plantin.

LIBRARY OF CONGRESS CATALOGING-IN-PUBLICATION DATA

Befeler, Mike.
    Mystery of the dinner playhouse / by Mike Befeler. — Large print edition.
        pages cm. — (Wheeler Publishing large print cozy mystery)
    ISBN 978-1-4104-7828-3 (softcover) — ISBN 1-4104-7828-9 (softcover)
    1. Murder—Investigation—Fiction. 2. Large type books. I. Title.
    PS3602.E37M97 2015b
    813'.6—dc23   2014049300

Published in 2015 by arrangement with Mike Befeler

Printed in the United States of America
1 2 3 4 5   19 18 17 16 15

For all the people in my family
who taught me about theater:
Roger, Kim, Dennis, Laura, Paige,
and the love of my life,
my wife, Wendy.

ACKNOWLEDGMENTS

Many thanks for the assistance from Wendy Befeler and my online critique group and the support from the fine people at Five Star: Deni Dietz, Alice Duncan and Tiffany Schofield.

CHAPTER 1

"You need a murder to solve," Angie Tremont said to her husband, Gabe, on Friday night after they finished dinner. "I can't stand to see you moping around here being bored. Retirement isn't working for you."

Gabe ran his tanned hand through the few remaining strands of gray hair on the back of his polished head and adjusted his gold-rimmed glasses. "I'd been looking forward to spending my days sitting on my chaise longue. But you're right. After only a week of retirement I'm ready for something else."

Angie gave the full-lipped smile that had first captivated Gabe over forty years ago. "I have the perfect activity for my restless retired detective. I'm taking you to the Bearcrest Mystery Dinner Playhouse Sunday night."

"That isn't one of those places where the actors get all chummy with the audience ahead of time and then stage a murder mystery, is it?"

A glint appeared in Angie's eyes. "Exactly. And they involve the audience in solving the crime. Clues are given during the performance, and tables compete against each other to figure out who the murderer is. You can test your skills against all the amateurs in attendance."

Gabe groaned.

Angie crossed her arms in her wife-knows-best fashion and planted herself inches from him. "Don't give me that. You'll have something to concentrate on for an evening — other than how bored you are."

Gabe suddenly realized this retirement gig wasn't all it was cracked up to be. He had thought he could do whatever he wanted. Now he was being drafted into some crazy performance at a theater. Still, it seemed to be something that Angie wanted to do. "I suppose."

Angie picked up her dinner dishes to take into the kitchen. "With that wholehearted endorsement, you're committed to an evening of fun and frolic. I'll call to reserve seats for us."

Gabe also rose, picked up his plate and followed Angie toward the sink. "I don't have to dress up, do I?"

"I wouldn't suggest bedroom slippers and

the undershirt you've been lounging around in, but you won't have to put on a coat or tie."

"Phew." Gabe set down the plate on the sink counter and put his hands around his throat like he was choking himself. "That's one thing I'm not going back to."

She wagged a finger at him. "You'll eventually need to put on a tie again when the grandkids get married."

"We still have a few years before that happens. Cal's only eight years old and doesn't even like girls yet."

"On the other hand, Allison is quite a young lady. She'll have all kinds of beaus proposing to her in a few years."

"That's because she's as pretty as her grandmother."

Although she pretended to ignore his compliment, Gabe saw her faint smile return. "They grow up so quickly. Seems like she was just a baby, and now she's thirteen. She'll be dating soon, going steady and getting engaged."

Gabe glanced again at his wife, seeing the sparkle in her eyes, the soft wave of her blond hair and her still-perfect rosy cheeks. She was quite a woman. And she had put up with him and his crazy hours for the forty years he had worked for the Bearcrest

Police Department. He never did figure out why this attractive woman had agreed to marry him.

They had started dating at the University of Colorado. Gabe had been one of dozens of guys chasing her. He had felt like he was competing with half the footfall team, the whole business school and several teaching assistants.

For whatever reason, she had discarded her other suitors and settled on him. Angie had been the most amazing person in his life and one for whom he gave thanks each day he woke up to find her lying beside him in bed.

Everyone always kidded Gabe because he looked more like a nerdy, antisocial accountant than a detective. And the irony — Angie was an accomplished accountant who looked like a movie star.

Angie put a stopper in the sink, ran hot water and added dishwashing soap. "Back to the main subject: you're now committed for Sunday night. So don't try to back out on me."

Gabe looked out the kitchen window and spotted a deer nibbling on their neighbor's tomato vines. This gave him an idea for a diversionary tactic. "Maybe we could go up to Rocky Mountain National Park for the day instead. I bet we could watch all sorts of wildlife."

"No way. I want to see the show, and you need something to concentrate on. Think of all the clues you can track down, the suspects you can watch, the conclusions you can draw. A taste of murder will be just the thing for you."

Gabe picked up the dish towel and began drying the plates that Angie had washed. "You may be a theater buff, but you know I've never had the bug. I prefer a good old-fashioned movie."

"That's why we get along so well. We each have our separate interests." She gave him her award-winning smile that still made his heart thump against his ribs. "And this may be the perfect combination for us — theater for me and crime solving for you."

"It'll probably be some corny whodunit."

Angie waved her arms in the air. "Actually, it will be a sophisticated setting — an English country inn, replete with a maid, butler, proprietress and guests."

"And snobby accents?"

"British accents, my dear. You'll have to see if you can figure out who committed the murder. It will be a good challenge for you."

Gabe dried the remaining silverware and

regarded Angie with his best detective stare. "I can tell you ahead of time. The butler did it."

CHAPTER 2

On Sunday evening Gabe parked his old blue Crown Victoria on a side street. He had circled blocks on two sides of the theater before finding an open spot. Dashing around the car, he opened the door for Angie.

"Thank you, sir."

They strolled arm-in-arm in the pleasant summer evening toward the theater, a Victorian mansion that reminded Gabe of the house in the old *Mork and Mindy* television show with its gabled roof, blue and white exterior and wooden steps leading to the front door.

On second thought, the place also reminded him of the Munster house. He could almost picture Herman Munster and his family of misfits appearing on the porch and scaring away passing pedestrians. Gabe shook his head. He had been watching too many 1960s and 1970s television reruns this last week.

That had been the problem. After the last five years of looking forward to retiring, once he had left his job behind, he felt completely at a loss. He had slept late only one morning and then became restless at six-thirty the next day.

He thought he would enjoy kicking back, leisurely reading the newspaper and watching the morning news, rather than his old routine of grabbing a cup of coffee and dashing out of the house, but it hadn't worked. Each morning he skimmed the paper, gobbled a bowl of shredded wheat and became disgusted at an ongoing exposé of police brutality in Denver. On Friday he had channel surfed, found an old Gary Cooper movie, but that only kept his interest for ten minutes. He couldn't picture himself watching soap operas and eating bonbons all day.

"A penny for your thoughts." Angie leaned on his arm as they headed up the stairs to the theater.

It would take more than a penny, Gabe realized as he let out a deep sigh. "I'm not cracked up for this retirement world."

Angie snuggled close. "You need a hobby. After your first week of so-called lounging around, find something you really want to do."

Angie had that right. But what did he really want to do? He started building a mental list. Golf? Many celebrities and sports figures who retired turned to golf. He'd tried it but couldn't imagine spending half a day whacking a little white ball. Gardening? Maybe he could grow prize-winning flowers or vegetables. Volunteering? There were always groups looking for assistance and he had skills that could be utilized. He'd have to give the subject more thought.

A middle-aged brunette wearing a long, flowing dress greeted them at the door and handed them a program. In an English accent she announced, "I'm Mildred Hanson, proprietress of the Hanson Country Inn. Thank you for coming to join us for dinner this evening. I can assure you you'll have a most entertaining evening. If I may assist you in any way, please let me know."

"All the actors play their roles when they mingle with the audience before the show," Angie whispered in Gabe's ear. "Another thing — all the actors use their real names for the parts. Mildred Hanson owns the playhouse and acts as well."

"You sure know the setup here." Gabe

17

arched an eyebrow. "Have you been sneaking to the theater?"

"Oh, bosh. I've been here twice before. Remember when I went with the garden club? And another time with my book club while you were in Colorado Springs for that law enforcement conference last year."

That would be a benefit of being retired. No more conferences. Although he had made some good friends in other agencies across the state, Gabe didn't enjoy sitting in a meeting room all day listening to lectures. He liked moving around.

Opening the program, Gabe found the Cast of Characters headed by the name Mildred Hanson, followed by five other names. Beneath the list appeared a short handwritten paragraph describing the Hanson Country Inn as the perfect retreat in the hills of Northern England, with lush meadows and hiking trails nearby. The description ended with the large, flowery signature of Mildred Hanson.

"Come on," Angie said, giving Gabe a gentle shove. "Let's circulate and meet the other actors."

"Care for a little liquid refreshment first?" Gabe asked. "I could use a cold beer. Do you want your usual?"

"Yes."

They stopped at the bar, where a man in a tuxedo with a mustache and Vandyke beard, brown hair, droopy eyes, probably in his late thirties, said, "I'm Peter Ranchard, the butler. What refreshments may I offer you, sir?"

"One beer — whatever you have on tap — and a glass of red wine. Preferably Merlot."

"Very good, sir." Peter poured the drinks, reached out with his gloved hands and gave the glasses to Gabe.

Angie accepted the wine from Gabe. "He's the one you've determined ahead of time must have committed the crime. Have you thoroughly checked him out, figuring out his nervous ticks and suspicious actions?"

"Of course. Can't you tell how guilty he looks?"

"Don't you think you should investigate the other four characters first before you make your final determination?"

Gabe shrugged. "Sure, I could waste my time doing that, but in these British mysteries it's always the butler."

Angie clicked her tongue. "When was the last time you actually read a British mystery?"

"I don't think I ever have. I saw one on

television by mistake once. Remember? You made me watch Agatha Christie's *Murder on the Orient Express.*"

She swatted him with her free hand. "And the butler didn't do it in that mystery. You enjoyed it as I recall. You should watch mysteries more often. And you call yourself a detective."

"Not any longer. Remember, I retired a week ago."

"And it's been a very long week." Angie sighed.

Gabe thought back to the retirement party put on by his police colleagues. The chief had given him a Fenwick Eagle GT fly fishing rod and a plaque now hanging in his den. Everyone had told their favorite Gabe stories, including the time he had been chased by a bear on the outskirts of town and had locked himself in his patrol car to escape.

Throughout the evening he had drunk too much Scotch while acknowledging toast after toast and had started his first Saturday of retirement with a hangover. He wouldn't do that again. One beer was enough for him tonight.

As they merged with the crowd of theatergoers in a large reception room, an older woman in a maid's outfit appeared with a plate of appetizers. "Good evening, sir and madam. I'm Clara Jager, the cook and maid. It's a pleasure to have you join us this fine evening. May I offer you hors d'oeuvres?"

Gabe reached for a water chestnut wrapped in bacon but bumped the tray.

Clara winced as if he had stuck her with a needle.

"Sorry," Gabe said. He regarded the short, stocky woman, who had red hair and a wrinkled face. The perfect image of a cook. She seemed to be in pain as she staggered off to offer food to other people gathering in the waiting area.

Gabe looked around the room. A bookshelf with old brown manuscripts covered one wall, and above a fireplace a row of colored bottles lined the mantle. The other two walls displayed old photographs of mining towns and men in baggy pants and suspenders holding picks.

Next, a tall, middle-aged man with wire-rimmed glasses and a white mustache accosted them. He wore breeches and boots and carried a riding crop. "Colonel Harold Coats, at your service." He bowed.

"Good evening, Colonel." Angie held out her hand.

Coats leaned over, a whistle dangling from a cord around his neck, and kissed her hand. "Ah, a beautiful woman to grace the evening. Welcome to our gathering."

Then Coats shook Gabe's hand.

Gabe was relieved that the Colonel didn't try to kiss it.

"And you, sir, are a fortunate gentleman to have such a fetching companion with you tonight."

Gabe smiled at Angie. "I certainly am."

Angie looked at the program. "We've met four of the actors. Only two left." At that moment a man in a crisp gray suit approached them. "I'm Arthur Buchanan." He held out a weathered hand that accompanied an angular face, large ears and a receding hairline. Gabe gauged him as being in his late thirties. "I'm one of the guests here at the Hanson Country Inn." He leaned toward them and whispered. "I'm here on government business, but everyone thinks I'm hiking through the hills."

"What kind of government business?" Angie asked.

He put his right index finger to his mouth. "I'm not at liberty to divulge my mission. Loose lips sink ships and all that kind of rot." He turned quickly and disappeared into the crowd.

"Five down, one to go," Angie said.

Finally, a young, slim woman in her twenties with long blond hair, a sparkling smile and wearing a slinky, gold-spangled dress greeted them. She held out a dainty hand. "I'm Sophie Elmira, and I'm delighted to make your acquaintance. This is a lovely country inn, don't you think?"

"Yes, it's charming," Angie replied.

Sophie winked at Gabe. "I hope to see you later."

Angie grabbed Gabe's arm and pulled him away. "She's the wicked ingénue, flirting with all the men. Watch out."

"Oh, I watched, but I still prefer more mature women."

"I'll take that as a compliment . . . sort of."

Gabe noticed a door with a sign informing patrons that restrooms were in the basement. At that moment a woman with frizzy black hair and thick glasses came up the stairs and pushed past them.

Gabe and Angie walked around the first floor of the house looking at framed photographs of reconstruction completed in the 1960s. Gabe read a plaque that described the house as originally being owned by a man who had made his fortune in the mines near Gold Hill in the mountains above Bearcrest. He had turned in his shovel and become a philanthropist, even bringing the first opera company to perform in Bear-crest. The house was later sold to a man who ran a commercial dairy, and it fell into disrepair when his son, who had inherited the house, disappeared during the Korean War.

"I imagine this place has seen a lot of history in its day," Gabe commented.

"May even be some dead bodies buried in the basement that a retired detective should check out." Angie pinched his arm.

"Hey, no violence."

"I'm trying to pique your imagination. Remember, you'll have a mystery to solve tonight."

"Nothing to it. I've met all the suspects. I still say the butler did it."

Angie *tsk*ed. "I think it's more likely to be that young wench. She's definitely a suspicious character."

"Go easy on her. You were a young wench at one time."

"I guess I don't need to worry about her as competition. You're too old for her anyway. Now that you're retired, you'll next be needing a seeing eye dog, hearing aids, Depends and a cane."

"No way. Maybe next week I'll start hiking to stay in shape. You're going to be stuck with me for a long time."

"Good."

They continued to stroll among the guests on the first floor. Gabe noticed that the woman with frizzy black hair came out of an office and disappeared into the crowd. This time he consciously registered her attire — a black pantsuit, with a vest and black leather gloves.

At that moment a whistle blew, and the background of conversations hushed. Colonel Harold Coats shouted, "At-ten-tion! Form a single file and march up the stairs and into the dining room to be seated."

They followed his directions and stood in line. As they passed, the Colonel, who guarded the doorway, asked, "Names and rank?"

"Mr. and Mrs. Tremont, citizens." Angie saluted him.

He checked a list. "You're assigned to table four. To the left. Step lively."

They made their way to the designated table and soon made the acquaintance of three other couples, one from Denver, one passing through on vacation from Ohio and one from nearby Longmont. Gabe still hadn't recognized anyone here — no one he'd investigated in the past.

Once everyone took their seats, the Colonel blew his whistle again. Mildred Hanson stepped to the microphone on the stage in front of the dining area and cleared her throat. "Welcome again to the Hanson Country Inn. It's nice to see all the smiling faces, and it's a pleasure to have all of you for dinner."

"Only cannibals could have all of us for dinner," someone shouted, followed by laughing and clapping.

"Dear me. Let me rephrase that. It's a pleasure to have all of you joining us here for one of the world-famous Hanson Country Inn meals. We will call you up to the buffet line by table number, starting with table number one. Now remember, follow your number."

The Colonel whipped his riding crop against his boot. "No loitering and no cutting in line."

"Yes, sir," came a chorus from the back of the room.

When table four was called, Gabe scraped back his chair, stood up and took Angie's arm to lead her to the back of the line. They then helped themselves to salad, rice pilaf, broccoli in cheese sauce, grilled chicken and toasty hot rolls. With their plates full, they returned to the table to eat and share casual conversation with the other three couples.

"I came to a performance here last year,"

the woman in a blue caftan who sat next to Gabe announced. "We'll be competing with the other tables to see if we can figure out who committed the murder, so pay close attention to all the clues."

"That won't be necessary," Angie announced. "My husband has already decided the butler did it."

"It's too soon to reach any conclusions," Caftan Lady replied, rubbing her hands together. "But let's see if we can whup the other tables."

"Mable always likes a little competition," her companion said. "Nothing like a contest to get her fired up."

"That's right. My two favorite things. Beating someone at a little competition and animals." She elbowed Gabe in the ribs. "You an animal lover?"

"Animals and I don't always see eye to eye," he replied.

Caftan Lady jutted her chin toward him. "What's that supposed to mean?"

Angie leaned across Gabe. "Gabe likes animals, but they don't like him."

"It must be how he treats them."

Angie shook her head. "No, it's an unexplained reaction that animals have to Gabe. Sometimes they run away, and sometimes they become aggressive. I've never been able to understand it."

Caftan Lady narrowed her gaze at Gabe. "Didn't you have pets as a child?"

"My parents brought home a cocker spaniel when I was five. It used my arm as a chew toy, so they gave it up for adoption."

Caftan Lady crinkled up her nose, took a bite of salad and turned to her companion to start a new conversation.

Once they had finished eating, the caterers cleared away the dishes and packed up everything. They left plates of cookies on each table and departed. After audience members had a chance to help themselves to a cup of coffee, Mildred Hanson came back on stage and a curtain opened. Sophie Elmira, Colonel Harold Coats and Arthur Buchanan sat on a large couch. Behind them stiffly stood butler, Peter Ranchard, and maid, Clara Jager.

"It may be a stormy night outside, but inside it's a lovely evening at the Hanson Country Inn," Mildred said, resting one hand on a table in the middle of the stage. Simulated lightning flashed backstage, and the sound of thunder could be heard. "My dear guests have now finished their evening meal. Would all of you care for a glass of claret?"

"Quite," Colonel Coats replied. Arthur

and Sophie nodded their heads.

"Peter, fill seven glasses. The twenty-three Bordeaux will do nicely."

"As you wish, madam."

"I'll assist him, mum," Clara added.

Peter and Clara disappeared through a backstage curtain.

"Why seven glasses?" Arthur asked.

Mildred put her hand to her brow. "I run a very egalitarian establishment, Mr. Buchanan. I insist that the staff always imbibe with the guests after dinner, so Peter and Clara will be joining us."

"If I count correctly, that would mean only six glasses," Colonel Harold Coats said as he tweaked his mustache.

"Oh, you're so clever." Sophie Elmira batted her eyelashes at the Colonel.

"Yes . . . uh . . . hmm." The Colonel covered his mouth.

"A good observation, Colonel." Mildred gave an indulgent smile. "I always have one additional glass poured in case any late guest arrives. It's also in memory of my poor departed husband." A wave of sadness crossed her face.

Clara returned, followed by Peter holding a silver tray with seven glasses of wine. He set it down on the table, and Mildred gestured for the others to gather around.

"Why, I think I do see a last-minute guest coming to the door." Mildred looked toward the audience and held her hand above her eyes as if searching the horizon for a wayward traveler. "Peter, please go welcome our visitor."

Peter stepped off the stage into the audience, approached one of the tables and reached for the arm of the woman with frizzy black hair and thick glasses. "Please join us for a glass of claret."

The woman looked confused and reluctant to stand, but Peter practically lifted her out of her seat and steered her up the steps. She tried to keep her face averted as Peter herded her to the table on the stage.

"Now each of you please place your hand on a glass but don't lift it yet. In a moment I will propose a toast to the tenth anniversary of the Hanson Country Inn."

Everyone reached for a glass, even the reluctant woman from the audience.

A large flash occurred offstage, a boom of thunder rolled through the house and the lights went off.

"Dear me, have we been struck by lightning?" Mildred's voice could be heard in the darkness.

A murmur ran through the audience.

"I can't see a thing," Angie said in Gabe's ear.

"Sshh," he replied. "They're setting up the murder."

Ten seconds later the lights came back on.

"What a close call," Mildred said. "Now, let's resume our toast. Please raise your glasses."

Everyone did.

"To another ten years at the Hanson Country Inn."

"Cheers," came the chorus. They clinked glasses and drank.

"A fine claret, madam," Colonel Coats said.

"We only stock the best."

Everyone returned their glasses to the silver platter on the table.

"Now, Peter, if you would kindly remove the glasses."

"Yes, madam." Peter reached toward the tray, stumbled and clutched his stomach. "I don't feel well." Without picking up the tray, he staggered toward the opening in the curtains and fell through, disappearing backstage. A loud crash ensued.

"Clara, go see what has happened to Peter," Mildred commanded.

Clara dashed through the curtains, and moments later a woman's scream shook the playhouse.

Clara came rushing back through the curtains, a look of horror on her face. "Peter's dead."

Angie leaned toward Gabe and whispered in his ear. "Wow, she's a good actress. She makes the murder seem so convincing."

"I'm not kidding." Clara gasped. "This isn't the play. The real Peter Ranchard is really dead."

CHAPTER 3

"What's going on?" Caftan Lady asked, a worried expression crossing her face as if someone had stolen her drink.

Then all hell broke loose.

Mildred Hanson raced toward the back curtain but smacked into Harold Coats, who had turned in the same direction, and both collapsed to the stage floor with legs flying into the air and flailing arms entangled.

Clara shouted, "Call nine-one-one!"

Angie calmly reached in her purse, pulled out her cell phone and punched in the three digits.

Clara staggered to the front of the stage, put the back of her hand to her forehead, groaned loudly and fainted into a heap as her skirt puffed upward and then settled like a deflated balloon.

The sound of chairs scraping could be heard as people in the audience stood to get a better view of the chaos. A plate of cookies crashed to the floor. People craned their necks and gawked like onlookers driving past an accident on a freeway.

Gabe had had enough of this.

He jumped up on the stage and raced through the back curtain. He found Peter's body, reached over to check for a pulse and determined the man was dead. Leaning over, Gabe noted the red discoloration of his skin. He put his nose close to Peter's face and sniffed, picking up the faint aroma of bitter almonds. A small table lay overturned, and additional wineglasses were strewn across the floor. Overhead a low wattage bulb provided minimal light, which reflected off a small silver bowl that had also been knocked over. Without touching anything, Gabe returned to the stage, where he found Harold Coats trying to sit up. "Blow your blasted whistle."

Harold reached for his whistle, but the cord was tangled around Mildred. He put the whistle to his mouth, momentarily choking Mildred as he blew a piercing sound.

People halted in their tracks.

Gabe stepped to the front of the stage. "Everyone please take your seats." Then he turned to the cast and the woman with black hair. "All of you sit on the edge of the stage, but don't touch anything and don't speak to each other."

Mildred extricated herself from the whistle cord, whacked Harold in the face with the back of her hand, stood up, dusted herself off and stomped over to Gabe. "Who do you think you are, ordering us around?"

Gabe sighed, pulled out his wallet and showed his police identification, grateful that he hadn't yet turned it in. "Ma'am, I'm Detective Gabe Tremont. Peter is dead, so nothing can be done for him. Further assistance should be here shortly. I want to make sure no one taints the crime scene. Please sit with the others."

Mildred looked like she wanted to argue, took a step toward Gabe as if she intended to swat a naughty boy, then seemed to think better of it. Her shoulders slumped as she exhaled loudly and plopped down on the edge of the stage next to the woman with the black hair.

The woman scooted next to Arthur Buchanan and away from Mildred, as much as the restricted space allowed. She turned her gaze downward.

With everyone contained, Gabe scanned the stage. He stepped toward the table where Mildred had stood and, without touching anything, leaned over the silver tray holding the seven glasses. He sniffed each glass. One gave off a faint almond aroma. Looking under the table, he saw a small blue vial and a tissue lying on the floor. He'd wait for the crime scene investigator before checking it further.

Two EMTs rushed into the room. Gabe showed them Peter's body, which by then only required the medical examiner. Instead, they tended to Clara Jager, who quickly revived after her fainting spell. Gabe helped her over to the edge of the stage to sit with the other cast members. When two police officers, Ken Sanchez and Janet Lyon, arrived, Gabe pulled them aside. "It appears the victim was poisoned. I've told all the potential suspects to sit on the edge of the stage. Do you know which detective will be coming?"

Ken scratched his head. "That's a problem, Gabe. No one's available right now. Brad's on vacation, Ned's down with the flu and the chief hasn't replaced you yet."

Gabe nodded his head. "Okay, I guess I can fill in. I'd like the two of you to take statements from the people in the audience and get their addresses and phone numbers where we can reach them. After that you can let them go. See if anyone noticed anything right before the death." He filled them in on the sequence of events he had witnessed. "I'll interview the cast members."

"Got it," Janet replied.

An assistant medical examiner arrived, and Gabe led her to where Peter's body rested. Gabe explained what he had seen and smelled.

She gave him a curt nod and set to work examining the body.

Gabe watched for a moment before returning to the front stage area. He regarded the sullen group of suspects sitting on the edge of the stage. At least they had followed his directions and not moved. Ken and Janet were speaking with audience members.

At that moment Mildred Hanson screeched. She reached over and pulled a black wig off the woman sitting next to her. "You . . . you . . ." she stammered.

The woman had short, pure white hair, which she tried unsuccessfully to cover with shaking hands.

Mildred jumped up and stomped over to where Gabe stood. She thrust a finger against his chest and threw the wig on the floor. "You can arrest that woman. Her name is Helen Lameuse. She owns the Creekside Mystery Dinner Playhouse. She came here to spy on my theater. She obviously killed Peter Ranchard to disrupt my show."

CHAPTER 4

"I'll be speaking to everyone who was on the stage at the time of Peter's death," Gabe assured Mildred. "Now, please, sit down."

Mildred gave a harrumph and slowly lowered herself to the edge of the stage as far from Helen as she could.

Gabe followed Mildred. "Where do the actors change their costumes?"

Mildred tried to ignore him.

"Ms. Hanson, I asked you a question."

Mildred scowled. "Backstage."

A young woman with brown hair tied back in a ponytail and holding a camera and large black bag wended her way through the audience and climbed the stairs to where Gabe stood.

Gabe pulled her aside. "Camille, we'll need photographs of everything on the stage and the body behind the curtain. Also, you'll find a vial under the table. After checking for fingerprints, test that bottle and each of the glasses on the table. Suspected cyanide poisoning. Also, thoroughly search the dressing area backstage."

"Anything else?"

"One other thing. All the people sitting here on the stage were in proximity to the victim right before he died. Fingerprint each of them."

"Got it, Gabe." She snapped on rubber gloves and began her work.

Gabe walked down the stairs from the stage and stood in front of the six people whose legs dangled over the side. "I'll need to speak with each of you individually. The rest of you remain here. As I stated earlier, don't talk to anyone else. Also, we'll be asking each of you to provide fingerprints."

"Are we suspects?" Clara asked.

"Fingerprints may lead to a suspect, but they can also be useful in eliminating those who aren't guilty. I'd appreciate your co-operation."

He scanned the group, and all grudgingly nodded their heads.

"But our show must go on." Mildred waved her hands toward the audience now being interviewed by the two police officers.

"I'm afraid the show is over for this evening."

"But . . . but, I'll have to refund part of

the ticket price. And it's all Helen's fault." Mildred sent daggers toward her competitor on the other end of the stage.

Gabe had an image of a catfight between the two women right on the floor in front of everyone. He could just picture fur flying. "You can take care of the business issues later. Right now I'd like to speak with you first, Ms. Hanson. Is there a private place where we can sit down?"

She scooted off the stage. "Follow me. We can use my office." She marched toward the side door, pausing once to glare back at Helen Lameuse.

Gabe caught up with her. They descended the stairs to the first floor and entered a small, cluttered office.

Mildred sat behind a desk covered with piles of paper and play programs. Gabe closed the door, removed a stack of newspapers from a battered wooden chair and took a seat.

"First, I'd like to get a list of everyone who attended tonight, the home addresses and phone numbers of your actors, and a contact at your catering firm."

Mildred reached into the stack of paper on her desk and extracted a sheet. "Here's the list for tonight's guests." She rummaged through the pile again and came up with

41

another sheet. "Here's a list with the addresses and phone numbers for the actors. Bearcrest Food Fashion catered tonight's dinner. You can speak with LaRita Jacobs. She's the tall woman who served the main course at the buffet. She and her two helpers provided all the food here tonight. Now how soon can we get this all cleared up?"

"We'll need to keep people off the stage and backstage area for several days until we complete the investigation of the scene."

Mildred performed an exaggerated eye roll. "Great. Just great. I have my regular midweek show scheduled Wednesday night, and I need to find a replacement for Peter, ASAP." She looked thoughtfully at Gabe. "You have any interest in acting?"

Gabe winced. "No." That wasn't anything he had ever contemplated and certainly wasn't what he would consider now that he was retired. "And besides, I'll be busy with this investigation."

"Too bad." She held her hands up with her thumbs touching and index fingers pointed upward to form a partial frame, which she looked through to study Gabe's face. "You have the right features for a character actor."

"You'll have to find someone else."

Mildred let out a loud sigh. "It's just as

well. Get things wrapped up quickly so I can reopen my show. I'll probably find a replacement on my standby list or at the community college. I can sometimes find students dying to do a theater gig."

"Bad choice of words, Ms. Hanson."

"Jeez. I guess you're right. Sorry. And you can call me Mildred."

"Now, Mildred, I have some questions for you. First of all, how long has Peter Ranchard worked here?"

She put her finger to her chin. "A year. He's been a very dependable actor. Never missed a show. In theater work that's a noble and cherished attribute."

"And how did you happen to hire him?"

"He showed up one day and asked for a job. I'm always looking for new talent. I put everyone through a role-playing audition, and he passed with flying colors. He started the next week."

"And did you check his references?"

She gave a dismissive wave of her hand. "In my line of work, I only care if someone can act. Peter was a very capable actor. That's all I needed to know."

Out of the corner of his eye, Gabe noticed a dusty pile of magazines on the floor. He wondered momentarily if any creatures had built nests or spun webs behind it. "Did Peter have any enemies among the other cast members?"

Mildred blinked. "I don't know. He kept to himself."

"What was your relationship with him?"

Her eyes flared. "What kind of question is that?"

"How did you get along?"

She straightened her back and narrowed her eyes. "Fine. I treat my actors with respect and keep a professional employer-employee distance between us. That's the way I always operate my theater."

"Never any arguments, problems during rehearsals, not following directions, disruptions, emotional outbursts?"

Mildred clenched her teeth. "No, everything was fine. Besides, I think Helen Lameuse is behind all of this. It was an interesting coincidence that she showed up tonight, of all nights."

"And you don't believe in coincidences, Mildred?"

"No. Grill her, Detective, and see if she confesses."

"I'll be speaking with her, but you might as well tell me what you know about her."

Her eyes lit up. "Now you're on the right track. She opened a knock-off theater in town two years ago. She's always trying to steal my customers. Even had the gall to stand outside on the sidewalk one night handing her brochures to people as they left my playhouse. She's sneaky, underhanded, and I wouldn't trust her one iota. Look at the way she showed up tonight. Wearing a black wig and those phony glasses. She spied on my show and killed Peter."

Gabe held up a hand as Mildred leaned across the table. "I understand your concern. Right now I want your opinion on several other questions. You said Peter kept to himself. When I speak to the other cast members, do you expect they'll say the same thing?"

Mildred dropped in her chair, and her gaze darted from side to side. "I don't know. You'll have to ask them."

"I will. Did you know anything of Peter's life outside of the theater?"

She gave a rueful shrug. "Not really. He had an apartment in town and showed up on time for rehearsals and shows. Nothing unusual."

"Did you ever see him other than in the theater?"

Mildred's eyes flashed. "Never. As I said earlier, I keep a clearly defined barrier between my employees and my personal life."

"Who opened the wine that was served on stage?"

"It's grape juice that Peter poured backstage."

"And where would the glasses have been stored ahead of time?"

"They're kept on a shelf backstage. Peter puts them on the serving tray and returns to the stage with them filled with grape juice."

"And who would have been the murder victim in the play tonight?"

Mildred waggled her eyebrows. "Haven't you figured that out yet, Detective?"

Gabe met her gaze without responding.

She gave him a pinched smile. "It would have been Peter."

"Now I understand. That's why the rest of the cast stayed in character when Clara found Peter dead."

"That's right. Clara was supposed to go backstage when Peter made dying sounds. It all followed the script up to the point of Peter really being dead."

"I found a small vial under the table. Is that a play prop?"

Mildred wrinkled her forehead. "No, that's not in the script."

"How do you handle the simulated lightning and thunder?"

46

She wagged a finger at him. "Ah, that's a trade secret."

Gabe glared at her.

"Just kidding. There's a button on the back of the table on stage. I push it the first time for the initial lightning and thunder. The second time I push it, lightning and thunder occur and the lights go out. The third time I push it, the house lights come back on. We don't have any stage crew other than the actors, so I had an electrician hook that up for me. Pretty clever, huh?"

"Yes. Are you aware of any of Peter's relatives we should notify?"

Mildred shook her head. "There aren't any. Peter was single and an orphan."

"How do you know that?"

"On the application form I have actors fill out, he indicated no emergency contact. When I asked him he told me he'd always been solo in the world."

"Thank you for your cooperation. I'll have more questions for you later. May I use your office to meet individually with the others?"

"Just as long as you don't let that conniving Helen Lameuse look at or touch anything. She's apt to try to steal something."

As Gabe walked back to the theater, he thought over what Mildred had said. She was definitely hiding something from him. He'd get to the bottom of it.

CHAPTER 5

Back in the dining area, Gabe noticed a dwindling number of people as a result of the two police officers interviewing members of the audience and dismissing them. The remaining people sat in silence awaiting their turn at being questioned.

Gabe handed the attendee list to Janet Lyon. "Here. You and Ken can use this to compare against the names of the people you're speaking with."

"Will do, Gabe. Any luck with the cast?"

"I'm just getting started. This may be a long evening."

Janet nodded and headed over to speak with another audience member.

Gabe approached Angie, who still sat at their table working a crossword puzzle. "I may be here for a while."

She looked up. "My, you've been busy."

"Yeah, and it won't let up for a while. You want to take the car home? I can catch a ride with Camille, Ken or Janet."

"I can wait. I have a whole new crossword puzzle book that will keep me occupied for hours." She signaled him with her index finger, and he bent close to her. "Besides," she whispered, "I'm watching the suspects. They're all acting very suspicious."

"Oh?"

"Furtive glances keep being exchanged. I'll keep my eye on them for you. Once I identify the murderer, I'll point the person out to you and you can wrap the case up just like that." She snapped her fingers.

Gabe gave her a kiss on the cheek. "If it were only that easy." But Angie did possess a strong intuitive ability, and he had always respected her view on things that affected his investigations. "You keep them under surveillance while I continue to work the crowd. And don't let any of them sneak away."

Angie saluted. "All under control."

Gabe next selected Helen Lameuse and asked her to follow him to the office. She dropped off the stage, wrinkled her nose at Mildred and joined Gabe in the trek down the stairs.

This time he went behind the desk and let Helen sit in the hard wooden chair.

"Now, Ms. Lameuse, what brought you to

the playhouse tonight?"

She scowled at him. "I wanted to see the show."

"It seems to be more than that. You wore a disguise, and Ms. Hanson obviously has some hard feelings toward you."

"Ha," she gave a derisive laugh. "Mildred is so full of herself. She can't take a little joke. Sure, I came here to check things out. It never hurts to keep informed on what your competitors are doing. No crime in paying to watch a show. Besides, I wanted to see what the food is like. Not as good as at my theater."

"Did you know Peter Ranchard?"

She winced. "Uh . . . ah . . . no."

Gabe stared at her.

She squirmed in her chair. "I had seen his name on the program and had heard mention of him in the theater community."

"Had you ever met him before?"

Helen shrugged. "I may have seen him at some theater events."

"You seemed surprised when Peter selected you to go up on stage."

"Well, yeah. Since Mildred and I aren't exactly best buddies, I wasn't anxious to be near her."

"Meaning you didn't want her to recognize you."

51

She let out a sigh. "Yeah."

"Do you know any of the other actors in the cast?"

"Not really. Same as with Peter. I may have run into some of them at theater gatherings. Nothing specific."

Gabe gave her his most intense stare. "In a small community like Bearcrest, I would think you'd know everyone in the theater world."

Helen fiddled with a piece of paper on the desk without looking at Gabe. "People come and go. Many actors pass through here. I can't keep track of all of them. Actors are like fleas. They're jumping around all the time."

Gabe remembered something from earlier in the evening. "Say, before the show I remember seeing you come out of the door that leads to the basement."

"Yes. I went to use the powder room. Can you believe it? Mildred makes the audience go down to that bleak basement to use the facilities. My playhouse has easily accessible restrooms on the first floor. And furthermore, in my theater, patrons don't have to climb stairs to a second floor to get to the dining room and stage. I make it easy for everyone. We're wheelchair accessible versus the climb in this joint."

"Thanks for the sales pitch, but I have another question for you. Why did I see you coming out of this office earlier?"

Helen reddened. "I was . . . uh . . . wandering around and came in here by mistake. Must have become disoriented by all the clutter around here."

Gabe regarded her carefully. "I notice you're wearing gloves tonight."

"Just part of my disguise. I have a scar on my right hand. I didn't want Mildred to notice it. Can't be too careful around that bit— . . . woman."

"May I see your scar?"

Helen gave an exasperated sigh. "I suppose." She removed her glove, revealing a jagged, calloused gash two inches long.

"Thank you. Tell me how your theater performances compare to this one."

Helen rubbed her hands together. "We put on excellent mysteries and have an elaborate buffet dinner. Rather than the skimpy plate of cookies, we serve homemade pie and cake. People always like a good dessert to go with outstanding theater. And we have much better acting than here. I also write all the scripts. I have an MFA in theater and put on a high-quality show. I act myself and have an incredible supporting cast." She smiled at him. "You'll have to come see a play. I'll be happy to comp you and a guest."

"Are you attempting to bribe me?"

She smiled again. "Goodness no. I just thought you'd enjoy seeing a really good performance rather than this amateur show."

CHAPTER 6

Next, Gabe invited Clara Jager to join him in the office.

She shuffled along beside him. "I hope this doesn't take long. I'm still pretty shaken up from finding Peter's body. I need to get some sleep."

"Once we complete the interview, you may leave."

She yawned. "That's good. This has been a stressful night."

Gabe sat behind the desk. Clara sank into the other chair and grimaced as she hit the hard wood surface.

"I have a few questions, and then you can be on your way, Ms. Jager. First of all, how well did you know Peter Ranchard?"

She rubbed the back of her right hand with her left thumb. "He was one of the . . . ah . . . other actors, that's all."

"Did you socialize with him outside of the theater?"

She winced. "Ah, no. Why would you ask that?"

"I'm trying to determine if Peter spent time with other cast members. How sociable was he with his fellow actors?"

"He was pretty much a loner. Some of us would go out for a beer after performances, but he rarely joined us."

"Did you speak with him much at the theater?"

Clara shook her head. "Not often. Only when practicing our lines or playing our roles. As I said, he tended to keep to himself, and I'm not much of a social butterfly either."

"Did he get into arguments with others in the cast?"

Clara continued to rub her hand. "No. I never noticed him confronting people."

"Are you in pain?" Gabe asked.

She dropped her hand. "I suffer from arthritis. It's acting up tonight. Stress makes it worse."

"I'm sorry to hear of your discomfort. Did you notice anything unusual with the grape juice or glasses on the tray tonight?"

She shook her head. "No. Peter opened and poured the grape juice backstage as he usually does. Then he brought out the seven glasses. Everything proceeded according to script, with Peter selecting someone from the audience to come up on stage, the fake lightning and thunder, the lights going out and Peter staggering offstage. But then he really died." She snuffled. "I still can't believe it."

Gabe offered her a handkerchief, but she waved it away.

He returned the handkerchief to his pocket. "And according to the script, you would be the one to go backstage to find Peter."

"Correct. He makes a crashing noise backstage, and that's my cue to go see what's going on. I'm to wait a moment, and then come screaming through the curtain saying he's dead. I did exactly that tonight, but I wasn't acting." She colored slightly. "Fainting wasn't in the script either. That's never happened to me before."

"I can understand. It must have been quite a shock."

"You can say that again. Usually Peter's sitting in that easy chair backstage. When I show up, he winks at me. Once he was picking his nose to see if he could make me laugh. I never expected to find him sprawled on the floor. I knew immediately that something bad had happened."

Gabe watched her again rub her hand.

"Who decides on the guest to invite up on stage?"

"If one of us notices an especially loud and obnoxious person in the audience, we mention it to Peter. Our objective is to find someone we can humiliate a little. We never have a shy person come up on stage. They clam up and don't add to the humor of the show."

"Any suggestions tonight?"

"No. If none of us recommends someone, Peter decides for himself. He's usually pretty good at finding a live wire."

"It's interesting that Peter picked a woman who owns a competitive theater. Do you know Helen Lameuse?"

"No. I've never met her. I've heard of her theater because Mildred always badmouths her shows, saying how juvenile her performances are and how she gouges her customers. I was expecting she'd have horns and a tail."

"So no love lost between Mildred and Helen."

For the first time Clara showed some animation. "For sure. Helen is public enemy number one on Mildred's list. If someone so much as mentions Helen's name, Mildred goes ballistic, bouncing off the walls."

"Yet, tonight, Mildred didn't recognize

her at first."

Clara worried her hand again. "That's the trouble with actors. They know how to use disguises. That woman looked completely different with black hair and glasses."

"You mentioned earlier that Peter wasn't confrontational with other cast members. Did he have any particular friendships with anyone?"

Clara bit her lip. "No-o-o. Except, one time I saw Mildred and Peter at a restaurant in town, and they appeared engaged in an intimate conversation."

Gabe wrote this revelation on his pad. "Did they show any affection around the theater?"

"Not at all. Mildred's all business at the playhouse and, as I said, Peter pretty much kept to himself." Clara grimaced and began rubbing her hand again.

"I won't keep you any longer this evening. Why don't you go get some sleep, and we can talk again at another time."

"Thanks. I'm pretty wiped out."

Gabe opened the door and watched as she left. Clara seeing Mildred and Peter together presented an interesting twist. No hint of that given by Mildred herself.

CHAPTER 7

Gabe asked Sophie Elmira to join him in the office. On the stage she had looked young and attractive. Up close, Gabe noticed hard lines on her face and around her eyes that conveyed the impression of a difficult life. He also saw the edge of a bruise on her arm that wasn't completely covered by the sleeve of her dress. Around her neck, she wore a gold necklace with a bright green stone, probably an emerald.

Before Gabe could ask his first question, she said in an exasperated tone, "I suppose you want to ask all about Peter and me?"

"Why, yes. That would be a good place to start."

"Well, I had broken things off. I don't know why I ever let it get started. It was a disaster. The guy was too into himself for me. It wasn't working out. Never would have. Over. Kaput. Done. You know —"

Gabe held a hand up to protect himself

from the machine gun barrage. "Please, Ms. Elmira, slow down."

She finally came up for air.

"Why don't you start at the beginning?" Gabe asked.

She clenched her teeth and closed her eyes for a moment. "Sorry. I tend to jump in too quickly and get ahead of myself." She took a deep breath. "Peter and I joined the cast within the same week. There was electricity between us, a mutual attraction, but I had been burned before by actors, so I remained cautious. I told him if anything were to happen between us, it would have to be kept secret. I had no desire to let a romance get in the way of my acting career. Consorting with another member of the cast can lead to problems if the director becomes aware of what's going on."

"So you two had a relationship?"

Sophie looked around as if checking to make sure no one overheard. "Yes. I finally gave in to the inevitable, but as I said, we kept it to ourselves."

"Were the other actors aware of your relationship with Peter?"

Sophie threw her head back and laughed. "Peter and I are excellent actors. We feigned indifference at the theater and spent our time together at my apartment. We avoided public places as well. No sense letting something slip that would bite us."

"Tell me about Peter."

A thoughtful expression passed over Sophie's face. "Well, at the outset he seemed very caring. He was attentive to me during our private moments together." Her eyes turned downward, and she balled her fists. "But then again, he was an actor. His true colors came out later. I came to hate him and broke off the relationship."

"Let me be blunt," Gabe said. "I noticed the bruise on your arm. Did Peter do that to you?"

She shrank into her chair. "Yes. His loving ways turned very dark. I couldn't take it anymore. That's when I called it off."

"How did he react when you broke up with him?"

"He became very angry." Sophie rubbed her arm. "This is the evidence of our last time together."

"And when did that happen?"

"Last Tuesday night. After he hurt my arm, I ran out of my apartment. When I returned two hours later, he had disappeared. I had the landlord change my lock the next day."

"Others have described Peter as not socializing much with the cast. Did you share that impression of him?"

Laughing casually, she said, "Oh, we socialized a great deal in bed, but he did tend to keep to himself when around other actors. He came across as a very private person and didn't mention details of his background. I would say he was compartmentalized. He kept our affair quiet. He could also brood. Several times when we hooked up, I knew something was on his mind, but he never shared his feelings. Peter had a dangerous, dark undercurrent about him." She grimaced and looked at her bruised arm.

"Do you know if he was seeing other women besides you?"

Sophie bit her lip. "Interesting question. I never had any direct evidence of being two-timed."

"But you suspected something."

"Yes. Sometimes he wouldn't show up at my apartment for most of a week. And he never invited me to his place. Used the excuse that he hadn't taken the time to clean up the place. As if that mattered."

"I heard that Peter was seen at a restaurant in the company of Mildred Hanson on at least one occasion."

Banging her palm on the desk, Sophie glared at Gabe. "How could I have been so naïve? The signs were there. That jerk." She slammed her hand again. "He was probably having an affair with the boss as well. He got what he deserved."

Gabe's eyes bore into hers. "What do you think happened to him?"

She met his gaze with large doe eyes. "Don't look at me that way. I didn't kill him. I wanted out of the relationship, so I broke it off. I didn't need to do anything more drastic. If he messed around with Mildred, she may have found out about Peter and me. She holds grudges. Just look at how she and that Helen Lameuse go at it. Like two banshees fighting."

"Is there anyone in the cast who might have held a grudge against Peter?"

"He wasn't that popular, if that's what you mean. I know that Arthur really hated him, but I never found out why."

"How do you know that?"

"I heard Arthur swearing at him in the alley behind the theater last night after the show. Arthur had Peter by the collar in one hand and had his other fist pulled back like he intended to punch him. When they saw me, they both took off."

"Did you ask Peter about that incident?"

"Yeah. I questioned him today before the show. He just sloughed it off saying Arthur had had a bad day. And it was true. Arthur flubbed his lines several times during the show last night. Pretty pathetic performance."

Gabe tapped his fingers on the desk. "Did you notice anything unusual during the scene with the wineglasses tonight?"

Her head tilted as she narrowed her gaze. "No, it went as staged until the fake death turned out to be real."

A thought occurred to Gabe. "Did Peter do drugs?"

Sophie laughed. "His drug was bourbon. He didn't use the hard drugs, at least that I ever saw. But he did turn into a mean drunk. That's when he became abusive."

"Why did you wait so long to break up with him?"

She shrugged. "I guess false hope. I thought I could reform him. Then it became obvious he was set in his ways. He'd get in his dark mood, drink and become violent. The pattern didn't change. He wouldn't give up the booze, so I gave up on him."

"Was he a public drunk?"

"That's the strange part. He didn't drink around others. Even when the cast had a bash, he wouldn't even touch the beer. Only late at night. Then — watch out."

"Any other observations about Peter?"

"No. I think we've covered the territory."

Gabe looked at his watch. "I need to speak with two others, and don't want to keep everyone here all night. We'll continue our conversation at another time."

As he walked back with Sophie, he thought over what he had learned. Mildred might have a motive of passion, Sophie clearly could have sought revenge, and Arthur had an altercation with Peter that would be worth exploring.

CHAPTER 8

Arthur Buchanan sat down in the office, nervously rubbing his hands together. A bead of sweat formed on his forehead.

Gabe decided to go directly after him. "I understand you didn't like Peter Ranchard very much."

Arthur recoiled. "Where'd you hear that?"

"You were observed having a heated argument with him last night. Would you care to elaborate?"

"No big deal." Arthur's casual wave of his arm looked more like an epileptic seizure. "We actors have lots of emotions and release them at times."

"To the point of being ready to assault him?"

Arthur let out a sigh. "Okay, okay. The guy's a slimeball. I got fed up and was pretty pissed at him."

"Angry enough to murder him?"

Arthur gawked in disbelief. "So that's

what this is. Do you think I killed him?"

Gabe didn't say a word.

Arthur waved his arms in a crossing motion. "No way."

"You can cut out all the theatrics. I want to know if you argued with Peter."

"Yeah, I wanted to bash his face in last night, but I wouldn't go farther than that. He wasn't worth it." Arthur wiped the back of his hand against his now dripping forehead. "Do you know what that creep did to me?"

"No. Why don't you tell me?"

"He stole my fiancée. I met this wonderful woman in Denver. We were engaged for three months. Peter saw her at a cast party and started chasing after her. She broke off our engagement yesterday and told me she loved Peter and not me."

"And her name?"

Arthur slumped as if the air had been let out of his lungs. "Kendra Jamison."

Gabe jotted a note. "Peter must have been quite a womanizer."

"He went after anything wearing a skirt." Arthur sank back in his chair and brought his hands up to his face. "That jerk had to interfere with me and Kendra."

"Were you aware of any other affairs he had?"

Arthur paused and then looked up at Gabe with bloodshot eyes. "He was probably nailing Sophie. I saw looks exchanged between them. Why didn't he stick with her and not mess with Kendra?"

"Did you notice anything going on between Peter and anyone else at the theater?"

For the first time, a glimmer of a smile crossed Arthur's face. "There's an interesting thought. Maybe Mildred. The SOB jumping the boss. It's possible."

"Did you ever see the two of them together?"

"No, just with all of us during rehearsals and the show."

"Did Peter have anything to do with Clara Jager?"

"Nah, she's too old for Peter. But now that you mention it, I did see them off in a corner talking in hushed tones a few times." Arthur flicked his hand. "No, that had to be something else. Peter had enough other women without going after Clara."

"Some of the cast members described Peter as a loner. Do you share that opinion?"

"Hah. As I said, he became too friendly with the women. He kept away from the men, though. Didn't socialize. No male bonding with that jerk."

"Did you notice anything unusual on

stage right before Peter died?"

"Let's see." Arthur tweaked his chin. "He brought in the wineglasses as he was supposed to. Mildred hit the button on the table to activate the recorded noise and lightning and turn off the lights. Hmm. The only other thing . . . I remember the sound of something falling on the floor after the lights went out."

CHAPTER 9

Gabe dismissed Arthur and sat there thinking. So far, Arthur and Sophie had motives associated with crimes of passion. Although neither had admitted killing Peter, they both had the means and opportunity to knock off the guy.

Mildred might have had a relationship going with Peter that she didn't admit. Gabe would have to poke at that one tomorrow.

And Clara. She claimed to have never even spoken with Peter, but Arthur had reported seeing them have an occasional tête-à-tête backstage. Another topic to explore.

Helen Lameuse had a motive to disrupt her competitor and had worn gloves that would have conveniently kept her from leaving fingerprints. On the other hand, she seemed genuinely surprised to be brought up on stage, but then again, she was an actor. And why would Peter select her to go on stage unless she knew Peter and they had planned this? Another avenue to explore. But if Helen was conspiring with Peter, why would she poison him? To eliminate him as a witness? Gabe tapped his fingers on the desk as he considered. Lots of possibilities.

Now he needed to speak with Harold Coats.

After escorting Harold to the interrogation room, Gabe assumed his position behind the desk.

"Now, Mr. Coats, or should I say Colonel?"

"No formality required. You may call me Harold."

"Did you notice anything unusual during the performance tonight?"

Harold ran a finger over his mustache. "No, things played out as scripted . . . until Peter showed up dead."

"Harold, how long have you known Peter?"

"Let's see. I've been employed here a year and a half. I first met him when he arrived a year ago."

"And your opinion of him?"

Harold arched an eyebrow. "I didn't like him."

Gabe waited, but Harold said nothing more. "Don't keep me in suspense. Why didn't you like him?"

"He was a bloody cad."

Gabe saw that this conversation would take all night if he had to drag each sentence, one at a time, out of Harold.

"Harold, look at me."

He twitched, and his eyes met Gabe's.

"I need you to give me more information. I know actors can give longer speeches than a few words. Please share some details."

"Jolly good."

Another pause.

"Well?"

Harold looked around the room and then finally focused above Gabe's left shoulder. "I'll attempt to do better. I disliked Peter because he didn't associate with his mates. In theater, we operate as an ensemble. We're on stage with each other nearly every day, including rehearsals and performances. We have to work together. Peter kept to himself like he was too good for the rest of us."

"There must have been more to it than that."

"Well, yes. There was the way he operated. He always slunk around. I don't like dodgy people."

Gabe clenched his fist. Harold knew something and was holding back. Might as well shake him up. "Did you kill him?"

Harold's eyes widened. "Good heavens, no. I must admit I have no regrets over his demise, but I wouldn't resort to murder. That isn't the type of person I am."

"And what kind of person are you?"

Harold straightened as if ready to review his troops. "I'm a military man with dignity and integrity."

"Did Peter have relationships with any of the women in the cast?"

Harold cleared his throat. "He had an eye for the ladies."

"Anyone in particular?"

"I'm sure he was chasing Sophie."

"Any specific reasons to think that?"

Harold gave out a burst of air as if trying to clear his lungs of smoke. "She's young and attractive, and Peter wasn't gay."

"Did Peter show any interest in Mildred?"

"She's the boss. He'd be bloody stupid to make a pass at her . . . unless she encouraged him."

"How did Peter get along with Arthur Buchanan?"

Harold gave a dismissive wave of his hand. "Not good. Not bad."

Tamping down another bout of frustration, Gabe leaned forward. Why wouldn't this guy elaborate? "Who do you think killed Peter?"

74

"Someone who disliked Peter more than I did."

"Who do you think that might be?"

Harold looked furtively over his shoulder to make sure the door was closed. "I hate to speak out of school, but I overheard a conversation earlier this week. Peter and Clara had huddled over in a corner and didn't know I was nearby. Peter said, 'You have one week to pay me or you'll face the consequences.' I think he may have been blackmailing her."

CHAPTER 10

So, a clean sweep, Gabe thought as he returned to the theater area. All the people on stage at the time of Peter's death remained viable suspects. Harold was holding something back, and Peter may have been blackmailing Clara. He'd have an interesting conversation with her the next day.

After Harold marched out of the theater, still trying to maintain the role as a military man, only the police contingent and Angie remained, as all the audience members had been interviewed, and Mildred had headed downstairs. Gabe approached Camille as she packed up her crime scene kit.

"Whatcha find?" he asked.

"Everything so far supports what you told me at the outset. Possible cyanide residue in the blue vial under the table and in one of the wineglasses. The lab will confirm that tomorrow, but I'm ninety percent certain with the sniff test. We'll await the coroner's report on the body, but I also agree that all indications point to cyanide poisoning."

"Any fingerprints on the vial?"

"One clear set. I'll be checking it against the prints I took from the people sitting on the stage." She wrinkled her forehead. "But I wonder about the tissue found next to the vial. It could have been used to hide prints, but if so, it didn't smudge the one set I found."

"Or it could have been there for another reason," Gabe added.

"I suppose. And I found one other thing backstage in Peter Ranchard's cubbyhole under a pile of clothes. This." In her gloved hand she held up an index card with three letters that read, "DIE."

"Any fingerprints on the card?"

"Nope. Clean."

Gabe looked closely at the card. The letters appeared to be cut out from headlines of a newspaper. The *D* and *I* came from one piece of paper, and the *E* had been snipped separately. The edges of the cut paper appeared jagged, as if small fingernail scissors had been used. Clear tape held the letters to the card.

An idea occurred to him. He jogged downstairs to find Mildred collecting brochures from the entryway. Satisfied that she wouldn't bother him, he returned to her office where he had seen a stack of newspapers. He began sorting through the pile. Part way down, he lifted out a front page section from the *Bearcrest Gazette.* Letters had been cut out of a headline. He scanned the article that described a proposed expansion for the Denver International Airport. The headline now read: (snipped-out-space), "A," (snipped-out-space), "xpansion."

He went out to where Mildred was still cleaning up in the lobby. "Who has access to the stack of newspapers in your office?"

She looked up. "Everyone. I have a subscription to the local paper that the cast reads. They drop the paper back in my office when they're done."

"So your office always remains open?"

"Absolutely. People can stop there any time."

Gabe thought over who could have made the note. Any of the actors. And he had even seen Helen Lameuse coming out of Mildred's office. Then the bottle that had held the poison. One set of fingerprints on the vial, but a tissue may or may not have been used to hold it. Pretty clear picture of what had killed Peter. But who had been involved in his death? He hadn't yet put all the pieces together in a logical fashion.

Gabe mounted the stairs to the dining room, where officers Ken Sanchez and Janet Lyon sat, completing their notes. "Let's all get together tomorrow at nine to go over all the interviews. That work for you?"

They both nodded.

"Anything immediately catch your attention?" Gabe asked.

"No one saw anything out of the ordinary," Ken replied. "A few people had too much to drink to notice anything, some were too shaken up to provide useful observations, and the rest acted like they were too tired to remember much."

"Same with the ones I spoke to," Janet added. "Everyone expressed shock but no useful witness statements. We matched all the names on the list you gave us with our completed interviews except for two. You, Gabe and one other witness I missed." She chuckled and pointed to Angie, still sitting at a table doing her crossword puzzles.

"I'll grill her on the way home," Gabe said. He strolled over to Angie. "You ready to blow this joint, or do you want to do puzzles all night?"

Angie closed her puzzle book. "I guess I'm set for a break."

After they sat down in the car, Gabe

asked, "Did you notice anything significant while waiting there?"

"In addition to completing a number of difficult puzzles, I picked up one intriguing thing." Angie gave him a devilish smile.

"You going to torture me or tell me?"

"I just wanted to make sure you were listening. As soon as you took Helen Lameuse into the room, Mildred gave her cast a lecture to speak openly with you. When she thought no one was looking, she slumped like she had been slugged in the stomach. I'd say once her game face came off, she was pretty upset over Peter's murder. There's more to her reaction than meets the eye."

"I'll have to work on that tomorrow. I think there may have been some relationship between Mildred and Peter. She didn't admit anything to me, but I heard some other indications that the two may have had something going."

"Wouldn't surprise me," Angie replied. "Well, the one thing you can say for the evening. You now know the butler didn't do it."

CHAPTER 11

The next morning Gabe jumped out of bed, feeling better than he had in a week. The previous Wednesday he had experienced some pains in his chest, and Angie had insisted he go to the doctor immediately.

Gabe hated visiting the doctor. Dr. Denton always found something that warranted a lecture, and the sawbones had poked and prodded before giving Gabe a speech that began, "You appear in good physical condition, but I'd like you to have an EKG and do some blood work. We'll check your cholesterol levels. I do have one piece of advice for you. Statistics show that people who stay involved after retirement live longer then those without a purpose. I can't see you wandering around aimlessly after your active career. Decide on something you want to pursue and do it. I'll give you a call when I get the lab results back, and we can schedule a follow-up session if required."

Gabe smiled to himself as he drove to the police station. Maybe Dr. Denton was right. It was important to find something he wanted to do. He now had a focus in his life — figuring out the cause of Peter Ranchard's death.

After parking his car, he strolled into the office of Police Chief Bradley Lewis. The chief sat in his swivel chair with a thick padded cushion on the seat. A husky man with red hair and freckles, Lewis had been a farm boy turned football player turned excellent cop, now turned donut chomper. The ever-present crumbs indicated that something chocolate had met its demise. Several weeks ago Gabe had come into the chief's office when Lewis wasn't there; the cushion had looked as if it had been squashed by an elephant.

The chief looked up and waved him toward a chair.

Gabe took a seat in the middle one of three visitor chairs on the other side of the desk from the chief. "It seems I stumbled into helping on a case last night."

Bradley leaned his large body forward as a twinkle came into his eyes, which were set below bushy red eyebrows. "Maybe you're having second thoughts about retiring. I haven't processed the paperwork yet.

There's time to reconsider."

"No, I'm going to retire, but I'll definitely help on this case until Brad gets back and Ned recovers from the flu."

"Tell you what. Since the paperwork hasn't gone through, we'll keep you on the payroll a little longer."

"Okay, but I'm really retiring after this case is wrapped up."

Bradley's gaze met Gabe's. "I don't know. Maybe we'll have to keep dangling new investigations in front of you. I suppose I should ask for that fishing rod back that we gave you for a retirement present. Have you used it yet?"

"No, I haven't had a chance."

"We'll have to wait to see if you hook a fish before I hook you into coming back full time."

"No way. I'm only filling in during this emergency."

Bradley laughed. "I knew you couldn't stay away. Investigation is in your blood. Maybe we could talk you into continuing on a consulting basis. Gun for hire type of thing."

Gabe flicked a piece of lint off his sleeve. "I'll consider that later. Right now I have an investigation to complete."

"Okay. Here's the deal. If you're so insistent on retiring, I'll put you on a thirty-hour week during this investigation. Then you can have at least ten hours a week to figure out how to spend your retirement time. I understand you haven't been too successful at it so far."

"How do you know that?"

The chief gave his enigmatic grin. "I have my sources."

Gabe thought over the proposition. Given the workload he had carried for years, thirty hours a week to dedicate to one case would be a piece of cake. Then, as the chief said, he could try out some other activities during his spare time. This would be a better way to ease into retirement than going cold turkey, as he had tried unsuccessfully the week before. And he wasn't doing this for the pay. If he spent more than thirty hours a week on this case, it would be on his own nickel. He could handle that. "Okay, I'll go with it."

The chief pushed his paw into the donut bag lying on his desk and only retrieved a piece of wax paper. He gave a snort, balled up the bag and tossed it toward the wastebasket. The shot missed by a foot.

Gabe noticed another crumpled bag resting near the wastebasket.

The chief apparently was having a two-bag morning. He wiped his hand across his mouth. "Good. Now give me a rundown on what you have so far on this theater situation."

"All signs indicate cyanide poisoning. We'll have that confirmed with the coroner's report and Camille's lab work. Six persons of interest had an opportunity to put poison in the victim's glass, and three of them have confirmed motives — an abusive relationship, a broken engagement and a competitor possibly trying to damage the playhouse business. From comments made to me last night, two of the other persons of interest appear to have lied to me regarding their relationships with the victim, so I have some things to check out, including possible blackmail. I'll be debriefing in a little while with Ken and Janet, who interviewed audience members last night. Then I'm going to visit the victim's apartment and plan to speak with the catering staff. Also, I want to make another pass through the theater today and re-interview several of the people on stage at the time of the death."

"Sounds like you're on top of it."

"I'll keep you apprised."

Over large mugs of steaming coffee, Gabe sat down with officers Ken Sanchez and Janet Lyon in the break room. "After thinking it over, any new observations on what the audience had to say?"

They both consulted their notes. Janet went first. "The folks I spoke to were paying attention to the play. They all recounted the action on stage leading up to the death of the victim. No one noticed anything suspicious. A number of them said they were watching carefully because they wanted to figure out the mystery in the play."

"Goes for the ones I spoke to as well," Ken added.

"I suppose no one noticed the vial being dropped on the floor." Gabe took a gulp of coffee and set the mug down.

"Nope. No mention of that."

Janet nodded her head in agreement with Ken.

"I wouldn't expect anyone to have seen that," Gabe said. "With the lights going out and a skirt on the audience side of the table, the perp had no trouble hiding it. Still interesting that the killer didn't dispose of the bottle. Why leave it where we could find it so easily versus taking it to stash somewhere completely out of sight?"

"Maybe figured he or she might be discovered with the vial," Janet said.

"Possible." Gabe rubbed his chin. "Drop

it in plain sight using a tissue. But the person messed up, because Camille found fingerprints on the bottle. We'll have to see what turns up when she completes her work."

Next Gabe tracked down Camille. "Any luck with the fingerprints you found on the vial last night?"

"Yup. Direct match with the right thumb and index finger of the prints I took from Mildred Hanson."

"Very good. I'll have a little chat with her. How soon will you get Peter Ranchard's fingerprints?"

"The coroner should let me collect those today."

Gabe looked at his notes. "Then we'll have everyone who was on the stage last night. What about the fake wine?"

"As suspected, I've verified that cyanide was in the one wineglass and the vial from under the table. We'll know more when the coroner completes tests on the body."

Gabe returned to his old office, entered and closed the door. The place looked the same, yet different. First of all, no pictures hung on the walls, and nothing remained on the desk except for the telephone and the computer. He ran his fingers over the keyboard. Part of the "A" was worn away.

His left pinky had left its mark.

His years of memorabilia had all been carted back to the den of his house over a week ago. Angie had immediately grabbed all the certificates to add to the family scrapbook. The tchotchkes he had collected over the years still remained packed in a cardboard box he had lugged home.

Gabe looked up the phone number for Bearcrest Food Fashion and made an appointment to meet with LaRita Jacobs and her two staff members at one that afternoon at their office. Next he called Mildred Hanson at her home.

A sleepy voice answered.

"Ms. Hanson, Detective Tremont here. I need to meet with you and some of your actors today."

"Why did you call in the middle of the night?"

Gabe looked at his watch. It was ten minutes after ten. "Will all of you be at the playhouse today?"

"Yes. We're having a rehearsal at two this afternoon and tomorrow as well. I called one of my standbys last night, and he'll be taking Peter's place, so we need to work him into the show. As they say, the show must go on . . . even when there's a police investigation. Speaking of which, when will you have that yellow tape removed from the stage?"

"You'll need to stay off the stage today. We want to check one more time."

Gabe heard a long sigh. "I guess we can rehearse in the dining area. We'll move some tables away. I hope we can use the stage tomorrow. I'll need at least one full rehearsal before our show Wednesday night."

"We should be able to accommodate you."

"Good. You're welcome to watch the rehearsal today, and we'll take a break around three-thirty, so that will be a good time for you to speak to cast members you want to harass . . . I mean interview."

"Thank you. I'll be there this afternoon."

Before leaving the office he initiated a background check on Peter Ranchard and the six suspects.

CHAPTER 12

Gabe drove to Peter Ranchard's apartment on Hill Street. The place looked like a tenement from the 1930s, replete with a rusty fire escape on the alley side of the building. Although it could have used a fresh coat of paint, at least there was no bare siding showing. He rang the bell for the building manager.

A skinny, gray-haired man holding a movie magazine answered the door. He had the decency to be wearing a plaid shirt rather than just an undershirt.

Gabe held out his police identification. "I'm pursuing an investigation and need to look at Peter Ranchard's apartment."

The man eyed Gabe skeptically. "Ya got his permission?"

"That won't be necessary. He's dead."

Rather than being shocked, the man licked his lips, and his eyes grew wide with excitement. "What happened?"

"The details haven't been released yet. He died at his place of employment. Now would you be kind enough to let me into his apartment?"

"Don't you need an okay from his next of kin or something?"

"Actually, Peter has no relatives, so I'd appreciate your assistance."

"Sure. Sure." The manager dropped the magazine on a table in the entryway, stepped out and closed the door behind him. "Follow me."

As they took the stairs to the second floor, Gabe regarded the wooden railing that didn't look strong enough to hold if someone fell against it and asked, "How well did you know Peter Ranchard?"

"He was already here when I took over as manager. I saw him in passing. He kept to himself and paid his rent on time. That's about it."

"Do you know how long he's lived here?"

The man shrugged. "I'd guess three or four years."

"Have you been in his apartment?"

"Nope. All the people here take care of minor maintenance, so I don't go in unless there are big emergencies, and I try to avoid those."

Gabe recalled others he had met like this

guy, who wanted to collect a pay check with the minimal amount of effort. That didn't work in the police department.

When they reached the apartment, the building manager pulled out a set of keys and unlocked Peter Ranchard's apartment. "Can I help?"

Gabe grabbed the doorknob to prevent the door from being opened more than a crack. "That won't be necessary."

"Okay, let me know if you need anything else. Dead. Jeez."

Gabe waited to hear footsteps fading before he opened the door the rest of the way. It swung two feet and then encountered something that blocked it from moving. Gabe pushed again, but the door didn't budge. He stuck his head through the opening, and a musty smell assaulted his nostrils. Pitch black. He put on gloves and ran his hand along the inside wall and found a switch. He flicked it, and a light came on. He stuck his head in again and flinched at the sight that met his eyes. Trash three feet deep cluttered the whole entryway. He sniffed. At least he didn't pick up the aroma of anything rotting or dead.

Gabe had investigated one other case involving a hoarding disorder. That woman's house had looked as trashed out as Peter's apartment.

Gabe squeezed through the door and tried to shove back a pile of magazines, newspapers, fast food bags, unopened mail, play scripts, hats, eyeglasses, walking canes, smoking pipes, a stuffed bird, fake flowers and wigs — things that Peter must have valued and saved for theater props or for whatever reason. As soon as he pushed something away from the entrance, another part of the trash mountain collapsed against the back of the door.

Giving up the futile effort, Gabe climbed on top of the mound to survey the living room. He couldn't discern any furniture. The whole room was stacked high with trash. He clumped toward the kitchen and turned on a light switch. Same thing. No sink in sight or any open surface. Empty cups, bags of chips, discarded brown paper bags covered everything.

He returned to the living room to find a slight indentation that served as a trail through the rubbish. He slid down the last part of it into hall refuse, maybe six inches lower than the living room. He tromped into the one bedroom, items crunching underfoot, turned on the main light switch and saw a bare mattress with trash around it to the height of the bed. Peaking above the mounds of refuse stood a dresser with a foot of junk on top. A desk with a personal computer and a stack of papers appeared to be the only relatively neat surface in the room. No chair was in sight.

Peter must have sat on the pile of trash when he used his computer. Gabe retraced his steps into the hall and stuck his head in the bathroom and turned on the light. Surprisingly, this one room in the house remained clean and neat. A pair of slacks and a shirt on hangers hung from the shower rail. Back in the hallway, Gabe found one other spot not covered with trash. A vertical washer/dryer combination mounted on one wall had nothing on top other than a box of laundry detergent.

Again slogging back into the bedroom, he found the closet door wedged two feet open; trash on both sides kept it from moving. Gabe stuck his head inside and found a light switch. Turning it on, he saw the floor covered with magazines and CDs, but above, clothes hung neatly on hangers attached to a wooden dowel.

Gabe shook his head in amazement. Peter was a classic hoarder, but he had kept his clothes in order. Probably why no one knew of his disorder. And he remembered Sophie saying she had never been to his apartment, although they had been lovers. One look at this place would have driven away any female, screaming her head off.

Peter had taped black garbage bags over all the windows. No wonder the place had been so dark when he first looked in. The covering must have kept out the sunlight since Peter, being an actor, probably stayed up late and slept during the morning. Gabe couldn't imagine living in this dark cave of crud.

Back in the bedroom, he leaned over the desk and began sorting through the stack of paper. Utility and rent bills, *People* magazines, a head shot of Peter marred by a speck of dried goo and more play scripts. Gabe opened the top center drawer and found the typical office supplies, from pens to envelopes. The pencils all looked as if they had been gnawed by a beaver.

The right top desk drawer contained a number of letters wrapped in a rubber band. Gabe removed the band and glanced at the letters. The first one was a love letter signed Sophie. After several other letters from Sophie, he found three with the signature of Kendra. Then in a distinct handwriting with large looping *g*'s, *l*'s, *b*'s and *d*'s, and circles rather than dots above the *i*'s, he read a very intimate account of what this woman wanted to do with Peter and various parts of his anatomy. Gabe had read much during his career, but still he felt the heat of a blush rush through his cheeks. No signature. The handwriting didn't match either Sophie's or Kendra's. Gabe checked the dates. This guy had been quite the stud. He had been stringing along three women at the same time.

Under the letters he found a stack of cash. Gabe counted it. Twenty fifty-dollar bills, an even thousand. Interesting.

Gabe next found a checkbook with an attached transaction record. He thumbed through it and noticed a cash deposit of nine hundred dollars during the first week of every month over the last year. Gabe concluded that the cash he found would have been for this month's deposit. If Peter hadn't died, he probably planned to keep one hundred dollars for pocket change and deposit the remaining nine hundred dollars. *Very* interesting.

Further inspection of the transaction record indicated that Peter hadn't spent much money. He made out checks for the rent, utilities, a VISA bill and little else. No spendthrift ways for Peter Ranchard.

The only other transactions were direct deposits from the Bearcrest Mystery Playhouse, near the end of every month over the last year. Going back to the previous year, Gabe noticed direct deposits from the Creekside Mystery Playhouse. Peter must have worked there for Helen Lameuse. She hadn't mentioned this little pertinent fact. To the contrary, she said she hadn't even known Peter. More and more little pieces of the puzzle that needed clarification.

In the second drawer down he found an appointment book with scheduled rehearsals and performances. The only other entries showed the name of Dr. James Viceroy, one entry as recently as the Friday before Peter's death. Apparently, he didn't keep records of his trysts with his harem of females.

One final surprise: a plastic supermarket bag contained over a dozen bottles of pills. Gabe picked up one container and inspected it closely. No pharmacy label, but it looked like one had been scraped off. He opened the bottle and peered inside. Then he shook a tablet out onto his palm and noticed the Percocet brand identification. He continued to inspect the other bottles and found more Percocet as well as Vicodin and Oxycontin. Quite a pain pill collection, and none of the bottles had any labels attached. Gabe had seen collections like this on several drug busts.

Trash blocked the bottom drawer of the desk. Gabe could only open it an inch. The inside appeared empty.

Gabe powered on the personal computer and waited for it to boot up. To his relief, it asked for no password. He found Peter's email program, also not password protected, and began scanning through recently received messages. He read postings from several actors' Yahoo email loops, an inquiry from a fan and several Facebook notifications. There was also the usual spam for travel discounts, Canadian pharmaceuticals, body part enlargements and Nigerian scams. All these messages remained unopened. Peter hadn't read his email messages for a week, and there was no indication that he ever deleted the old ones. What a set of dichotomies: messy with his computer system and apartment, but neat with his clothes.

Then one communiqué caught his attention. With no subject listed, the body of the message read, "DIE." It had been read but not deleted. Gabe jotted down the email address that had sent it the previous Tuesday night.

CHAPTER 13

Gabe stepped out of the apartment, closed the door and exhaled to free his lungs of the musty air. He itched all over and wondered what critters he might have picked up. Pulling out his cell phone, he called the office and asked Camille to have the department's computer geek check on the email address that had sent the death threat to Peter. Finally, he called the department admin, Shirley, to have a cleaning service take care of Peter's apartment.

"Place could use some scrubbing?" she asked.

"No, a flamethrower. But they'll first have to help me look through all the mess for any other papers that may be useful to the investigation. Then a lot of trash will have to be lugged out and thrown away. Several years ago we used a company that sorted through a murder victim's house, trashed by the perp. See if you can line up that same outfit."

"I'll see what I can find. How soon do you want them?"

"I need this stuff gone through within the next week. The sooner the better."

Gabe returned to the manager's office and asked if he had an extra key available.

The guy put down his magazine. "You're in luck, Detective. I keep a spare for each of the residents."

"I'd appreciate the use of it. We'll have to do some further work and cleanup in Peter's apartment."

"How soon will you have it ready so I can rent it again?"

"Probably next year."

Gabe stopped at home to scrub his hands and grab a sandwich with Angie.

"What new information have you turned up on the murder?" she asked.

Gabe chewed a moment, savoring the tuna, relish and mayonnaise before swallowing. "Peter Ranchard was a pretty unique character."

"Oh?"

"He suffered from a hoarding disorder and had a thousand dollars hidden in a drawer. There's evidence of his receiving this amount every month. He also had a

100

stash of illegal pain pills."

"So he may have been selling drugs."

"That's one part of it. From a statement made by one of the other cast members, Peter could have been extracting blackmail money as well."

"Not simply 'the butler did it' after all," Angie said.

"No. And in spite of the mess he lived in, he was quite the ladies' man. He had three women on the string at the same time, one a cast member and the second Arthur Buchanan's fiancée, who broke off the engagement because of Peter."

"And the third?"

"I haven't confirmed it yet, but as we discussed last night, it could have been Mildred Hanson." Gabe thought over the letter he had read. If it had been sent by Mildred, she had a very explicit imagination regarding sexual encounters.

Angie wiped her mouth with a napkin and stood to clear the dishes. "Quite a convoluted set of relationships."

"It goes deeper. Peter also used to work for Helen Lameuse at her competing playhouse. Helen wore the black wig, and Mildred confronted her last night. When I interviewed Helen, she claimed not to know Peter. If I go through the list of suspects,

Mildred Hanson might have had a relationship with Peter that she didn't admit when questioned, and her fingerprints were found on the vial that contained the poison used to kill Peter. Clara Jager claimed no contact with Peter, although Peter was overheard demanding money from her. Sophie Elmira admitted an abusive relationship with Peter. Arthur Buchanan hated Peter because of the broken engagement Peter supposedly caused. That leaves Harold Coats. He also claimed no contact with Peter, but acted very suspiciously. These people were all standing close to Peter when he received a lethal dose of poison, and nearly all had motives to get rid of him."

"Quite a list."

"That's not all," Gabe replied, his gut tensing at all he needed to solve. "I found a death threat on his computer, and Camille discovered one backstage in his cubbyhole."

"Sounds like a case for a good detective to solve. One who isn't retired." Angie lifted an eyebrow.

Gabe scraped back his chair. "I'll sort it out. I should learn more this afternoon."

Angie sent him on his way with a kiss.

As Gabe closed the door he savored Angie's affection and her intention to keep him well fed.

When Gabe arrived at the caterer's establishment, LaRita Jacobs ushered him into an office. She wore a white apron and stood approximately five-foot-ten with dark brown eyes and a well-tanned complexion.

"I need to speak with you and your entire staff present at the Bearcrest Mystery Dinner Playhouse on Sunday night," Gabe said.

"You got it." LaRita turned her head and shouted, "Jean and Ned. Get in here."

In a moment two college age kids appeared. They both wore the same type of white aprons as LaRita. Jean was a plump girl with freckles and displayed a wide grin. Ned stood a few inches taller than Gabe with a pointed chin, angular features and unruly blond hair. He reminded Gabe of a scarecrow.

"Whatcha want, boss?" Ned asked.

"Detective Tremont wants to talk to us." She pointed her right index finger at each of them in turn. "You answer all his questions, you hear?"

"Yes, ma'am," they chorused.

Gabe looked around the room. One wall displayed three photographs — one of a banquet table covered with salmon, roast

103

beef, chicken and vegetables, another of three smiling people holding pastry trays, and the final one, an elaborate three-tiered wedding cake about to be cut with a fancy knife jointly held by a beaming young bride and groom.

"Are the three of you the regular catering crew for the Bearcrest Dinner Playhouse?" Gabe asked.

"Yes," LaRita replied, flicking a strand of black hair away from her eyes. "We've been the food service crew for the last six months. Mildred has provided us a steady job four nights a week. We know all the actors at the playhouse."

"As I mentioned to you on the phone, Peter Ranchard died during the last performance. Did any of you notice anything unusual at the playhouse on Sunday night?"

The three of them shook their heads, and LaRita said, "The news came as quite a shock to us since we had seen Peter so often. It's hard to imagine the playhouse without him."

"Since you've been working there for the last six months, did any of you observe anything unusual in the relationships among the cast members, possibly something you overheard or saw while doing your job?"

The three of them exchanged glances.

Then Jean slowly raised her hand like a kid in class who was embarrassed to give the right answer to the teacher.

"Yes?" Gabe said.

"Well . . . uh . . . one time I spilled some food and went to the sink behind the stage to get some paper towels. They didn't notice me, but I saw Harold Coats give a wad of money to Peter Ranchard."

"You never mentioned that before," LaRita said.

Jean shrugged. "I didn't think anything of it at the time. The detective's question triggered my memory, and I thought I should say something."

"Thank you," Gabe replied. "That's very helpful. Anything else? For example, romantic involvement between cast members or any arguments?"

"Now that you ask," Ned said, "sometimes our customers don't pay much attention to us. Kind of like servants in the old days. As I carried food in one evening, I spotted Mildred Hanson and Peter standing very close together. He put his hand on her cheek and they kissed."

"Wow," LaRita said, slapping her forehead. "You two really observe stuff. I never picked up on any of that."

"As I said," Ned replied, "we're often

ignored." Then he smiled. "Plus, I tiptoed and stayed in the shadows."

"Remind me to watch my behavior around you two," LaRita said.

But Ned and Jean's anonymous snooping suited Gabe just fine.

CHAPTER 14

As Gabe drove to the Bearcrest Mystery Dinner Playhouse, he thought over what the caterers had told him. He'd need to spend some time with Harold Coats to find out what had been going on between him and Peter. And the evidence of a romantic link between Peter and Mildred seemed to be accumulating. In addition, Mildred's fingerprints had showed up on the vial containing the poison. Gabe watched a car cut off another car in the lane to his left. As a patrol officer, he would have pulled over the jerk, but now traffic wasn't his responsibility. The offending car had a bumper sticker written in script that he couldn't quite make out. But it gave him an idea.

When he entered the playhouse, he picked up one of the programs and turned to the page with Mildred's handwritten note. Sure enough. The large loopy letters and the circles over the *i*'s matched what he had seen in the unsigned love letter found in Peter's desk drawer. Gabe knew for sure Mildred hadn't been upfront with him, and he'd have to confront her about her relationship with Peter as well as the fingerprints found on the vial.

Mildred was sitting behind the desk in her office. He surveyed the room, still stacked with bills, newspaper and flyers. Was hoarding a common theater disorder?

She looked up and waved him in.

"May I speak with you in private?" he asked.

Mildred regarded her watch. "We have fifteen minutes before rehearsal starts. Fire away."

Gabe eased the door shut and sat down. "Last night you told me that you only saw Peter here at the playhouse and didn't socialize with him on the outside."

A worried expression crossed her face. "That's correct."

"I've had two reports of intimate conversations between you and Peter. In addition, I found a love letter from you to him in his apartment."

She glared at Gabe. "How'd you know I wrote that letter? I didn't even sign it." She slapped her hand over her mouth. "Uh-oh."

"Yes, uh-oh. Now that you've admitted it,

I expect to hear a complete account of your relationship." Gabe tapped his fingers on the corner of the desk and gave her his most intense detective stare.

She hung her head. "It shouldn't have happened. I never allow myself to fall for someone in my cast, but something sparked with Peter. Yes, I tried to keep it quiet. Then two days ago the jerk broke it off. I'm sure he hooked up with some younger honey. He said he'd had enough of me."

"How'd you react to that?"

"I threatened to fire him. He laughed and said it would make a great sexual harassment lawsuit if I fired him, because his boss had seduced him and he now wanted out of the relationship. I knew I was screwed in more ways than one."

"Did you kill him?"

Mildred's lip trembled. "Of course not. I still loved him even if he didn't love me. I found it hard to be around him after he dumped me, but I'm an excellent actor and can put up a good front."

"Are you acting now?" Gabe asked.

Mildred let out a choking half laugh. "Very perceptive, Detective, but no. Peter's betrayal and death both devastated me."

"Did you ever go to Peter's apartment?"

"No. We only met at my place. Peter

always begged off, saying his apartment needed to be cleaned."

That's an understatement. Gabe regarded Mildred carefully and then dropped the next bombshell. "Under the table on the stage we also discovered a vial that contained the poison put into Peter's wineglass. That bottle had your fingerprints on it. Care to comment?"

Rather than acting upset or surprised, Mildred pursed her lips. "Was it a small blue bottle?"

"Yes."

"When I came in today, I noticed one missing from the shelf in the reception area. You may have seen my collection of small glass decanters."

Gabe nodded his head. "Let's go take a look."

Mildred led him into the reception area and pointed to the shelf. "Right there. Yesterday there were six blue bottles, and now one's missing. See the empty spot second from the left? Someone removed one."

Gabe examined the shelf and saw dust circling where a container had rested. "And how would you explain your fingerprints on the vial found under the table last night?"

"That's pretty obvious. I collected all of

them and put them on the shelf. My fingerprints are probably on all these bottles. It
would have been odd to not find my fingerprints on that one. Now, in spite of all this,
I have a show to rehearse. If you'll excuse
me, we can talk more later. And please take
that yellow tape down so we can use the
stage tomorrow."

She stepped past Gabe and stomped away.

Gabe followed her up the stairs and into
the dining area where the other actors had
gathered. He watched as Mildred gave
instructions and moved everyone into position to begin the rehearsal. She appeared
completely unfazed by what they had discussed. On with the show. So either she
presented a very good façade or someone
else had poisoned Peter. Would Mildred
have been careless enough to leave fingerprints on the vial? And the tissue found with
the bottle. Was someone else hiding their
own fingerprints while leaving Mildred's to
incriminate her? He'd have to see if he
could find anything that had been missed
the night before.

Next, he decided to check the stage and
backstage, so that the areas could be released for use again. He threaded his way
through the furniture, carefully examining
the stage floor and finding nothing new. He

parted the curtains and repeated his inspection of the backstage, confirming that no new evidence could be found. Then he proceeded to the dressing area, which consisted of one room divided by a curtain. Both sides contained clothes racks and cubbyholes. Each cubbyhole had a name over it, and clothes on the rack were separated by spacers also with names. He sorted through all the clothes as Camille had done the night before. Satisfied that nothing had been overlooked, he removed the yellow crime scene tape and returned to watch the rehearsal.

As he sat down, Sophie shouted at Harold, "What's with you? You messed up that line again!"

Harold scrunched up his nose. "Well, if you wouldn't dawdle so much, my timing wouldn't be off."

"Enough, you two!" Mildred roared. "We need to familiarize Alex with the script and blocking, so no bickering."

Both Sophie and Harold glared at her.

The new guy, Alex, performed the part Peter had played Sunday night. He was slightly taller than Peter and what the ladies would call a hunk, except for his glum expression. How would it be to replace an actor who had been killed here the day before?

They continued with the rehearsal, and after Alex "died," he returned in the role of Inspector Whodunit, an incompetent detective. Gabe clenched his teeth at the antics of this supposed investigator. He hated when people made fun of his profession. He felt like going up and shaking Alex, but Mildred had probably written the script. He wanted to shake her as well, both for the portrayal of the detective and to see if he could loosen any more useful information from her.

CHAPTER 15

After Alex, as Inspector Whodunit, had incompetently interrogated each of the suspects, tripped into a potted plant and lost his shoe, Mildred held up her hand. "Stop. Alex, you need to put more feeling into your role. I want to see your desire to solve the murder. You have to project the aura of an experienced investigator."

"But I'm supposed to act like a jerk."

And he certainly was succeeding at that.

"No. Think of Inspector Clouseau in *The Pink Panther.* He thinks he's competent. Look at each clue and put feeling into questioning the suspects. You have to come across as believing that you're the best detective in the world."

Gabe rolled his eyes. *Right.*

They rehearsed the scene again, and afterwards Mildred clapped her hands together. "Let's take a thirty-minute break." She picked up a water bottle and sucked it dry.

Gabe asked to speak with Clara Jager and received Mildred's permission to use her office again.

Once they were seated, Gabe looked thoughtfully at Clara. "Why were you paying money to Peter?"

Clara recoiled, looked wildly around her as if seeking an escape route, and began rubbing her hand. "I . . . I don't know what you mean."

"Yes you do. Peter demanded money from you. Witnesses overheard a conversation between the two of you. Was he blackmailing you?"

She relaxed, and a smile crept across her face. "Is that what you think? Where would you come up with such a crazy idea?"

Gabe returned her smile. "I can see it wasn't blackmail. Were you buying pain pills from Peter?"

She jerked like a marionette on a string and nearly fell off her chair. Righting herself, she began rubbing her hand again.

Gabe narrowed his gaze at her. "Okay, you've all but admitted the drug connection. I'm not going to bust you for buying illegal prescriptions, but I want you to fill me in on the details of what transpired between you and Peter."

"I can't. Mildred will fire me."

"Mildred has more on her mind right now than your use of pain pills. Since you're implicated in a murder investigation, I'd suggest you be forthcoming and make it easier on yourself. We can do this here, or I can take you to the police station for questioning. Think it over. Your choice."

Clara took out a tissue from her purse and dabbed at her wet cheek. "No, that isn't necessary. I guess you would have found out in the long run. As I told you last night, I suffer from severe arthritis." She held out her hand. "Look at my fingers. I can't even straighten them anymore. Over-the-counter medication doesn't help, and I began using prescribed painkillers a year ago. My doctor became concerned with the amount I was taking and refused to give me a prescription for the number of pills I needed to control the pain. Peter found out and started selling me enough to supplement my prescription. It was the only way I could reduce the pain enough to keep working. And I needed the job."

"Isn't a thousand dollars a month pretty steep for pain pills?"

Clara rubbed her hand. "A thousand dollars a month? No, Peter sold me the pills for a hundred dollars a week."

"Did you give him cash?"

"Yeah, and I fell a little behind in payments. I owed him two hundred dollars. He shouted at me to pay up and threatened to tell Mildred about my drug problem. That may be what someone overheard. Then last week he showed up at my apartment. When I opened the door, he burst inside and threatened to expose me if I didn't double the payment amount. He wouldn't leave until I gave him some money, so I went in my bedroom and found a small amount of cash to calm him down."

"Did you kill him because of his threats?"

Clara's mouth dropped open, and then she gulped. "Are you kidding? I need the pills. I was hoping that once I paid him back what I owed, he'd be reasonable about future payments. Now how am I going to get medication?"

"I suggest you seek professional help for both your arthritis and addiction to pain medication."

Clara's hand trembled. "What am I going to do? I can't afford a high-priced doctor."

"Bearcrest County Services has an excellent substance abuse treatment program. You can give a counselor a call to make an appointment. I'll write the number down for you." Gabe regarded her thoughtfully before taking out a pen from his pocket, jotting the information on his notepad, tearing off the page and handing it to Clara.

"You won't say anything about this to Mildred, will you?"

"I'm afraid what you've told me will come out as the case progresses. Remember, you were one of six people with Peter when he died. I'm investigating all relationships between him and people in that group. None of you has been cleared yet."

"I guess I couldn't hide my addiction much longer anyway. Maybe Peter's death will provide the impetus for me to do something about it."

"Go get professional help. I'll need to talk to you again."

Gabe walked back upstairs with Clara. He wondered if she was just blowing smoke up his posterior or if she would really deal with her problem. With actors it was hard to tell when one of them was making a sincere statement or playing a role.

Clara took a chair with the other cast members, and Gabe tapped Harold Coats on the shoulder.

He spun around as if he'd been burned. "What do you want?"

"I have some further questions."

"What? We just spoke last night."

Gabe pointed to the door. "Come with

118

me to Mildred's office."

"We'll be resuming rehearsal in a few minutes."

"This won't take long."

Reluctantly, Harold followed Gabe to the office and sat down across the desk from him, scowling intensely.

"Last night you mentioned a suspicion that Peter was blackmailing Clara. I found out that wasn't exactly the case. Any chance Peter was blackmailing you?"

Harold twitched. "Why would you think that?"

"Peter received payments from someone. Everyone on the stage last night with Peter had some reason to hate him. You mentioned your dislike for him but didn't divulge any specifics. I think it's time for you to come clean."

Drops of sweat glistened on Harold's forehead as he fiddled with the stapler on the desk. "No . . . no, there was nothing."

Gabe continued to stare at Harold without saying anything. He had learned this poker move with other reluctant witnesses and perpetrators.

Harold squirmed and then stood up. "I need to return to the rehearsal." He opened the door and shot out of the room like a dog stuck with porcupine quills.

Gabe sat thinking over the afternoon's work. He had established the link between Clara and the drugs in Peter's apartment. There was something going on with Harold. He'd find it out in short order.

CHAPTER 16

Gabe had one more stop for the afternoon. He drove to the Creekside Mystery Dinner Playhouse. He parked in front and regarded the building, a converted warehouse that had been painted in half a dozen shades of blue. It reminded him of ocean waves meeting the sky with flocks of bluebirds flying by.

Inside he passed through a neatly carpeted foyer leading to a reception area with modern art on the walls. He inspected one painting that looked like tadpoles swimming into a cave. It was titled "Conception." He shook his head. He and modern art didn't get along that well. He had done some painting in his time. A few landscapes of meadows and mountains. Nothing abstract. He might even try his hand at painting again as a retirement activity.

Nobody was behind the reception counter, so Gabe headed down a hallway past two empty offices until he came to one with Helen Lameuse's name surrounded by stars on a placard above the door. He could hear her voice as she talked on the phone. He waited until she hung up.

He stepped inside to find her madly scribbling notes. The stack of paper on her desk rivaled what he had seen in Mildred Hanson's office. "Ms. Lameuse, I need to speak with you for a moment."

She looked up over a pair of glasses a fourth the size of the ones she had disguised herself with the night before. She wore a gold blouse and had a dozen gold bracelets around each wrist. Gabe couldn't figure out how she could work while carrying around all that weight. It appeared as convenient as having handcuffs dangling from her wrists.

Helen tapped her watch that somehow she found amid all the bracelets. "Ah, Detective. Make it snappy. I have a rehearsal to conduct in twenty minutes."

Gabe shut the door. "This won't take much of your time. Last night you told me you didn't know Peter Ranchard."

Helen fiddled with her glasses. "That's correct."

"How do you explain the fact that he worked for you here last year?"

"Oh, that."

"Yes, that."

She flicked her hand as if ridding herself of a pesky fly, setting off a jangling sound. "You have to realize what a crazy business this is, Detective. Things change all the time, and my day is a constant blur." She put the back of her hand to her forehead dramatically. "So many actors come through here, I guess I forgot."

"Awfully convenient to forget a former employee who dies under suspicious circumstances with you present. I find that very hard to believe. Why did Peter select you to come on stage last night?"

Her eyes grew large. "How would I know?"

"It's interesting that of all the people attending the show, Peter should pick you, Mildred Hanson's competitor, to join the cast on stage."

Helen hung her head. "You're right. It wasn't a coincidence. Peter and I stayed in touch after he came to work for Mildred. He kept me informed about her performances." Then Helen's head shot up. "But I had nothing to do with his death. In fact, I was surprised that he called me up on stage. That wasn't the plan. I came to the Bearcrest Playhouse to observe, not to be involved in the show."

Gabe regarded her carefully, trying to detect a lie. She seemed sincere, but she was an actor and had lied to him earlier. That bugged him with these people. They were trained and paid to play parts. He thought back to the night before. Helen had definitely looked surprised when Peter selected her out of the audience. "If that's the case, I still don't understand why Peter brought you on the stage."

Helen sucked on her lip for a moment. Then she snapped her fingers. "Here's a thought. Peter could be very vindictive. He may have been trying to foment trouble between Mildred and me."

"Is that why you tried to hide your face up on the stage?"

Helen took her glasses off for a moment and then put them back on. "Yes. I didn't want Mildred to recognize me. It would have led to a nasty scene. I wanted to get off the stage without any commotion."

"Were you aware of any romantic liaisons Peter had?"

"Yes. One of the problems I had with Peter — he was always hitting on the women in my cast."

"Including you?"

She laughed. "He tried, but I set him straight. Nothing was going to happen

124

between us. I'm not interested in men."

Gabe nodded. "But Peter decides to involve you in the show at the Bearcrest Playhouse, and then he's found dead shortly thereafter."

"Look, Detective, even if I had wanted to hurt Peter, which I didn't, I wouldn't have known that I'd be selected from the audience. Suddenly I'm being pulled up on stage, I try to hide from Mildred and the next thing I know, Peter's dead. It's as simple as that."

"None of this is simple."

She let out a sigh. "You're right. I don't know what Peter was really up to or who killed him."

CHAPTER 17

When Gabe returned to the police station, Shirley, the mid-forties, plump department administrator, waved at him.

"You flirting with me again, Shirley?"

She rolled her dark brown eyes. "I don't flirt with thoroughly married men." She handed him a note. "I finally reached the cleaning outfit you asked for. Here's the phone number for the head guy, Tom Buelson."

"Thanks. When can I see him?"

"He said he's swamped this week, but he could meet you on Friday afternoon to size up the job, and they're available next Monday to start."

Gabe scowled. "I'd hoped he could start sooner, but I guess this will have to do. I'll take it from here."

He went to his office and called Tom to set up an appointment at Peter's apartment. He hoped Tom had a crew with a strong tolerance for dust and crud. Then he decided to track down Dr. James Viceroy. Finding no listing in Bearcrest, he checked Denver and came across the needed phone number.

"Dr. Viceroy's office," a pleasant female voice announced.

"I'd like to speak with him, please."

"I'm sorry, Dr. Viceroy is on vacation. He can't be reached but will be back on Thursday."

"Please have him call Detective Gabe Tremont in Bearcrest when he returns." Gabe left his number. "And what is the nature of Dr. Viceroy's practice?"

"He's a psychiatrist. I'll give him the message when he gets back."

When Gabe returned home, Angie had a pot roast waiting for him. "The almost-retired warrior returns."

"A week of retirement was enough for now. The chief's putting me back on thirty hours a week."

"Why only thirty?"

"He says I can handle one case with that schedule and should spend the rest of the time figuring out how to be retired."

"Good advice. And have you decided what you want to do with the time you're not working?"

Gabe bit his lip. "Actually, no."

"After last week, I thought you'd become more proactive about your future." She slapped the back of her right hand into her left palm. "You need to get cracking."

"You sound like my high school guidance counselor."

Angie put her hands on her hips. "I'm not going to go through another week like the last one. You make a list and start trying some new hobbies."

"After dinner."

Once the meal was complete, Angie took out a piece of paper and a pen and handed them to Gabe. "All right. Get started. I want you to list all the retirement activities you can think of."

"But I don't know what I want to do."

"That's just the point. Make a list."

He let out a resigned sigh. Angie wasn't going to back off, so he might as well get started. Taking the paper and pen, he sat down at the cleared-off dining room table and started writing.

He felt like he was back in high school taking the English and math SAT. At least then he had known most of the answers.

After five minutes Angie looked over his shoulder and then grabbed the list. "This is all you have so far? Golf, gardening, painting and volunteering? What about fixing up the house? What about that old set of model trains in the attic? What about more bridge since we play periodically with the Schillings?"

Gabe let out a loud groan. "Not bridge with the Schillings."

"You could join a duplicate bridge group and play with other people as well."

"Okay, okay. I'll add those to the list." He picked up the pen again and began writing. After fifteen minutes of squinting at the sheet of paper and periodically jotting something down, he had added house projects, model trains, bridge, cribbage, poker, photography, hiking, reading mystery novels, starting a Facebook page, writing stories about his years on the police force, Sudoku puzzles, crossword puzzles, stamp collecting, getting a pet and fishing. He proudly held up the list for Angie's examination.

"That's better." She scanned the list. "Now where are you going to start?"

Since he had a lot of work to do with the investigation, he would ease into this. "I'll do the crossword puzzle from this morning's newspaper."

"That's pretty safe."

So Gabe retrieved the paper out of the recycling box in the kitchen and sat down to do the crossword puzzle. After filling in the capital of Afghanistan, snack for cops and the Beatles' drummer, he became stuck on unicycle component, since "wheel" and "seat" didn't fit. He tossed the newspaper aside. He couldn't imagine spending time doing this. He took his list and lined through "crossword puzzles." He'd try something else on the list the next day.

He was saved further thought on the matter when the phone rang. Angie answered it and handed the receiver to Gabe. "It's your brother."

Gabe eagerly grabbed the phone. "Hey, Nick. It's good to hear your voice. Caught any ambulances lately?"

A loud laugh came over the line. "Ah, big brother. Always the humorist. My law practice is thriving. So what's this rumor that you've retired?"

"It's not a rumor. I hung up my badge a little over a week ago."

"I can't imagine you sitting around as a retired gentleman with nothing to do. I bet you're driving Angie nuts."

If you only knew. "Actually, I'm back to working part time on a case."

"Hah. I knew it wouldn't stick. You're getting sucked back into police work again. You'll never retire."

"This is only temporary. Once I complete this one investigation, it's back to full time retirement. Then I'll be living the life of Riley again."

"Yeah, a likely story. And then what will you do?"

Good question. "Angie helped me develop a whole list of alternatives. It's only a matter of picking the most interesting ones."

"Such as?"

"Model railroads, playing bridge, cribbage, painting, doing some writing . . . those sorts of things."

"Give me a break, Gabe. I can't see you doing any of those for more than an hour before you'd jump up out of frustration."

"We'll see. Right now I have a murder to solve."

"Murder? In the little burg of Bearcrest?"

"Hey, this may not be like your Los Angeles, but we have crime."

"Someone fall off a cliff or drown in a lake?"

"Actually a murder by poisoning in a theater."

"Well, at least that should occupy you for a while. I wouldn't want you to be bored in the outlands of Colorado. And remember

131

what I always tell you: If you want to find the killer, follow the money."

And that might be right. Gabe made a mental note to follow up on one item in the morning.

They bantered back and forth for another ten minutes and caught up on family doings. Gabe always liked calls from Nick and hearing what his nephews were up to with their soccer games, choir concerts and Boy Scout trips. They had plenty of hobbies. Why didn't he have at least one that he was dying to do? But speaking of dying, he did have an investigation to complete.

After he hung up, he heard banging noises from the kitchen, and Angie appeared with her deranged housewife expression on her face. "It's the garbage disposal again. You need to do something."

"Me?" Heat rose up his neck.

"Yes, you. Do something useful."

"I've had a busy day. I was looking forward to relaxing. I don't want to be hassled right now." He clenched his fists. "Can't you just leave me alone?"

"Well, I'd like to relax and not be hassled too, but the sink is full of carrot and potato peels because the garbage disposal is clogged up again. Go fix it." She stomped upstairs and slammed the bedroom door.

Gabe let out a deep sigh. He shouldn't have gotten mad at Angie. Maybe retirement was having a debilitating effect on him. He went out into the garage to retrieve the cut-off broom handle he used for this situation. Their garbage disposal was at least thirty years old and on its last leg. Once a month or so it got stuck, and it was Gabe's responsibility to return it to operating order.

He placed the handle of the broom down the drain and thrust it around in a circle. After a grinding sound, the broom handle gained traction, and the blades in the disposal started moving. He ran water and flipped the switch. The appropriate whirring sound split the air, and the water and vegetable remains circled the drain and disappeared. He shook out some cleanser and wiped the sink with a washrag as the water continued to run. This whole activity reminded him of Peter's trashed-out apartment. He'd have to stir that mess and see if he could make something happen.

After putting the broom handle back in the garage, he climbed the stairs and knocked on the bedroom door.

"Go away!"

"Come on, honey," Gabe said. "I'm sorry I was a jerk. The disposal is fixed."

The door opened a crack.

Gabe's eyes brightened. Making up was always the best part of their fights anyway.

In the morning Gabe dashed off to the police department to review the preliminary coroner's findings. Death by potassium cyanide poisoning. He called Camille into his office and showed her the report.

"This all matches my investigation, Gabe — a potassium cyanide solution in the vial found on the floor and also in one of the wineglasses."

"But only one glass."

"That's right. Someone very deliberately put the poison in only Peter Ranchard's glass."

Gabe considered this again. "Six people on stage with Peter. The lights go out and someone pours the cyanide into his glass."

"Any prime suspects yet?"

"Of the six, five have either lied to me or had a strong reason to hate Peter. There's something going on with the sixth that I need to track down. All of them had an opportunity to poison him. I still have to figure out where the potassium cyanide came from and see if it links to anyone in particular."

Later in the morning Gabe received the background checks he had requested. No criminal or arrest records for Peter or five of the suspects. He learned one new piece of information though. Harold Coats had served time for stealing money from a theater three years earlier. He was currently on parole. This was right in line with the thought Gabe had when talking with his brother on the phone the day before.

CHAPTER 18

Gabe stopped home for lunch. As he strolled up the walkway, a black ball of fur hurled itself at the neighboring fence and began yapping at him. Gabe looked into the Schillings' yard and shook his head. That cockapoo could sure make a racket. "Easy, Gracie. After all this time you should recognize me."

Ignoring his comment, the little dog kept barking and leaping against the fence. It was a good thing she was so small. A larger dog might have knocked it clean over.

Once in the kitchen, Gabe collected the makings for a sandwich. He gathered mayonnaise, mustard, wheat bread, pickles, lettuce, pieces of American and cheddar cheese, and thick slices of turkey. That gave him a thought. He found his list of retirement activities and added cooking. Maybe he'd become a gourmet chef. He could just picture himself in a tall white toque, whipping up some luscious sauce to put on grilled salmon. Or maybe steak tartare or beef Wellington or lobster bisque? The possibilities were limitless.

Angie stuck her head through the doorway. "What brings you home, and why are you dripping mayonnaise all over the floor?"

"My stomach brought me home." He looked down and noticed that while daydreaming he had made a mess. "Sorry about the spill. You want a sandwich?"

"Sure, I'll join you. Just make sure you clean up afterwards. When you prepare food, it's like a tornado hit the kitchen."

After they finished eating, Angie said, "Just a reminder. We have bridge at the Schillings' tonight."

Gabe groaned. "You know I'm out of practice."

"Come on, Gabe, you even put bridge on your list of potential retirement activities. This will be a chance to check it out again."

"But their dog Gracie hates me."

"Gracie doesn't hate anyone. She's the sweetest dog. Always comes right up and licks my hand."

"Maybe she does that to you, but she always barks and growls at me. When I got home today, she tried to attack me."

"Are you kidding? That little rag mop

couldn't hurt a flea. But if you're concerned, I'll protect you from Gracie tonight, and a bridge game will be a good break for you after two days back on the job."

"Maybe I'll check out some leads on my case instead."

"No way. Besides, Henrietta always serves that peach cobbler you like. That will be your reward."

"But before eating the cobbler, I have to put up with Al's dumb jokes." Gabe put his hands around his throat. "That's pure torture."

"Now, now. He probably says the same about your police stories."

"But mine have a punch line. Al has the most complete list of inane, pointless jokes in the world. I think I'll pass on the bridge tonight."

Angie glared at him. Then a sparkle came to her eyes. "I'm not going to let you off that easily, but I'll give you a sporting chance. Since you like poker and that's on your list as well, I'll make you a little wager. I'll play you a game of Texas Hold'em. If you win, you don't have to go to the Schillings' house tonight. If I win, you have to come with me cheerfully — and no further complaints."

Gabe rubbed his hands together. "You're

on. I'll get out the cards and chips." He went to the cupboard and brought his poker kit back to the kitchen table. "Blue chips will be worth ten, red at five and white just one. We'll each have one hundred to start and play until someone runs out of chips."

"Fair enough. No ante and we take turns dealing. I'll go first." Angie shuffled the deck and dealt out two cards to each of them.

Gabe regarded his king and queen off-suit, and dropped a red chip in the middle. He thought back over all the times he had played poker with the guys from work. He had held his own pretty well, winning more than losing. He figured he could whup Angie.

"I'll call," she said. Then she flopped three cards faceup.

Gabe threw in another red chip and Angie called again.

After the "turn" card, Gabe checked and Angie did likewise. Angie pulled one more card from the deck and put it faceup for the "river."

Gabe bet a red chip and Angie called him. He showed a pair of queens to beat her pair of jacks.

"This should be over soon," Gabe said, winking at Angie.

"Don't be so sure."

139

Angie won the next hand and took the lead by one red chip. "I think the worm has turned," she said with a smile.

"Beginner's luck. Your deal again."

Angie shuffled and gave each of them two cards.

Gabe snuck a peek at his cards and saw a pair of kings. He threw a blue chip onto the table.

Angie called and then flopped a six of hearts, ten of spades and jack of diamonds.

Gabe studied his hand. Nothing that helped him, but no real threat that the board helped Angie either. He threw in another blue chip, which Angie called. On the "turn" a king of clubs came up. This gave Gabe three of a kind with no chance that Angie could make a flush. She still could end up with a straight, but he remained in good shape. She couldn't have a higher three of a kind and even if she held two aces, he had her beat. He flipped in two blue chips, and this, too, Angie called.

Then Angie dealt out and showed the "river" card, a ten of clubs. Now he had her. No concern if she had a straight, since he had her beat with a full house, kings over tens. "All in," he announced and pushed his chips toward the center of the table.

"Are you sure you want to do that?" Angie raised an eyebrow.

"You betcha."

"I'll call."

Gabe threw his cards down triumphantly. "Full house."

"That's a very good hand," Angie said, wrinkling her brow. Then she smiled. "But not quite good enough." She turned over her two tens, which gave her four of a kind. She pulled all the chips toward her.

Gabe opened his mouth to protest, thought better of it, and shook his head in resignation. "Card shark. Remind me in the future to stick to my murder investigation."

After his humiliating defeat, Gabe looked up Harold Coats's address on the sheet given to him Sunday night by Mildred Hanson. He found an address in the north end of Bearcrest and drove there, hoping to catch Harold before the day's rehearsal. Pulling up in front of a two-story building that needed a new coat of paint, Gabe went inside, found the right apartment and rang the bell.

Harold opened the door and blinked at Gabe.

"I have a few more questions for you."

Harold glanced at his watch. "Come in. I have thirty minutes before my presence is required at the playhouse."

They sat down in a living room that held a couch and two chairs plus a stack of magazines on a coffee table — a normal room after the unbelievable chaos of Peter's apartment. Harold wore pressed slacks, loafers and a long-sleeved shirt.

Acting on a hunch, Gabe said, "I'd like to ask you if you'd voluntarily show me your bank records."

"Pray tell me why'd I want to do that?" Harold's eyes narrowed.

"Because I could get a warrant, and I'm sure your parole officer wouldn't like hearing of you being uncooperative during a murder investigation."

Harold slumped. "So you know about that."

"Yes, but I suppose you've hidden it from Mildred."

"I'd never get a performance job if I went around telling everyone I'd been caught stealing."

"Right now I'm not concerned with your past, but with the case at hand. Now, please show me your bank records."

Harold raised his hands. "I'm bloody well done for. Okay." He went into the adjoining bedroom, returned with a manila folder and threw it on the coffee table.

Gabe looked through the statements. "Over the last year, I see you've made a cash withdrawal each month for exactly one thousand dollars."

"Quite so."

"I imagine you took that in twenty fifty-dollar bills."

"How'd you know . . . what the — ?"

"Let's cut to the chase. Why were you paying Peter Ranchard a thousand dollars every month?"

Harold clutched the sides of his head. "I guess you'll find out anyway. Peter was blackmailing me." Then the floodgates burst. "He uncovered the indiscretion from my past. I had once nicked money from a cashbox at a theater where I worked. I was caught and spent time in jail for it. It took me a year to get an acting job again. I kept my past hidden from that employer, but eventually the theater went bankrupt. When Mildred hired me, I felt fortunate to be employed again and kept my history to myself. Mildred makes quick decisions if she wants to hire someone, so fortunately she didn't check my background. But Peter did. He tracked down my theft conviction and confronted me. He said he'd notify Mildred if I didn't slip him a little cash every month. I went along with it, figuring

143

it was a small price to pay to stay employed at the playhouse. Then last Saturday Peter informed me that I needed to double the size of the payment. I didn't know what to do. That would have milked me dry."

"Sounds like a good reason for murder."

Harold waved his hands in a crossing motion. "No. I'm glad Peter's gone, but I'm done with crime. I learned my lesson. I've been clean since leaving jail."

"You mentioned to me Sunday night that you'd overheard Peter demanding money from Clara. You suspected blackmail."

"If the bloke extracted money from me, no reason why he wasn't blackmailing others, the cad."

"But you don't know that for a fact."

Harold shook his head. "I made a supposition, but I never approached Peter or Clara with my suspicions."

"How did Peter act when he discovered your theft?"

"He gloated over my criminal past for days. He'd pass me in the theater, wink and whisper how Mildred would love to hear that I served time. He was driving me nuts. Then he put the squeeze on me."

"And this has been going on for almost a year."

"My only out was finding a new job, but

then Peter would probably threaten me there. I took the path of least resistance and paid up."

"So now you're safe from Peter's threats and saving a lot of cash each month. Quite a motive."

Harold stood erect and looked Gabe in the eyes. "I didn't kill him."

CHAPTER 19

Next on his agenda, Gabe headed over to the Bearcrest Mystery Playhouse. If nothing else, he could keep an eye on the majority of the suspects. This was an elusive crowd, and he needed to keep after them. He found Mildred in her office frantically searching through a pile of documents.

"I'd like to watch part of your rehearsal and look around the playhouse this afternoon," Gabe said.

"Sure, sure." She continued to shuffle through paper.

"Anything new to tell me?"

Mildred grabbed a piece of paper and gave a triumphant laugh. "Aha. Got it. No, nothing new to report, Detective. But *mi casa es su casa*. You can wander around to your heart's content as long as you don't disrupt the rehearsal." She wagged her right index finger at him. "And no arresting anyone. I need my whole cast."

"I'll stay out of your way."

Gabe did his fly-on-the-wall imitation for the first half-hour of the rehearsal, sitting quietly in a folding chair in the back of the dining area. He watched for any facial tics or other signs of nervousness from the actors, but all appeared oblivious to his presence. He had met some criminals who were pretty good actors in his day, and he suspected that one of these actors might be a pretty good criminal. He'd have to watch himself around this crew.

No arguments today between cast members, and Peter's replacement, Alex, seemed to have his part down to Mildred's satisfaction as she didn't harass him at all this time. He played the incompetent detective with gusto, much to Gabe's disgust.

Satisfied that he would learn nothing new by studying stage blocking or listening to Clara, Harold, Sophie, Arthur and Alex repeat their lines, he rose from the chair and wandered down the stairs to the reception area. The place was deserted. He checked the row of blue glass bottles. Nothing had changed. Still the one spot where the vial had been taken.

Which one of these characters had removed it?

Gabe strolled past Mildred's office and

then came to the door leading to the basement restrooms. He flicked on the light switch and descended the rickety wooden stairs, guiding himself along an equally flimsy wooden railing that threatened to fill his hand with splinters.

He thought back to Helen's comments comparing her playhouse to Mildred's. Sure, the Creekside Playhouse resided in a more modern building, but you couldn't beat the atmosphere of a Victorian house. Provided no vermin, human or otherwise, scurried around in the basement.

At the bottom of the stairs he came to a small passageway with restrooms on either side. Sticking his head in the men's room, he verified that nothing was on the floor other than a wastebasket. He knocked on the women's room door and, when no one answered, did an equally quick inspection.

The hallway led to a large room, the floor being a cement slab covered with boxes and costume racks. He expected music from *Phantom of the Opera* to be playing in the background and dripping water to be forming stalactites and stalagmites. The basement smelled like wet dog.

He shivered in the cool, dank air and came to a complete stop, wondering if he'd pick up the sound of rats scuttling through the collection of props. Instead, he could only hear his own heart thudding in his chest. He took a deep breath, which caused him to sneeze. Tweaking his nose to suppress another sneeze, he turned on a light switch, walked past a wooden post supporting the ceiling and peered into a mildewed cardboard box that contained a collection of tiaras. Other boxes contained shoes, swords, hats and costume jewelry. He lifted a pair of dark blue swim fins out of one of the boxes. If he ever needed a Halloween costume, this would be the place to come.

After navigating the whole room, he came to the only other door. It was opened a crack. He pushed on it, but it didn't budge. Putting his shoulder into it, the door finally gave way and slammed into the inner wall. A yellowed newspaper had been bunched under the door, impeding his attempt to open it.

He entered a small storage room with a dirt floor and wooden shelves. Finding no light switch, Gabe had to suffice with ambient light from the adjoining larger room. He made out the outline of a miner's hat on a shelf. He picked it up and took it back to the main room. He blew off dust, which led to another round of sneezing. Deep gouges lined the crystal of the light attached to the helmet.

Gabe remembered that a miner had originally lived in this house. Maybe he'd found a relic from the original owner.

Returning to the small room, Gabe replaced the hat on the shelf. As his eyes adjusted to the dim light, he spotted an old burlap bag in the corner of the dirt floor. White crystals had spilled out of a torn corner of the bag. This was interesting.

Gabe retraced his path through the main room and up the stairs. He went out to his car and opened the trunk. Finding his emergency kit and extracting a Ziploc bag that contained a granola bar and a package of peanut butter crackers, he emptied the bag and took it with him into the house. Back inside the small basement room, he turned the bag inside out, put it over his hand and collected some of the white crystals in the same manner as someone picking up dog poop. Then he sealed it.

Without bothering the rehearsal, Gabe left the playhouse and drove to the police station. Traffic was light, and thoughts of what he'd found swirled through his head. He went to Camille's office and dropped the plastic bag on her desk.

She looked up from her computer screen, a hint of a smile crossing her face. "A present for me? Gabe, you shouldn't have."

"Analyze these crystals. I think they may be pertinent to our playhouse investigation."

CHAPTER 20

When Gabe arrived home, Angie met him at the door with a big grin on her face. "I have a present for you."

He gave her a peck on the cheek. "Something to do instead of going to the Schillings' for bridge tonight?"

"No, silly. Not to replace bridge but another activity on your list to try. I bought you a Sudoku book at the grocery store today. While I get dinner ready for my hard-working detective, you can do a puzzle."

Gabe gave an eye roll but sat down at the dining room table. He had done one simple puzzle several years ago when the fad first hit. He licked the pencil and began jotting down possibilities in the open squares. It took him fifteen minutes, but he completed an easy level puzzle. He looked at the result while rotating his shoulders. Yeah, he had finished it but so what? He pushed the book aside. This wasn't for him either.

He picked up his list of potential retirement activities and stared at it for five minutes. Nothing leaped out begging him to do it. The phone rang, and he picked it up to hear his daughter, Cindy, on the line.

He perked up at the sound of her voice. "How are things in the wonderful world of Colorado Springs?"

"We're all fine, and your grandson is growing like a weed. When are you and Mom coming for a visit?"

That was a good question. "I'm back to working part time on a murder investigation. Maybe after I wrap up the case."

"What? I thought you retired."

"This is just temporary."

"I don't know. I bet you're driving Mom nuts."

"Why does everyone keep saying that?"

"Because anyone who knows you realizes that you can't stand sitting around doing nothing."

"For your information, your mother has helped me compile a whole list of things to do in my retirement."

"And I bet you haven't found one that you want to pursue."

Was he that transparent? Did his family know him better than he knew himself? "Well . . . uh . . . I'm still looking at possibilities."

Cindy laughed. "And you'll be looking at them until the cows come home. Get with the program, Dad. You need to pick something and go with it."

Gabe could picture the sparkle in his daughter's blue eyes, the same eyes she'd passed on to her son, who possessed the dark hair of her husband. "Eventually. Right now I have my hands full with an investigation."

In the background Angie shouted, "Who's on the phone?"

Gabe put his hand over the receiver. "Cindy."

"Good. I need to speak with her."

Gabe uncovered the receiver and spoke into it again. "I'm going to put your mom on. She wants to harass you about something."

While Angie and Cindy chatted, Gabe sat at the table and reviewed his list. What did he really want to do?

After dinner Gabe put on his tan slacks and a sports shirt and was pushed out of the house by Angie, who accused him of dragging his feet.

"I'm not stalling," he insisted. "I needed to peruse my retirement activity list again.

Besides, we don't have to be right on time."

"We're already fifteen minutes late, and this isn't a party. Only the Schillings and us. It's hard to explain being late when we're walking next door."

"It's a beautiful evening. We could take a nice stroll instead. Look at the sky. Ah, the beautiful outdoors."

"Gabriel!" She only used his full name when treating him like a little boy or when she was really upset with him. Tonight she had reason for both.

"I think I'm coming down with the flu."

She swatted him on the arm. "You'll be suffering from more than the flu if you don't get with it. Don't be such a big baby. You can survive an evening of bridge. Suck it up, big guy."

"Maybe I should stay home and do the laundry."

"Right. You haven't done the laundry in thirty years."

"No time like the present to learn."

"You're impossible. Brave it out like a man. Pretend you're working on an important investigation."

"Speaking of which, maybe I should stay home to review my notes. I still haven't cracked the mystery playhouse case. I have six good suspects but haven't narrowed the list down yet. I might make a breakthrough tonight."

"And you never would have been involved if I hadn't insisted that you go to the playhouse Sunday night. Consider this the same. You may come up with some insights tonight."

"Like remembering why I don't like bridge at the Schillings'."

Angie came to an abrupt halt and tapped the toe of her shoe. "You don't intend to welsh on your bet, do you?"

Gabe let out a sigh. "You're right. You won fair and square. Time to face the music."

At the Schillings' house Al opened the door, and Gracie ran up, skidded to a stop and growled at Gabe. Angie reached over and scratched her head, and Gracie licked her hand. "See, she's friendly. You try it, Gabe."

Gabe braced himself and reached his hand toward Gracie. The little cockapoo snarled while trying to nip him. Gabe yanked his hand back as if being attacked by a vicious beast, which, now that he thought about it, he was.

"Down, Gracie," Al commanded. "I can't understand what got into her. She loves everyone."

Angie smiled. "Gabe has a strange effect

on animals."

Gabe shrugged. "I do better with people."

Al ushered them in. "Have you heard the one about the rabbi, minister and priest in a rowboat?"

"Yes," Gabe replied.

Ignoring him, Al pressed on. "See, this rabbi, minister and priest are out in a boat on a lake and the minister says, 'I forgot the lunch. I'll have to go back and get it.' "

Gabe plastered a fake grin on his face and listened while Al butchered the punch line and then broke out laughing, slapping his hand on his thigh as if it was the best joke he had ever told.

Gabe exchanged a plaintive glance with Angie, who only smiled and pushed him toward the bridge table in the living room, whispering in his ear, "Remember: You lost the bet, but you'll get peach cobbler."

Gabe remained unconvinced that even Henrietta's peach cobbler would make up for an evening of suffering through bridge and Al's jokes. He willed himself to be a good sport and not insult his neighbor.

They played two rubbers of bridge, and then Henrietta announced, "Time for dessert. And I have Gabe's favorite. Peach cobbler."

"Are you going to desert us?" Al guffawed.

"Say, Gabe, have you heard the one about the cobbler who ran out of leather?"

"You can tell that later, Al," Henrietta said. "Right now I need you in the kitchen to serve the à la mode part of dessert."

Al headed to the kitchen looking as sad as a kid whose favorite toy had been taken away by his mother.

With a sigh of relief, Gabe stood up to stretch. Then he wandered around the living room looking at the framed mountain scenes on the walls. Al had a good photographic eye in spite of his other shortcomings.

Al returned from the kitchen and whacked Gabe on the back. "Now that you're retired, you should join me for bridge. I'm only working three weekdays in my jewelry shop. I let my assistants cover the rest of the time, and on Tuesday, Thursday and Saturdays I play in the bridge group at the Bearcrest Community Center. That should allow you to bridge into your retirement." Al winked at Gabe and started yukking.

That's all he needed. "I'll keep it in mind, Al. Right now I'm pretty busy. I'm filling in on a case."

"So you didn't really retire after all."

That's when it struck Gabe. Maybe he didn't want to retire. After one week with nothing to do but laze around, he was glad to be back on an investigation. He'd see this case through and then figure out something meaningful to pursue instead of turning into an old codger sitting around on his butt, playing geezer bridge, butchering punch lines to jokes and watching reruns on television. No, he wanted more from his remaining years than that.

As Gabe and Angie headed home, he said, "Maybe I should cross bridge off my retirement list. I definitely know that isn't where I want to put my time."

Angie hugged his arm. "Don't be so hasty. You played well tonight, even making a small slam."

Gabe smiled to himself. He hadn't done so badly in spite of being forced to listen to Al's dumb jokes. Still, he wanted to challenge his mind some other way, like he always had — solving crimes. He continued to be good at it and enjoyed outwitting the bad guys. As he put the key in the lock of their front door, he let out a loud sigh.

"What's on your mind?"

"Retirement isn't turning out the way I expected."

Chapter 21

The next day Gabe awoke and did a double take when he discovered he had slept until nine. Angie was already up. This was unusual since he was typically the early riser. Apparently the bridge and Al's dumb jokes had exhausted him. He stretched and peered through the opening in the curtains to find a bright sunny day awaiting him.

After a leisurely breakfast consisting of a cheese omelet, bacon, toast and coffee, he looked at his retirement activity list. Most of the items were activities to entertain himself. Why not do something useful? He underlined the entry of volunteering. He could help other people and have a purpose for his life. That would be a good use of his time and get him away from navel inspecting.

He thought of all the volunteer opportunities to tutor kids, help at the homeless shelter, build trails in the open space or assist senior citizens. Older people were the fastest growing segment of the population. And wait a minute — that included him. But he was in good shape, had all his mental faculties and was fully independent. Helping elders might be a good place to put some of his time.

He remembered a friend of his, Fred Jackson, who delivered meals to homebound senior citizens. Fred had raved about the interesting characters he met and how appreciative people were who received the food. He told Gabe that people often invited him in for a chat and recounted stories of their interesting lives.

That would be something Gabe could handle and would provide a needed service. He went on his computer and found the phone number for the local Meals on Wheels. He called and asked for information regarding their volunteer program. The receptionist transferred him.

"Thanks for calling," a pleasant woman's voice said. "We're always looking for drivers as we've recently added thirty-five new clients."

"I have some time on my hands and would like to help out," Gabe said, not getting into the details of his aborted retirement. "How soon do I start?"

"Let me look at the schedule." There was a pause on the line before she returned. "You're in luck. There's an orientation session this afternoon at four. Come to the Bearcrest Community Center, Front Range room."

After hanging up, Gabe got in the car and headed to the police station to check for messages. He had been in his cubicle no more than ten minutes when Camille came racing in.

"You nailed that one right," she exclaimed.

He arched an eyebrow. "Meaning?"

"Those white crystals you brought in yesterday check out as potassium cyanide. I think you've found the source of the poison used to kill Peter Ranchard."

Gabe regarded Camille thoughtfully. "It's a step in the right direction, but everyone in the cast had access to that basement. Helen Lameuse is the only suspect not at the playhouse all the time."

"Then you've eliminated one of the six."

Then Gabe recalled something. "No, I can't even do that. I saw Helen coming up from the basement right before the show started. She said she was using the restroom down there. So even she could have had access to the potassium cyanide. I still can't eliminate any of the suspects."

"So what was potassium cyanide doing in the basement of a dinner theater?" Camille asked. "I never went down there when I was checking the crime scene."

"A remnant from early mining days. It was used in the process of extracting gold. A mining executive originally owned the house. Still it's interesting that the bag never had been removed."

"Waiting there for someone seeking a method for murder."

"Mildred Hanson, of all the suspects, should have come across the burlap sack in the basement. Why would she have left it there in her theater?"

Camille scrunched up her nose. "If she's the one who killed Peter, she couldn't have been planning this for very long. You're right. She should have cleaned out the basement a long time ago."

"And Peter Ranchard received the lethal dose from someone who wanted him out of the way. I've now established that all six suspects had the means to kill him with access to the cyanide, the opportunity from being on the stage when the lights went out and a motive."

"Any favorites?" Camille asked.

"Not yet. Here's what I know. Mildred Hanson could have sought revenge for an affair turned sour. And her fingerprints were on the vial containing potassium cyanide found under the table on stage. Helen Lameuse could have wanted to disrupt a competitor. Sophie Elmira had suffered through an abusive relationship with Peter. Peter threatened Clara Jager over nonpayment of money owed for illegal painkillers. Peter blackmailed Harold Coats, and Arthur Buchanan was angry over a relationship ruined by Peter. Each one had reasons to benefit from Peter's death. I just haven't found the link to the one particular person who planted the poison."

"Come on, Gabe. A good detective like you has to have a hunch or two," Camille said.

He chuckled. "I told Angie ahead of time that the butler did it. Since making that statement, I've kept my opinions to myself."

"You'll figure it out. I'll go back and see if I can find any fingerprints or other evidence on the burlap bag in the basement."

Then Gabe realized what had been nagging at him. "But there's one strange part to all of this. When the lights went out, seven glasses rested on a tray. If one of the six other people on stage wanted to kill Peter, given that it was pitch black, how did the murderer know which glass to put the poison in?"

CHAPTER 22

After Camille left his office, Gabe thought over all the suspects again. There was one other explanation, given the uncertainty of what happened in the dark. Was the wrong person killed? Did the murderer mean to poison someone else on stage, but Peter drank from the wrong glass as an unintended victim? Could either Mildred or Helen have wanted to kill the other but instead knocked off Peter? Maybe Mildred had recognized Helen after all. Could she have gone into the basement to get the poison and then told Peter to select Helen to come on stage? Possible, but not likely.

Maybe Helen found the poison when she went into the basement. But she wouldn't have known that she'd be selected to come on stage. Her accidently poisoning Peter wasn't a probable scenario.

Did pain pill–addicted Clara, blackmailed Harold, abused Sophie or unlucky-at-love

Arthur mean to kill someone else? Gabe had found no indication of another grudge among cast members. Peter still seemed the most likely intended victim given his strange behavior and the way he manipulated people.

One other thing still bothered Gabe. Helen Lameuse had lied to him, first claiming not to know Peter and only later admitting that Peter had helped her spy on Mildred's operation. Gabe decided to check further on the Creekside Dinner Playhouse. Time to make his fingers fly across the keyboard.

As he looked through computer records, one interesting item caught his eye. A year and a half ago, a theft had been reported at the Creekside Theater. In scanning through the report, he found that money along with a gold and emerald necklace had been taken. Gabe remembered where he had seen a necklace matching that description.

Gabe looked up Sophie Elmira's address and found she lived in the foothills on the edge of Bearcrest. He drove there and pulled up to the curb in front of a small house that looked like a renovated log cabin. As he turned off the ignition, he heard a loud thump that shook the car. He jerked his head, encountering the yellow eyes of a mountain lion. The cat on the hood had teeth the size of paring knives. It thrust its face up against the front window and snarled. With his heart pounding, Gabe pressed himself as far as he could into the seatback. He'd never seen a mountain lion this close and couldn't believe its aggressive behavior.

Gathering his nerve, Gabe made a shooing motion. The snarling beast remained planted in place, staring at him.

Gabe leaned on the horn, but the loud honk had no effect.

The cat clawed at the window.

When it became clear it was Gabe or this animal, he restarted the engine, applied the gas, yanked the car into reverse and drove backward. The animal lost its balance, rolled off. With a last snarl it disappeared into the woods.

Gabe sat there for a moment, allowing his breathing to return to normal. He looked toward the trees to make sure the large cat had really taken off. Then he slowly exited his car and inspected the hood. He saw a dent and five-inch long claw marks in the paint. He'd have an insurance claim, but wouldn't want his old cohorts at the precinct to hear about this wildlife encounter.

With one more furtive glance over his shoulder, he hurried to the door of Sophie's house and knocked. She obviously hadn't heard the commotion outside.

After a moment she answered. "Yes, Detective?"

"May I come in? I have something to ask you."

"Sure. Why not?"

As opposed to Peter's trashed apartment, Sophie's place was in immaculate condition — simple furnishings but in good taste. He even smelled the aroma of bread baking.

"Did you know you have a mountain lion in the neighborhood?" Gabe asked.

"There have been a number of sightings lately. Everyone in the neighborhood has been concerned. That's why I keep Sammy inside."

A Siamese cat came prancing up to Gabe. Gabe stiffened.

The cat sniffed his cuff, hissed and dashed off into the kitchen.

"I've never seen Sammy act that way," Sophie remarked. "He likes everyone."

"I have that effect on animals. Nothing unusual."

"The reason for your visit, Detective?"

"The other day you were wearing a gold necklace with a green stone. Do you have it handy?"

"It's in my bedroom. Wait a second."

She disappeared and then returned with the requested item.

"Where did you get this?" Gabe asked.

She placed the necklace on the end table next to her. "Peter gave it to me as a present when we started seeing each other."

Gabe handed her the report he had printed off. "If you look at this, you'll see that a necklace meeting the description of yours was stolen."

She put her hand to her cheek. "Oh, dear."

"Peter used to work at the Creekside Dinner Playhouse. Did he ever mention that to you?"

She shook her head. "He never told me anything about his past. He was a very private person."

"I would guess he stole the necklace."

"When we broke up he said he wanted it back, but I told him no deal." She regarded the necklace longingly. "I guess I'll have to give it to you if he stole it."

"Yes. I'd like to show it to Helen Lameuse to see if she can identify it conclusively as the missing necklace."

"How do you know she won't automatically claim it as hers?"

Gabe smiled. "I'll make arrangements

with a jeweler I know to borrow several similar necklaces. I'll have Helen look at the line-up to see if she can identify this one."

Gabe next drove to Al's jewelry store, knowing this would be one of the days he'd be working.

Al greeted him with a huge grin. "Hi, buddy. You here to buy a present for your bride? I have a special on tennis bracelets."

"No, I need to ask a favor." Gabe held out the necklace. "I'd like to borrow several necklaces that look similar to this one."

Al took out his loupe and examined the stone. "Nice emerald. Let me show you what I have." He pulled four necklaces out of the glass cabinet and lined them up on the counter. "All gold necklaces with similar-sized stones."

Gabe selected three of them. "I'll fill out a consignment form. I'd like to show these and the necklace I have to an individual. I'll be able to return them within two days."

"No problem. Get them back when you can. You ready to join me for a game of bridge at the Community Center?"

"I'm pretty busy on this case right now. Also, I'm signing up to be a volunteer for Meals on Wheels."

Al punched his arm. "Come on, Gabe. All

work and no play. You can take a break for a little entertainment."

Gabe rolled his eyes. Bridge with Al wasn't his idea of entertainment. "Maybe when I wrap up this part-time job. Thanks again for the necklaces."

"The least I can do to help the fraternal order of police. As long as you're here, have you heard the one . . ."

With his collection of jewelry, Gabe next drove to the Creekside Dinner Playhouse. He found Helen Lameuse in her office and on the phone. She waved at him to take a seat. Once she hung up she asked, "What can I do for you, Detective?"

"I found a report that money and a necklace were stolen from your theater some time ago."

Helen frowned. "Yes. I lost three hundred dollars in cash and a valuable emerald necklace. It had been my grandmother's and was the one thing she left me when she died three years ago."

"Please describe it to me."

"Gold link chain with an emerald this big." She curled her index finger alongside her thumb.

"Anything distinctive that would help identify it?"

She furrowed her brow. "Well, there was a scratch on the back of the mounting. Looked like a small zigzag lightning mark."

Gabe brought the four necklaces out of his pocket. "Take a look at these and see if one matches the stolen item." He lined them up on the desk in front of her.

Helen's eyes widened as she leaned over to inspect the first one. "No, not this one." Then she went down the line. "No, this emerald's the wrong shape . . . and this one doesn't have the right type of setting."

"And the fourth one?"

Helen looked closely. "The emerald looks familiar." She picked it up, turned it over and a huge smile crossed her face. "Looky here. This scratch."

Gabe bent over, and sure enough, he saw a zigzag mark. And this was the necklace Sophie had given him.

"I assume Peter Ranchard was working for you at the time of the theft."

"Why, yes." She narrowed her eyes. "Do you think he stole it?"

"The evidence supports that suspicion. Did you ever have any misgivings about his honesty?"

"Peter always looked out for Peter. I never had any problems with him, other than his hitting on all the females in the cast, but he never did anything to help anyone other than himself. The police questioned everyone working here at the time. Nothing implicated Peter. Do I get to keep the necklace?"

"Not yet. It's still evidence."

CHAPTER 23

That afternoon at five minutes before four, Gabe dutifully showed up at the Front Range room of the Bearcrest Community Center. As he left the car, he received a call from Camille.

"No fingerprints or other evidence on the burlap bag in the basement of the dinner playhouse," she reported.

"Too bad." Gabe signed off and proceeded into the building. A woman in black slacks and white blouse, her brown hair tied back in a bun, greeted him and handed him an information packet. He took a seat in a folding chair along with half a dozen other people. He didn't recognize anyone in the room — no one he had seen, met or arrested.

At exactly four, the woman cleared her throat. "I'm Vicky Johnson, and I want to thank you for coming to our Meals on Wheels orientation. There are many older citizens in our town who are unable to drive to this community center where meals are served for those who can't cook for themselves. People suffering from disabilities or sickness may be homebound for periods of time, or permanently. Our county is dedicated to provide meals to those who can't afford them or who have difficulty obtaining food and cooking on their own, and our program has been chartered to assist those people. Let's go around the room, and please introduce yourselves and say why you're here."

Five of the people were his age. The sixth was a young man. The kid explained that he was a college student who wanted to help in the community. Gabe nodded at the kid's interest in civic engagement. The others were retired and said they now had time to give back to others. When Gabe's turn came he said, "I recently retired and found myself bored out of my mind."

This brought a chuckle from several of the other retired folks.

"I'm looking for something to help others and thought this would be a good place to start."

Vicky smiled. "Well, we can use all of you. The information sheet I handed out explains our procedure. You can choose days and times of day to make deliveries, whatever works for your schedule. You have to provide documentation of a valid driver's license and automobile insurance. We'll have a background check conducted, and once you pass, you'll be given a list of names. Food packages can be picked up here at the community center a half hour before your delivery times. Any questions?"

"How long will it take for the background check to be done?" a woman in a flowered dress asked.

"We should have it back within a week. We work with the local police department on that."

Gabe could have his completed within the hour.

"Other questions?"

"Can we sample the food?" the kid asked.

"Sure. If you stick around for an hour, I'll let you taste what we're sending out for dinner tonight."

When Gabe returned home, he found Angie in the kitchen. He gave her a kiss and said, "I hope you haven't started anything for dinner yet."

She pointed to an unopened package of noodles, cheese and an empty bowl. "I planned to make a macaroni casserole."

"Put everything away. We're going out to-night."

Angie's eyes bored into him. "Why do I think this has something to do with your investigation?"

He gave a sheepish smile. "I can't put anything over on you. Go get your party shoes. We're going to the Bearcrest Dinner Playhouse to see the performance we missed on Sunday night."

"If you're offering to go to the theater for the second time in one week, I'll have to take advantage of it."

"I've already been there too many times in the last four days, but I need to watch the show, and you'll have a dinner and some entertainment out of it."

"Are you sure we'll be able to get in at this late notice?"

"Yes. I made reservations."

Angie put her hands on her hips. "What if I hadn't wanted to go?"

Gabe shrugged. "I guess I would have had to look for another date."

She whipped the kitchen towel at him, and he scampered away, chuckling.

While Angie changed into theater garb, Gabe sat down to look at his list of retirement activities. Once again, nothing caught his eye. He realized he hadn't spoken with his only son, Hank, in two weeks, so while waiting for Angie, he decided to call him.

Hank picked up. "Hey, Dad. Good to hear from you."

"Your mom and I are going out to the theater in a few minutes, but I thought I'd check in. How's the construction business?"

"Things are finally picking up again. I've got two new houses going up in Tacoma. It's keeping me pretty busy. How's retirement?"

"I'm back working part time on a murder case."

"I figured you wouldn't stay retired long."

"That's what everyone keeps telling me."

"Why don't you and mom take a long road trip? You could visit all the national parks and come stay with Gretchen, Heather and me for a while. Your granddaughter would enjoy seeing you and Mom."

Gabe liked his daughter-in-law but wished Hank had met a girl from Colorado and not Washington. Then he could see his only granddaughter more often. "That's a possibility, after I wrap up this investigation."

Hank chuckled. "You'll end up getting pulled back in on other cases. Anyway, if you ever really retire, plan on traveling."

As they drove to the theater, Gabe said, "I

signed up to volunteer for Meals on Wheels today."

Angie hugged his arm. "Good for you. That will work much better than bridge, crossword puzzles or Sudoku."

"You got that right. I expedited my background check for them, so I can start delivering meals tomorrow if I want. I'll just see how my schedule works with this investigation."

"Any other thoughts on retirement activities?"

"I've had several suggestions that we should do some traveling. We could drive around the country. What do you think?"

"I'd enjoy visiting the kids and grandkids more, but that can't be a permanent activity for you. You still need to find something that you can really focus on when you wrap up this current case you're on."

They arrived at the dinner playhouse and went through the same rigmarole with the actors welcoming them, although Mildred and Sophie both gave Gabe a jaundiced eye. He merely smiled in return.

After they met Alex Newberry, the new butler and Peter's replacement, Angie leaned close to Gabe's ear. "He's even more handsome than Peter. Tonight, will you stick with the theory that the butler did it?"

"No. I expect Alex to be the victim, but I hope he's only acting."

They took their seats with three other couples. One man, who owned an antique shop in Nederland, looked the part of a mountain man complete with deerskin jacket. His wife, who co-managed the store, dressed as if she should have a role in the play as an evil seductress. Another man was a local doctor whose wife directed a non-profit artists' cooperative. The third man proceeded to bore them all with inane jokes while his wife ignored him and talked loudly about her golf game.

Gabe grimaced as each joke became worse than the one before. Then he had a thought and turned to the joke-teller. "Do you play bridge, by any chance?"

The man puffed up. "Why yes, I'm an excellent bridge player."

"In that case I have a contact for you. Give him a call. I think you two will hit it off." Gabe wrote Al Schilling's name down on a sheet from his ever-present notepad and handed it to the man. "He's listed in the Bearcrest phone directory. You two can play bridge together and swap stories."

"Great. I hope he appreciates good jokes."

"If you only knew."

Angie looked at Gabe askance.

"What? I thought he and Al would enjoy each other's company."

The golfing lady cleared her throat so loudly that everyone else at the table stopped talking. "Did you hear that a murder happened here recently?"

"That's why we came," her obnoxious husband said. "This is a mystery playhouse, and we're here to witness a murder."

She glared at him. "No, not a pretend murder. This was a real one."

Gabe and Angie exchanged glances.

"That must be why there's such a large crowd here tonight," Golfing Lady continued. "Do you think anything like that will happen again?"

Her companion gave a dismissive wave. "Nah. You probably just heard a rumor."

At that moment Mildred announced dinner and began calling table numbers to head up for the buffet. Gabe grabbed Angie's hand and raced to the line.

"I detect that you wanted to get away from the table." She squeezed his hand.

"Very perceptive. It's enough to put up with the actors, but to have that jerk performing at our table is too much. I never thought I'd find someone more annoying than Al Schilling, but with this guy, it's a toss-up."

182

"Now, now. Remember, this is a business dinner for you but entertainment for me. Suck it up."

Gabe let out a sigh. "Let me at the chicken."

He loaded up his plate and returned to the table in time for the jokester to ask, "Did you hear the one about the three nuns in the beauty parlor?"

"Yes," Gabe replied.

"But I bet everyone else hasn't." He proceeded to tell the joke and was the only one at the table to laugh at the punch line. This guy even surpassed Al Schilling on the oblivious ranking scale.

"Do you know the one about the guy who couldn't shut up?" Gabe asked him.

The man looked puzzled. "No. Haven't heard it."

Angie gave Gabe a poke in the ribs, but it was worth the pain. "I guess I'll save it for another time."

"In that case I'll tell you the one about the three circus clowns who go into a bar. The first one had a red nose . . ."

Gabe shook his head in disgust and buried his fork in the chicken. During the rest of the meal he tried to tune out the annoying jokester and was finally saved when Mildred stood up to begin the play. Everything proceeded as it had on the previous Sunday night. When the lights went out, Gabe listened carefully. He heard a reverberation as something struck the stage floor.

When the lights came on, the cast members reached for the glasses of wine.

Then a realization struck Gabe. He jumped up from the table, knocking his napkin to the floor and shouted, "Don't anyone drink from the wineglasses!"

The obnoxious joke-teller chuckled. "We have an actor planted at our table. Hey, everyone look at this guy."

Gabe dashed forward and climbed up onto the stage.

Mildred glared at him and in a thinly veiled stage whisper asked, "What are you trying to do?"

"Prevent another poisoning."

Murmurs rippled through the audience. Gabe could hear Angie explaining to people at their table, "He's a real detective. There must be something wrong here."

Gabe pulled aside the table skirt and peered under it. An overturned vial rested on the floor.

CHAPTER 24

It was déjà vu with the exception of there being no Helen Lameuse on stage. Instead a skinny, anemic-looking man had been selected by Alex Newberry as the recipient of the extra glass of wine.

Gabe retrieved the crime kit from his car, snapped on rubber gloves and checked the silver platter containing the wineglasses. He sniffed each one but detected none of the almond aroma. He carefully picked up the vial. The stopper had not been removed, and he found no accompanying tissue this time. He had to work to get the stopper out and caught a whiff of the distinctive almond aroma.

Camille soon appeared, and Gabe asked her immediately to check for fingerprints on the vial.

"I have the fingerprint cards from each of the people on stage Sunday night. I'll see if I can make a quick match," Camille said.

"Good. I don't think there's any poison in the wineglasses but check them thoroughly just in case."

Once Ken Sanchez and Janet Lyon arrived, they divided up responsibilities as on Sunday night. Gabe, again, interrogated Mildred Hanson.

"This is becoming a very disturbing pattern," he said.

"Someone's trying to ruin my theater. Helen's behind this somehow. Did she sneak into the theater? I didn't see her, but she may be in one of her disguises again. She either did something or hired someone to disrupt our performance again."

Gabe jotted a note on his pad. "I doubt she's here, but my fellow police officers will be interviewing everyone. Now, regarding the people on stage, in addition to you, I want to speak with Clara, Sophie, Harold and Arthur this time. I'll need to use your office again."

Mildred let out a long sigh. "I suppose. Let's get on with it."

On the way to Mildred's office, Gabe checked the shelf with the small blue bottles displayed in the lobby. Two distinct empty spots.

Gabe followed Mildred into her office and closed the door. "I heard the bottle hitting the floor this time. Did you?"

"No. My full attention was focused on operating the switch for the lightning, thunder and lights."

"The vial looks exactly like the one used Sunday night, and there's another bottle missing from your lobby display. Did you notice anyone around there earlier this evening?"

"No, but all the actors pass through that area during the pre-show when mingling with the audience."

"I wish I had looked earlier," Gabe said, inwardly chastising himself. "Do you go into your basement often?"

Mildred flicked her hand toward Gabe. "What kind of question is that? I sometimes use the restroom, and we have some old props stored there."

"What about the small room off the very back?"

"That door's jammed shut. I haven't been there in years."

"What was inside the last time you looked?"

Mildred gave a dismissive wave of her hand. "Just some mining paraphernalia. Nothing we ever use."

"But you hadn't cleaned it out?"

"Never got to it. If we ever need some ad-

187

ditional storage space, that will be my next spot."

Gabe continued with the questioning, finding nothing useful from Mildred or Sophie. When he returned to the dining area, Camille pulled him aside and whispered in his ear, "I have a match on two sets of fingerprints — Clara Jager and Mildred Hanson."

Gabe thought over how Mildred's fingerprints had been on the vial used Sunday night and her explanation of how she had originally collected all the bottles and put them on the shelf in the reception area. The new piece of evidence here — Clara's fingerprints. Gabe trotted over to where the actors sat on the stage and signaled for Clara to join him in descending the stairs to Mildred's office.

As before, she rubbed her hands.

"Clara, we previously discussed how you bought illegal drugs from Peter."

"Yeah, we've been over that."

"I also found evidence of the pain pills in Peter's apartment. You admitted that he threatened to raise the price of the medication. You obviously had a motive to want him out of the way. But what were you trying to do tonight?"

She twitched in her seat. "What do you mean?"

"We found your fingerprints on the bottle under the table on the stage. I suspect it contains poison."

She turned white, and her hands shook.

"You'll need to come with me to police headquarters." He then read the Miranda rights to her.

She looked wildly around the office.

Once he finished, he sat back calmly. "Do you understand your rights?"

"Yes."

"Do you want an attorney present now?"

Clara gulped. "That won't be necessary."

"Why don't you save us both time and trouble by explaining what you did tonight?"

She put her head on the desk and sobbed. "You're right. I planned to put poison in a wineglass tonight."

"But the vial didn't have the stopper removed."

"My arthritis. I couldn't get it out, and it slipped out of my hand and rolled under the table."

"Who did you intend to kill?"

"It's not important."

"Did you kill Peter?"

She looked up at Gabe with red eyes and scrunched up her nose. "Whatever."

"Where'd you get the poison?"

"In the basement. I found it two weeks ago."

"And where did you keep it?"

Clara now rubbed her hand at a frantic pace. "I put it in two baggies and kept them in my apartment. One I brought tonight and mixed into the vial."

"And the other baggie?"

Clara frowned. "I couldn't find it this afternoon. I seem to have misplaced it."

"If you couldn't open the vial during the performance, how did you open it earlier to put the poison inside?"

"I had to use a pair of pliers. When I put the stopper back in, I thought I'd be able to get it out again, but apparently I pushed it in too hard. When the lights went out and I tried to open the bottle, it slipped out of my hand and fell under the table."

"Did you tell anyone else that you had found poison in the basement?"

"I mentioned it in passing to the rest of the cast."

Gabe stared at her. "Why'd you do that?"

"I thought they'd find it interesting that something left over from mining days had been stored in the basement."

"And you recognized potassium cyanide?"

Clara resumed vigorously rubbing her

right hand with the palm of her left hand. "Of course. I worked in a supply store when I was younger. I've handled potassium cyanide before."

"I'd like to repeat what I asked earlier. Who was the poison meant for tonight?"

Clara glared at him. "I've already told you; it doesn't matter."

"And the death of Peter Ranchard. Did you poison him?"

"I have nothing more to say. My hands hurt. Can you get me some pain medication?"

CHAPTER 25

After Clara was escorted away, Gabe pulled Mildred aside near the stage. "Clara is the primary suspect in Peter's death, but I have to tell you that you aren't cleared yet."

"What do you mean?"

"We discussed before your fingerprints being on the vial containing the poison used to kill Peter. Well, we found your prints on the bottle tonight as well."

Mildred gave a disgusted sigh. "Do we have to cover that same ground again? I placed all those glass containers on the shelf. As I've told you, if you check, I'm sure you'll find my fingerprints on every one of the bottles up there."

"I understand."

She wagged her right index finger at him. "But you. Every time you come to my show, it's a disaster. I'm not sure I want you to attend any more performances."

Gabe laughed. "I can assure you I had

nothing to do with Peter's poisoning nor this second attempt."

"An interesting statement coming from you of all people, Detective." Mildred gave him a wry smile. "I don't believe in coincidences."

"Touché."

"How soon will Clara be returning?"

"I'm afraid you can't count on her again in the foreseeable future. You'll have to find another replacement."

Mildred threw her hands up in the air. "Great. Just great. Now I have to bring in another new actor by Friday night. Do you know how difficult it is to find someone on such short notice? I jumped through hoops to find a replacement for Peter and now . . ." She stopped with her mouth open, which then slowly curved into a smile. "Say. Here's an idea. How about your wife? Does she want to act?"

Gabe gawked at Mildred. Angie as an actor? "I don't know. Why don't you ask her?"

Mildred marched over to where Angie sat doing her crossword puzzles and cleared her throat loudly.

Angie looked up. "Yes?"

"Since your husband seems bent on doing everything possible to shut down my playhouse, I thought you might be able to help me."

Angie closed her crossword puzzle book and set her pencil on top. "What do you have in mind?"

"It seems I have a little staffing problem. How'd you like to take Clara's place this coming weekend?"

Angie blinked with surprise. "What?"

"I need someone to play Clara's role since your husband has arrested her. Have you had any acting experience?"

Angie smiled. "Why, yes. I played Lady Macbeth in high school and was in several summer stock performances of *South Pacific* after my sophomore year in college."

"You're hired."

"But do you think that's a good idea with Gabe investigating Peter Ranchard's death?" Angie asked.

"Oh, pooh." Mildred wrinkled her nose. "The show must go on."

"You really want me to fill in?"

"The job's yours."

Angie looked toward Gabe. "What do you think?"

He shrugged. "It's up to you."

Angie gave a determined nod of her head. "I think I'll do it."

Gabe studied his wife for a moment.

"Fine. Just don't drink from any of the wineglasses."

As Gabe and Angie drove home, she bounced up and down in the seat. "I'm going to be in a play."

"You never mentioned to me you had any acting experience."

"A brief hobby, but then I became sidetracked with other college activities and a certain man who caught my eye."

Warmth spread through Gabe's chest. "And I'm eternally grateful you even noticed me among all the competition."

"Don't be so modest. I knew immediately what a good man you were, and as they say, a good man is hard to find."

"I'm glad you thought so."

"And I still do."

Gabe tapped the brake pedal as a squirrel charged across the road. "I'll have to come watch your performance on Friday night."

Angie reached over and took his right arm. "I'm not sure Mildred will want you in the playhouse."

"I'll have to sneak in. I can't miss this opportunity to see you on stage."

"I'm surprised that you approve of me doing this."

"Why do you think that? If it's something

you really want to do."

She hugged his arm again. "You're the best."

"And I'll have a spy on the inside."

She released his arm and gave him a punch in the shoulder. "I might have known you had ulterior motives."

"Besides, now I can say I'm sleeping with an actress."

CHAPTER 26

On Thursday morning as Gabe headed out to the car, Al Schilling came running down his walkway to intercept him.

"It's Thursday, Gabe, old buddy. Bridge at the Community Center. Is this the day you're going to join me?"

"Sorry, Al. I have a full schedule of investigative work."

Al sagged like a collapsed balloon. "Aw, gee. I'd hoped this would be the time you'd come along."

"We'll try again, Al."

Gabe drove away, wondering if Al would ever give up pestering him. The one thing you could say for his neighbor — the guy was persistent.

Along the way to the police station, Gabe saw an advertisement on a bus for a cholesterol-reducing medication. He shuddered. He hadn't heard from Dr. Denton regarding the results of his lab work. Had a medical problem been found, and was the doctor now hesitating before informing him? Usually he received a phone call right away. His stomach churned. Maybe this time something was wrong. Had he become a walking time bomb waiting for a heart attack or stroke to happen? He hoped not.

When Gabe arrived at police headquarters, the department administrator, Shirley, handed him an opened envelope with a letter inside. "This came in yesterday, but I didn't realize at first you should see it. It may be relevant to your case. I also left a message on your desk from a call a few minutes ago."

Gabe looked at the address. It merely said Bearcrest Police Department. Without an address or zip code, it could have taken extra time to get here. He unfolded the letter, which read, "Someone is following me. I fear for my life. I think someone is trying to kill me." It was signed Peter Ranchard.

Gabe counted days and realized it could have been mailed right before Peter's death.

Taking the letter to his office, Gabe picked up an unmailed check that he had found in Peter's apartment and compared the signature. Spot on. Why would Peter mail a letter to the police department? If he had concerns, why wouldn't he call and ask for help? Strange.

Peter died Sunday night. At the latest, he could have put this in a mailbox earlier in the day on Sunday. It wouldn't have been picked up until Monday. Normally it would have arrived on Tuesday, but with the lack of a complete address, that would have meant Wednesday. The timeline fit.

And Peter had received the email threat as well. When that was traced it would be an important piece of the puzzle.

After putting the letter and envelope into his manila folder on the case, Gabe picked up the message on his desk, which was to call Dr. James Viceroy. When Gabe returned the call, the receptionist asked him to hold the line, and in two minutes a pretentious male voice declared, "Dr. Viceroy here."

"This is Detective Gabe Tremont from the Bearcrest Police Department. Thank you for calling me back earlier."

"What can I do for you, Detective?"

"I'm trying to track down some information concerning one of your patients — Peter Ranchard."

Gabe heard a derisive laugh. "As you know, Detective, I can't divulge any information that's doctor-patient confidential."

"I understand, Dr. Viceroy. But I think

199

you'll want to help in this particular situation. Peter Ranchard has died under suspicious circumstances."

Gabe smiled to himself as the impact of his statement caused a momentary pause on the line.

"Well . . . uh, there are still HIPPA requirements to protect confidentiality."

"That's correct," Gabe said, "but I'll provide an authorization letter to you. In the case of a criminal investigation, you're allowed to provide information to me. I'm hoping that you may be able to shed some light on Peter and why someone might have wanted to kill him. Your assistance could be instrumental in bringing Peter's killer to justice."

Gabe heard a deep sigh. "I'll need to see a letter."

"Fine. I'll bring one with me. How soon can I meet with you?"

"I'm fully booked with patients today through mid-afternoon, but I should be able to see you late this afternoon. I'll have my receptionist schedule a time."

With an appointment set for four-thirty, Gabe drafted a brief letter stating that the individual in question, Peter Ranchard, had died under suspicious circumstances and that the Bearcrest police sought information in regards to a criminal investigation into the death. He signed it and put it into a manila folder.

At lunchtime, Gabe debated going home for a sandwich or stopping at Garcia's for his favorite Mexican food. Angie kept telling him to stay away from spicy burritos, but Gabe couldn't resist. Giving in to temptation, he went there and ordered the beef *grande* with the green sauce. As he savored the first bite, his mind raced through all he had discovered so far on his case. Clara was now in the county jail for the murder, but something still nagged at him. After sleeping on it overnight, he wasn't convinced that Clara had killed Peter. With a cast of characters all having reasons to see Peter dead, any of the others could have been responsible for the poisoning. And Gabe still had much to learn about the victim.

It was only after he drove away from the restaurant that Gabe felt the wave of heartburn seize his chest. He stopped home to grab two Tums.

"What are you doing raiding the medicine cabinet?" Angie asked.

Gabe hung his head. "I had lunch at Garcia's."

She planted her hands firmly on her hips. "How many times do I have to remind you that you can't handle the peppers anymore?"

"I think this is the last time. I got the message." He burped and popped the two tablets in his mouth.

That afternoon as Gabe drove into Denver hoping to beat rush hour traffic on the inbound leg, knowing he couldn't avoid it on the return, he considered again everything that had transpired. Of the five suspects besides Clara, he hadn't decided on another prime person of interest yet. All had links to Peter that provided a motive for murder, all could have committed the crime but none yet jumped out as more guilty than the rest.

Clara remained in custody, but as he again reviewed the evidence in his mind, he became more convinced that she hadn't actually killed Peter. Maybe learning more regarding Peter's behavior and the reason for seeing a psychiatrist would lead to further insight into the case. Some piece hadn't yet fallen into place.

Dr. Viceroy operated out of a small clinic near the medical complexes surrounding Colorado Boulevard, east of downtown

Denver. The office had the typical collection of outdated magazines, from children's to adult. He only had to wait fifteen minutes before the receptionist led him into a small office with the obligatory medical certificates lining the wall.

Dr. Viceroy, a plump, red-cheeked man in his fifties, held out a pudgy hand that felt like a sock full of sand.

"Thank you for agreeing to meet with me on such short notice." Gabe handed over the letter he had drafted. "Here's the legal document that gives you permission to speak openly with me about Peter Ranchard."

Viceroy read it through, nodded his head and dropped it on his desk. "I'm very distressed to hear that Peter Ranchard passed away."

Gabe studied the man, trying to decide if Viceroy felt real concern or merely regretted the loss of a paying customer. "Yes. I happened to be at the playhouse where he worked on Sunday night. He died from cyanide poisoning."

Viceroy crinkled his nose. "Not a pleasant way to die."

"You're correct. And as I told you on the phone, I'm investigating the case. I found your name on Peter's calendar and am hoping you can lend some insight into Peter's background, character, and anything he might have divulged concerning threats or concerns for his safety. First, tell me why you've been seeing Peter."

"I've been treating him for six months. He originally came to me because he had trouble sleeping."

"And why did he travel all the way to you in Denver when he lived and worked in Bearcrest?"

Viceroy puffed up. "Well, I don't like to brag, but I'm the leading expert on sleep disorders in the Rocky Mountain region. I've published the definitive treatise on sleep deprivation and have garnered recognition for helping a number of celebrities. Peter heard of my reputation and came here seeking treatment. He was concerned that his lack of sleep would affect his ability to stay awake during performances and might negatively impact his career. He thought he might lose his job if the problem wasn't resolved."

"Did you diagnose his sleeping difficulty?"

"Sleep disorders are complex and never have one simple cause. Peter had some . . . uh . . . unique problems. I'm not sure how much I should say."

Gabe gave his most reassuring smile. "I

understand, Doctor. But remember, the information you provide may be instrumental in leading us to the cause of Peter's death. You might provide that one link that clarifies everything."

"I suppose you're right. Well, to be blunt, Peter had an insatiable appetite for attention. He thrived on applause. When he felt he didn't receive adequate recognition, he would become frustrated."

"How did this manifest itself?"

Viceroy tapped his pen on his desk. "He thought people were out to get him. Consequently, he sought escape in sex and became angry."

"And his condition when you last saw him?"

"Interesting question. He complained as always of having difficulty sleeping, but he also felt that things were falling apart around him."

"Did he give any specifics?"

"He said that the relationships with his coworkers had become very stressful. This was his code for people not recognizing his acting ability. He described problems with his boss and several of the other actors."

"Did you ever see Peter in a show?"

Viceroy chuckled. "Yes, I once took my wife to see a mystery at the Bearcrest Dinner Playhouse. Peter was an excellent actor . . . also in the sense that he gave no indications of his underlying problems. At the time I attended, he claimed to be getting little sleep, but no one in the audience would have suspected anything because of his energetic performance, glib demeanor, humor and interaction with the cast members. He appeared completely relaxed and in control of his actions."

"So either Peter could hide the symptoms of his sleep deprivation . . . or might there be any chance he put on an act when he came to your office?"

Viceroy turned his head to the side and pursed his lips. "It's possible. I've had patients who try to con me, but I found no reason for Peter to put on an act with me. He liked to be the center of attention, but I could see no reason that he would pay my fees to try to entertain me. No, I think he suffered from a legitimate sleep disorder but had learned to conceal the problem from others."

"When investigating cases, I have to look at all possible causes of death. Did you consider Peter suicidal?"

Viceroy laughed. "Far from it. He thought too much of himself. He possessed a strong narcissistic streak and never gave any indications of wanting to harm himself. He once commented that he wanted to live forever."

"What about the possibility of drinking too much?"

"He never discussed any substance abuse, and when he came to his appointments, I never saw any indications that he was drunk or on drugs."

"One of his coworkers reported to me that Peter drank excessively but not in public. What's your thought on that?"

Viceroy now tapped his pen against his cheek. "It's possible. In our society many people over-imbibe at times."

"Did he ever mention any grudges, arguments or indicate he thought someone wanted to kill him?"

Viceroy smiled. "Peter exhibited a certain amount of paranoia. He often shared stories of people who disliked him."

"And the most recent time you met with him?"

"Yes, he did seem to be even more upset than usual. He said he suspected someone wanted to kill him."

CHAPTER 27

Gabe leaned forward. "You have my attention, Dr. Viceroy. Did Peter give any hint who wanted to kill him?"

"He thought a number of people were out to get him. He said he suspected all the people he worked with and a previous employer."

"Very interesting. I'd like to mention some names to you, and tell me if Peter ever talked about them to you. First of all, Mildred Hanson."

"Oh, yes. His current employer. He admitted a romantic encounter with her. He stated he felt uncomfortable with the affair and called it off. He feared that Ms. Hanson would find some way to get back at him. He said she was very vindictive and might try to punish him for breaking off the relationship."

"Did he give any specifics on what he thought she'd do to him?"

"No. Only that he no longer felt comfortable in her presence. I think fear of her might have contributed to his inability to sleep well."

"Let me mention another name. Helen Lameuse."

"Ah. The former employer. Peter said she coerced him into spying on Ms. Hanson. He said he had told her he no longer wanted to do it. She apparently threatened him unless he continued to cooperate."

"Did he divulge the nature of this threat?"

"No, he went into no further details."

"Does the name Clara Jager ring a bell?"

"Hmm." Dr. Viceroy snapped his fingers. "That may be the woman who forced him to provide painkillers."

Gabe leaned forward. "That's the one. What do you mean 'forced him'?"

"Peter explained that he helped her out with some pain pills once in the past, and then she continued to demand further medication from him. She paid him for a while and then refused to pay any longer, saying she'd get even with him if he didn't keep up with the supply. He didn't feel safe around her either."

"That doesn't make sense. She would have more to lose than he did."

Viceroy tapped his pen on his desk again.

"I'm only reporting what I heard."

"Here's another name. Harold Coats."

"Ah, the gentleman with a criminal past. Yes, Peter found out the man had committed a theft. He said he was afraid Mr. Coats would hurt him because of his discovery."

"Did he mention blackmailing Harold Coats?"

"No. That didn't come up."

"How about Arthur Buchanan?"

"Yes. The man who disapproved of Peter's relationship with a young woman. He said that Mr. Buchanan threatened him on several occasions."

"Did Peter tell you that the young woman and Mr. Buchanan planned to marry?"

"No, he didn't."

"One final name. Sophie Elmira."

"Uh-huh. Another girlfriend. Peter said she became too possessive, and he had to break off the relationship. He feared that she would become violent."

"But he never mentioned that he abused her?"

"No, he didn't."

"Did you consider Peter capable of abusing a woman?"

Viceroy sucked on his lip for a moment. "I would say that would not have been his normal pattern, but under sleep deprivation

210

he could have become angry and hurt someone if provoked."

"So in Peter's world, all these people had it in for him," Gabe said.

"That's exactly what he communicated."

"And they caused all the problems."

Viceroy smiled. "Very observant, Detective. Yes, Peter had an inability to take responsibility. He quickly blamed others."

"And all of this fed into his sleep problem."

"Apparently so. This also tied into the important aspect of his personality that I mentioned earlier. He thrived on being the center of attention, a desire that began as a child. Being an orphan, he sought recognition through putting on clever skits for his peers. This led to his choice to pursue an acting career. He adored the admiration of the audience when he stepped on stage. Between acting jobs, he craved to be back on stage. This also contributed to his sleeping disorder. He would toss and turn at night thinking back over past performances, trying to figure out how to be better, how to catch the attention of a major director. He wanted to be on a larger stage than a mystery playhouse. He often told me he dreamed of a grand dramatic role never achieved by any other actor."

"Didn't he audition for other shows?"

"Yes, but he hadn't been successful in achieving the next level in his career. He told me people undervalued his talent."

Gabe thought back to seeing Peter during the preshow at the Bearcrest Dinner Playhouse. "Do you think he had an overinflated view of his own ability?"

"I think Peter was an excellent actor, but his chosen career required patience, an attribute Peter did not possess."

"Did he ever mention stealing a necklace and money from a playhouse?"

Viceroy shook his head. "That never came up."

"Have you ever visited Peter's apartment?"

Dr. Viceroy gave an indulgent smile. "No, that's not the way I operate. My patients always come to my office."

"I discovered he suffered from a hoarding disorder."

"What!" Viceroy popped out of his chair.

"Yes. When I went to his apartment, I found one to three feet of accumulated trash and belongings covering the floor."

Viceroy's mouth dropped open. "That makes no sense whatsoever. He was a very meticulous individual."

"From looking at his apartment, I can tell

you that he took care of personal grooming and clean clothes, but other than that his place was a disaster area. Have you ever treated anyone with a hoarding disorder?"

"Why, yes. I have one other patient I'm working with. She came to me because she couldn't throw anything away."

"The same as Peter. I'm surprised that he never divulged this aspect of his behavior to you, or that you never picked up hints of it."

Viceroy shook his head vigorously. "Never. Very strange."

"Yes, it is. Did you give Peter any medication?"

"I'm not a big fan of drug therapy. That can easily be abused. But one time I did prescribe sleeping pills."

"Do you know where he would have filled the prescription?"

"He probably used a pharmacy in Bearcrest."

"And only one time?"

Viceroy adjusted the cuff of his long-sleeved shirt and then stretched his arms. "That's correct."

"Is there anything else that came up in your last meeting with Peter?"

"Yes. With all the people who had reasons to hate him, he feared that something bad might happen over the weekend. He didn't have any specifics other than feeling extremely paranoid."

CHAPTER 28

As Gabe crept along in the rush-hour traffic on Highway 270 between Colorado Boulevard and I-36, he contemplated what he had heard. Peter had certainly been selective in what he told Dr. Viceroy and what he omitted. Peter was a man with emotional problems, seeking acclaim in the theater but not achieving what he wanted. And he possessed a knack for alienating his fellow actors through misguided relationships and apparent illegal activities.

Peter had certainly snowed Dr. Viceroy. Gabe couldn't decide if Peter was that good an actor or if Viceroy was that bad a psychiatrist. Probably a little of each.

He again reviewed the conversation, trying to pull out any useful tidbits from the background noise. Dr. Viceroy indicated that Peter suspected six people hated him, and they all had good reasons to want Peter out of the way. Now Peter was dead. Everyone on stage had access to the wineglasses during the time the lights went out, and anyone on stage could have earlier acquired potassium cyanide from the basement. Gabe realized he needed to pursue another round of interviews with the six suspects. He would get on that first thing in the morning.

But for now he had to battle this heavy traffic.

When Gabe got home, he was eager to work off the frustration from the freeway traffic. Needing some exercise, he changed into hiking shorts, boots and a T-shirt bearing the picture of an eagle.

"You want to join me for a hike in the foothills?" Gabe asked Angie.

"You go ahead by yourself. I'm in the middle of a scrapbooking project."

Gabe took off on his own, grateful that he hadn't added working on scrapbooks to his list of retirement projects. Angie enjoyed it, but he would go nuts after half an hour of organizing old pictures and memorabilia.

He headed up Bearcrest Canyon, pulled off onto a dirt road and parked at a trail-head. The late-afternoon sun had dipped behind the Continental Divide, but at this latitude there would be another hour and a half of light with the long twilight.

Gabe strode along the trail and took in a deep breath of air, sniffing the scent of pine. There had been no other cars in the parking lot, and he cherished this time to himself with only the sound of wind rustling through the trees and the periodic squawk of blue jays. He climbed up a steep incline and came to a feeder stream that eventually combined with Bearcrest Creek. There was still a reasonable flow of water, and stepping stones provided a means of crossing without getting his boots wet. He planted his right foot on the first rock and stepped out into the stream. On the second rock his left boot didn't gain purchase. His foot slipped, and with his arms pinwheeling, he splashed facedown into the water.

Even in summer the water was still cold. He dragged himself out of the stream and used his hands to wring as much water from his shirt and shorts as he could. A gash on his knee accompanied scrapes on his hands.

He shivered. The gentle breeze now felt like an arctic blast. No sense getting hypothermia. He hadn't thought to bring a jacket. He should have known better. When hiking in the mountains, it was always advisable to bring extra layers. The weather could change in an instant, or he could do some-

217

thing stupid — like falling in a stream.

Gabe limped back to the trailhead, drove home and crossed hiking off his list of retirement activities.

That evening after dinner, Angie handed the script for her part as the maid at the Mystery Dinner Playhouse to Gabe. "I need you to help me rehearse my lines."

Angie might as well have handed Gabe a live grenade. He regarded the script in his hand. "What am I supposed to do with this?"

She *tsk*ed. "It's simple. Just read the part right before the lines I've highlighted with a yellow marker."

"I guess I can handle that." Gabe sat down at the dining room table and looked at the first page. He spotted the initial highlighted set of lines. Right before it was a short speech by Alex, whose name had been written in and Peter's struck out. Gabe cleared his throat. "As you wish, madam."

Angie bowed. "I'll assist him, mum."

"Spot on, Angie," Gabe said.

Angie tapped her foot. "Save the editorial comments. Just read the preceding lines. Go to the next line."

"Okay. Okay." Gabe scanned down the page. Nothing else highlighted. Turning the page, he came to the next prompt for Angie. The name Clara was scratched out and Angie's name written in. "Angie, go see what has happened to Alex."

Angie walked away and then ran back with her face scrunched up. She put her hand to her forehead. "Alex is dead."

Gabe nodded approvingly.

"You can skip ahead several pages to where Detective Whodoneit appears," Angie informed him.

"Got it." Gabe leafed through pages until he found the next highlighted section. "Okay, here goes." He simulated a British accent. "And who might you be?"

"I'm Angie, the maid."

"A simple maid?"

"No, sir. I'm not simple. I'm quite bright."

Gabe groaned.

"Hush." Angie glared at him.

"Let me rephrase that. Are you simply a maid?"

"Of course. I'm not the butler."

"Did you poison Alex, the butler?"

"No, sir. I don't make a practice of poisoning butlers."

"What do you make a practice of?"

"I don't have to practice at all. I'm quite proficient now."

Gabe stuck out his tongue and inserted a

finger in his mouth, garnering another glare from Angie.

"Don't leave this inn. I'll need to question you again."

"I promise not to go out of the inn."

They continued through the rest of the script. When they finished, Gabe threw it down on the table. "How can you memorize this dreck?"

"It's not that bad."

"And that gawd-awful detective. No law enforcement official would ever act that dumb."

"He's supposed to look stupid."

"Well, I resent that."

Angie reached over and patted his arm. "This is a mystery theater with an emphasis on humor. It's just a play, dear. Just a play."

"I guess you're right. It still riles me."

"Don't take it personally."

"Do you need to run through it again?" Gabe asked.

"Thanks for helping me. I'm good."

And she was. Gabe realized why Angie would be the theater person for the family and why he had never put acting on his list of potential retirement activities.

CHAPTER 29

On Friday morning Gabe grabbed a cup of coffee and a piece of toast, gave Angie a kiss on her cheek, headed outside and drove off to police headquarters. His banged knee from the hike the afternoon before felt better, and he hardly had a limp at all.

It was a sunny morning, one that could have pulled him into the mountains for a hike, if he hadn't struck that off his retirement list, or to try his new fishing pole, but today he needed to put more of the pieces together on his case. He took in a deep breath of fresh air and smelled the faint aroma of freshly baked bread from the Bearcrest Bakery. He imagined sinking his teeth into a hot bear claw, the local specialty. He lowered his window and felt the breeze run across the hairs on his arm. When he stopped at the intersection of Main and Pine, he heard birds chirp and then saw swallows swoop through the intersection, probably trying to catch insects for break-fast.

As he turned onto Pine Street, he saw the distinctive flashing red and blue lights of a police cruiser and an EMT van parked in the Bearcrest Shopping Mall. Given that he was driving his own car and didn't have a police radio, he had no clue as to what had happened. Curious, he pulled in and found Officer Ken Sanchez coming out of Bear-crest Hardware.

Ken looked up and nodded to Gabe. "You here to check out the scene?"

"No. I just happened to see the lights on your squad car. What's going on?"

"A robber struck the hardware store thirty minutes ago. Took all the money out of the safe, knocked Violet Kartagian to the floor and took off. She called nine-one-one, and here I am. I can use your help."

At that moment Gabe's cell phone jangled. He answered to hear Chief Bradley Lewis's distinctive deep southern accent. "Gabe, I need ya to help out."

"I'm at the hardware store right now," he replied.

"That's the one. Ned had a relapse and is back home sick again. Brad won't return from his vacation until Monday. You have to jump in on this one for me."

Gabe looked skyward. "I have my hands full with the Bearcrest Playhouse case and am only working part time."

"You have to cover this one. You can tack on extra hours for the next week."

Gabe let out a sigh. "Since I'm already here, I'll do it. But I don't want to get diverted from the other case."

"I know you can handle both." The phone clicked off.

"Great," he muttered. "Some retirement." Might as well get going on it. Then he realized that he really wasn't that disappointed.

He entered the hardware store and found an EMT tending to Violet, who sat on the floor.

"I'll take you to the hospital," the EMT said to Violet.

She ran her hand over her bleached blond hair. "That's okay. It isn't that much of a bump."

"You should see a doctor."

"No, I'm fine. I don't need any medical attention."

The EMT regarded her skeptically but finally packed his bag and headed back to his van.

Gabe bent over and said, "Violet, I need to ask you some questions."

Her large brown eyes met his. "Sure." She was in her late twenties, good complexion, on the positive side of plain with a rounded face.

Gabe took out his notebook. "Tell me everything that happened this morning since you arrived at the store."

She stroked the top of her head and winced. "We open the store at nine, so I got here at eight-thirty to unlock, turn on the lights, put out the daily specials signs and get some money from the safe to put in the cash register. I didn't notice anyone being here, but right after I opened the safe a man came out of the storeroom and pointed a gun at me."

"Did he follow you in or had he been in the store already?"

"No one could have followed me in without me noticing him. He must have been hiding from earlier."

"Who has keys to the store?"

"Only Mr. Madison and me. We take turns opening." She snuffled. "Today was my turn and look what happens."

"Describe the man with the gun."

She shook her head. "I didn't get much of a view of him and couldn't see his face. He wore a black ski mask."

"His clothes?"

She bit her lip. "I was pretty shaken up and didn't pay attention real well. I think jeans and a gray sweatshirt." Then she looked up at Gabe. "He wore some kind of gloves."

"Anything written on the sweatshirt?"

"Not that I noticed."

"How small or large of a man?"

She gulped. "He was big and tall. Maybe six-foot-five with lots of muscles like a football player or weightlifter."

"Could you tell his age?"

"Not really. I think he was maybe old, like in his forties."

Gabe realized how his perspective had changed. At his age, forties was practically a young pup. "What led you to that conclusion?"

"He had kind of a growly voice that sounded older."

"What kind of gun did he point at you?"

"I don't know much about guns. It was big and gray."

Gabe jotted a note. "So what happened after he pointed the gun at you?"

"He told me to empty the contents of the safe into a large garbage bag. I did exactly as he asked. Mr. Madison trained me never to argue if we have a robbery. He says life is more important than money."

"Good advice. Do you know how much money was in the safe?"

"It had to be a lot. Mr. Madison always goes to the bank on Friday afternoon, so the last week's proceeds were in the safe. Most of our customers pay in cash, and it was a busy week. There was probably thirty thousand dollars taken."

Someone who knew the store's operation, Gabe realized. Selecting the right day of the week, arriving at the right time of day to find only one person here and knowing it would be good pickings.

"And after you gave him the money?"

"He knocked me to the floor." She rubbed her head. "Then he left. I was stunned but pulled out my cell and punched in nine-one-one. Then I called Mr. Madison. He was in a meeting in Denver but is on his way back here."

"Did you notice any other cars in the parking lot when you arrived this morning to open the store?"

"There are always cars for the Bearcrest Café two doors away." She paused and wrinkled her forehead as if trying to replay the scene. "Nothing unusual."

"Have you recently seen anyone snooping around the store or asking questions about how you operate?"

"No, nothing like that."

Gabe looked up and noticed something that made him smile. "I see you have a surveillance camera."

Violet nodded. "Won't do any good. We keep a recording unit in the storeroom. The robber removed the tape. He made a point of telling me before he hit me."

Camille, the crime scene tech, arrived. Gabe gave Violet one of his cards and told her to contact him if she remembered anything else about the robber. Then he pulled Camille aside to chat. "I don't think you'll find any useful prints. Violet indicated the guy was wearing gloves. But check the storage room and around their surveillance recorder as well. The perp was in there and handled the recorder."

"Okay, Gabe."

He had one other thought. Camille also filled in as a crime scene artist. She had been a double major in college — art and forensic science. "After you complete the crime scene, spend some time with Violet and put together a sketch of the subject."

"Will do. I have my sketch pad and charcoal in the car."

He left Camille to do her thing and looked at the front and back doors but could find no evidence of the locks being tampered with. Then he went to the neighboring stores. Nothing was open on either side of the hardware store. At the Bearcrest Café, he interviewed the waitress, cook and half a dozen customers. No one had seen a man enter or leave the hardware store.

Gabe returned to the hardware store and found Sanford Madison had arrived. Gabe pulled him aside. "Have you seen anyone snooping around or asking about how you run your store?" Gabe asked.

"No. This all comes as quite a shock to me. All the years I've been in business, this is the first burglary."

"Actually, it's classified as an armed robbery and assault since Violet was confronted and struck on the head and the guy carried a gun."

He nodded. "We've never had any problems whatsoever. And I haven't noticed anyone acting suspicious."

"How long has Violet worked here?"

He smiled. "Three years. She's a pip. Great employee and very conscientious. Best and hardest worker I've ever had."

Gabe made one more pass through the store and left Camille to complete her work. He headed into police headquarters and went to his desk, where he found a note that had been left from Sid Axley, the computer guy.

Gabe moseyed over to Sid's office and knocked on the door.

Sid sat slumped over, madly pounding on his keyboard, but finally paused and looked up at Gabe. "Hey, man. I got something for you — the source of that email address Camille passed on to me."

"That's right. I've been so busy I forgot to check back with you."

Sid wagged an index finger at Gabe. "You're too young to have short-term memory loss."

"Thanks for the vote of confidence. So who sent the threatening email to Peter Ranchard?"

"The email account belongs to Sophie Elmira."

The plot thickens. Gabe immediately called Sophie and informed her he would be stopping by shortly.

When he pulled up to the curb, he scanned the neighboring woods to make sure no mountain lions wanted to use him or his car as a scratching post.

Sophie greeted him at the door. "What now, Detective?"

"I'd like to ask your permission to check the email history on your computer."

She shrugged. "Sure, why not? You'll find my computer in the bedroom. It's on all the time, so help yourself."

Gabe sat down, hit the space bar, and the screen popped up. "You don't use a password?" Gabe shouted.

From the other room came the reply, "No. I never bothered to set one up."

Gabe shook his head. She was as bad as Peter. He started scanning through sent email messages. He checked for the date that Peter had received the threat and found no record of a message having been sent.

"Do you delete email messages that you send?"

She shook her head. "No. I don't send very many, so I don't bother cleaning them out."

"Did you send any messages to Peter last week?"

She looked confused. "No. I never communicated with him via email."

Gabe watched her carefully. She appeared genuinely sincere. But then again, she was an actor.

"Did you know Peter was seeing a psychiatrist?"

Her mouth dropped open. "Are you kidding? He never mentioned that."

"Did he ever complain of trouble sleeping?"

"No way. He always sacked out like a dead man."

"Did you ever threaten Peter?"

Sophie gave him a scorching look. "Detective, it was the other way around. He threatened me."

As Gabe drove away, something else gnawed at him. He decided to stop by the Creekside Playhouse. He replayed in his mind what he had seen on the night he had first gone to the Bearcrest Playhouse. Helen had been snooping around her competitor's theater. She had been in the basement, in Mildred's office and then on stage at the time of Peter's death. And she had initially lied to him about not knowing Peter.

He found Helen in her office.

She looked up, giving him an exasperated sigh. "Now what?"

"I'm making the rounds today, checking with all the witnesses from Sunday night. I want to ask if you have thought of anything else you noticed on the night of Peter's death."

She shook her head. "We've been over all of it before. Nothing new."

"You wore a disguise that night. Is everything here?"

"Yes. I used a black pantsuit, vest, wig and glasses."

"Would you be kind enough to show them to me?"

"If it will get you to leave me alone." She stood up and led him to her backstage area. "Here's the clothes rack with the pantsuit and vest. The wig and glasses are on that counter over there."

"Have you worn this outfit since Sunday night?"

"No. It's been hanging here unused since then."

Gabe patted down the black pants and found nothing. Then he checked the vest, feeling something in the left pocket. He reached in and pulled out a sandwich bag with white crystals inside.

Helen gaped. "Where did that come from?"

CHAPTER 30

"Are you going to arrest me?" Helen asked after Gabe had informed her he suspected incriminating poison might be in the bag found in the vest she had worn to the Bearcrest Mystery Playhouse Sunday night.

"Not now. I have to confirm what's in the bag. But is there anything you want to tell me?"

She shook her head. "I have no clue how that ended up in my pocket. I never noticed it and if I had, wouldn't have left it there."

"Just don't go out of town," Gabe said.

"Don't worry. I have a theater to run. I'll be right here if you need me."

Gabe drove home to grab a ham sandwich with Angie.

"How's the investigation going?" she asked.

"I've been busy. Uncovered new information concerning Peter Ranchard's death, and the chief gave me an additional case this morning."

"Another case? But you're retired."

"So they tell me, but I need to help out. The Bearcrest Hardware Store was robbed."

Angie put her hand to her cheek. "Oh, dear. Was anyone hurt?"

"Violet Kartagian got a bump on the head, but she's okay."

"What about your main case?"

"It continues to become more complicated. The more I get into it, the more I think all six of the suspects are guilty."

Angie gave him a thoughtful smile. "Maybe they worked together like in Agatha Christie's *Murder on the Orient Express*."

"That's the one you made me watch." Gabe took a bite of sandwich.

Angie *tsk*ed at him. "For a detective, you sure aren't very familiar with mystery literature."

"That's one of the items on my retirement to-do list. One of these days I'm going to start reading mystery novels."

"In all your spare time?"

"Once these two cases are over, I'll be back to having lots of time on my hands. Then I can read."

Angie glared at him. "Anyway, do you even remember the plot of *Murder on the*

Orient Express?"

"No. Something with a bunch of people on a train."

She gave an exasperated sigh. "You either have a short attention span or are starting to suffer short-term memory loss."

"Give me a break. You're the second person today to question my memory. I remember important things. But TV shows don't stick with me. What's the big deal with this movie?"

"Like with your playhouse crime, a murder is committed, and a number of people have motives for killing the deceased guy."

"Similar so far."

"The punch line — they all took turns stabbing the victim. They had a pact to work together to kill him."

"Hmm. So you think my six suspects could have been working together to kill Peter Ranchard?"

Angie shrugged. "Just a thought."

"I'll keep that in mind, although I can't see Mildred and Helen cooperating on anything. But I did uncover an interesting clue. I found what I suspect to be potassium cyanide crystals in the pocket of the vest worn by Helen Lameuse on Sunday night."

"That sounds suspicious."

"Still, it doesn't make sense for Helen to keep evidence of poison after the murder." Gabe swallowed the last bit of his sandwich.

"Maybe Mildred committed the murder and put the bag in Helen's pocket. She would love to see Helen blamed for what happened."

"That's a possibility."

Angie picked up their plates and took them to the sink. "I take it you're not convinced that Clara committed the murder."

"No. She made a halfhearted confession but never outright admitted to poisoning Peter, and my gut isn't convinced she's the one."

"Do you have a favorite right now?"

"That's the problem. Everyone seems guilty with no one person jumping out as the prime suspect yet."

Back at the office, Gabe deposited the baggie of white crystals with Camille to verify the contents. "Also check for fingerprints. See whose you find besides mine. Did you discover anything at the hardware store?"

"Slim pickings. Most of the fingerprints matched Sanford Madison or Violet Kartagian. I couldn't find any shoeprints or useful fibers. The guy got in and out without leaving anything I could find."

"What about a sketch?"

Camille groaned. "Violet wasn't very helpful. She didn't see the guy's face. Here's all I could put together." She handed him a sketch that looked like a hooded wrestler on *WWE Smackdown.*

Gabe next called Mildred and reached her in her office at the playhouse. "I have a question to ask you."

"You've been full of questions this week. I hope this doesn't take long. I have a lot going on."

"I'll be fast. Did Peter ever display evidence of not getting enough sleep?"

"Are you kidding? That guy displayed more energy than all the rest of us put together. Clara would fall asleep between scenes, but Peter stayed wound up and hyper the whole time. He was like the Energizer Bunny on uppers."

"Thanks. I'll let you get back to work."

As he hung up, he wondered why Peter had sought treatment from Dr. Viceroy. Neither Mildred nor Sophie had seen indications of a sleeping disorder. What had Peter, the consummate actor, really been up to?

Gabe wrote up notes on all that had happened, still not reaching any conclusions.

Checking his watch, he saw it was time to go meet the cleaning guy.

After parking, Gabe strolled up to Peter's apartment, and moments later a lanky man in his thirties wearing work boots, a tattered denim shirt and worn jeans arrived. He introduced himself as Tom Buelson.

"I hope you're prepared for a disaster area," Gabe warned.

Tom opened his hands. "Hey, that's what we specialize in. Water damage, fires. You mess it up, we clean it up."

Gabe unlocked the apartment door, leaned in to flick on the light and then let Tom experience the sight.

Tom whistled. "You weren't kidding. What a trashed-out place."

"Have you seen something like this before?"

Tom nodded. "Yeah. We had one other gig with a hoarder. Let me scope out the place." He tromped through the apartment, took a number of pictures with a digital camera and jotted some notes on a pad.

"I want to work through the contents in here with you," Gabe said. "I'll need your crew to sort through everything and cart out the refuse, but I want to look at any paperwork that's uncovered."

"No problem. I'll have a Dumpster

brought in, and we can set aside anything of interest for you. I need to talk to one of my guys in the office and can have a quote for you in an hour. We could start mid-morning on Monday."

"How long do you estimate it'll take to clear out this place?"

Tom scrunched up his nose. "Two full days."

"Give me a call on my cell. If you keep the bid reasonable, I can give you authorization immediately."

"You got it."

After Tom left, Gabe snapped on a pair of rubber gloves. As long as he was here, he wanted to poke around a little. Surveying the chaos again, he decided to leave the living room, kitchen and hall to the experts. But there might be something useful around the desk area in the bedroom.

Gabe climbed the mound of trash and threaded his way toward the hall. On the downward side of one mound, his foot slipped out from under him as a magazine slid away. He landed solidly on his tailbone, fortunately not hitting anything harder than newspaper. He gingerly stood and navigated his way into the bedroom. Was he turning into a decrepit geezer? First falling in the stream and now this.

He pushed aside fast food bags and examined the trash close to the desk. Nothing of interest stood out. Then he remembered the bottom drawer he hadn't been able to open on the previous visit. He pushed aside a stack of newspapers and magazines, but the drawer still opened only a few inches.

This would take some work. He cleared off the top of the pile of trash closest to the desk and threw it toward the middle of the room. The more he shoved away, the more refuse collapsed into the empty space. It took him thirty minutes to finally clear aside a space so that the drawer could be opened all the way. He peered inside and spotted nothing but the back of a pad of paper. He reached in and retrieved it. Turning it over, he identified it as an unused portion of a prescription pad with the letterhead of Doctor James Viceroy.

CHAPTER 31

After discovering the prescription slips, Gabe took out his cell phone and immediately called Dr. Viceroy.

"He's with a patient at the moment and has a very busy schedule this afternoon," the receptionist informed Gabe.

"This is Detective Tremont. I'm following up on the meeting I had with him. How long will he be tied up with his current patient?"

"Another thirty minutes or so."

"I'd appreciate if you could have him call me after his appointment and before the next one begins. Tell him this is urgent."

Gabe continued to sort through paper near the desk. He found some old bills for telephone and utilities. Obviously, Peter didn't have a filing system other than tossing things on the floor. Intermixed were pages of scripts. Rather than disposing of them, Peter had just pitched them among his other piles of papers.

The job continued to be a challenge to keep a cleared area from being inundated from nearby debris. It reminded Gabe of trying to dig in dry sand as a kid and having the sides of his hole continuously collapsing.

He quit after fifteen more minutes, his head throbbing from the stuffy surroundings. He sneezed. Taking a handkerchief out of his pocket, he wiped his nose to eliminate the accumulated dust.

Escaping outside, Gabe took a deep breath of fresh air. He reminded himself to bring a surgical mask for the extended time in the apartment on Monday. It was either that or a scuba outfit with an oxygen tank on his back.

As Gabe plopped down on the seat of his car and put the key in the ignition, his phone rang.

"Detective, Dr. Viceroy returning your call. My receptionist informed me that you needed to speak with me urgently."

"Yes, thanks for the quick call back. I found several blanks from a prescription pad with your name on it in Peter's apartment. Why would he have that?"

Viceroy gasped loudly over the phone. "He shouldn't. I'll be darned. Peter must have taken part of a prescription pad from my office."

"Yes. He may have forged your signature and used the prescription slips to order illegal drugs."

There was a pause on the line. "This is a very troubling situation. Do I need to speak with a lawyer?"

"That's up to you, Dr. Viceroy. I'm only investigating the death of Peter Ranchard. But you may want to look into your procedure for controlling access to your prescription slips. If Peter got hold of them, someone else could as well."

After closing his cell phone, Gabe shook his head. How things had changed. Now, doctors had to guard their prescription pads just as they had to lock up their drugs. With all the black marketing in medication, stealing prescription pads had become an easy way to buy pills and resell them at street prices. That, plus the increased demand for all types of painkillers.

Gabe couldn't believe how careless Dr. Viceroy had been. Hopefully, he would rectify the situation.

Gabe now knew how Peter had obtained the pills he sold to Clara Jager. Forging prescriptions, stripping labels off the bottles, and then charging a premium to his good customer and fellow actor. Nice little side-line business. Peter had been a busy fellow before he succumbed to cyanide poisoning.

CHAPTER 32

On Friday evening Gabe stopped by Bear-crest Florists. What to buy? He regarded the display of chrysanthemums, daisies and carnations. No, these wouldn't do. It had to be a dozen roses. Scanning through the shop, he selected the freshest and most pristine ones available. Nothing but the best for his bride.

As he returned to his car with his purchase in hand, he thought of one of the items on his retirement to-do list — gardening. Could he grow roses as pretty as these? He had successfully tended a vegetable garden many years before, but the rigors of his job took over, and he abandoned the exercise after two seasons. He had never tried his hand with posies. He could imagine the front of their house lined with the colors of the rainbow. On the other hand, he could also picture shriveled and dead plants everywhere. He shook his head. He didn't think gardening would be his retirement magic bullet, but he might give it a try one of these days. You never could tell what would stick.

He hadn't seen much of Angie the last two days between his investigation and her rehearsals. And now he'd be having his third meal at the playhouse within a week. He was receiving a comp as a result of sleeping with an actress in the show. He smiled to himself. He looked forward to seeing Angie on the stage. This time he'd watch the whole show without anyone fooling around with cyanide.

He headed off to the Bearcrest Dinner Playhouse by himself and thought of Angie already there getting dressed in her maid's costume, jittery with excitement before her first performance.

When he entered the building, he hid the bouquet of roses in the alcove and then ran the gauntlet with the contingent of actors. Angie in her maid's uniform came up and propositioned him. He promised he'd take her up on it after the show.

He completed an uneventful meal with no bore telling stupid jokes. In fact, he sat with three couples who all knew each other and included him in their conversation on skiing and hiking. He even contributed recommendations on several hiking trails they had not been on before. He didn't mention the one with the stream he had fallen into.

During the chitchat he never divulged his occupation, merely indicating he was retired. Not exactly the case, but no need to bother going into details with strangers. Besides, the others in the group seemed content with telling their stories and life experiences. Gabe had learned to be a good listener and had no compulsion to talk about himself tonight.

After surviving the third chicken dinner in a week and resisting the urge to start clucking, Gabe sat back to watch Angie in action. After helping her rehearse, he knew the show cold. He could have even written a review for the *Bearcrest Gazette*.

Everything progressed as planned through the blackout. Alex Newberry staggered offstage, and Angie followed him, shortly thereafter letting out a blood-curdling scream before she raced back on stage to announce Alex's demise.

She did it so convincingly that Gabe had to restrain himself from dashing up on stage. That would have set Mildred off, screaming and shouting at him, accusing him of again disrupting the show.

Alex came back in a rumpled suit and

large shaggy mustache as the incompetent Inspector Whodoneit, who destroyed evidence, trampled clues and butchered his lines. Alex didn't match Peter as an actor, but Angie held her own. Gabe thought she performed even better than Clara. Maybe Angie had a new career here. She might have found her retirement niche, even if he hadn't.

At the end of the show, Alex, in his role as the inspector, came back on stage to tell each table to decide who had committed the murder and pick a spokesperson for the table. The three couples unanimously elected Gabe to present their results. Everyone debated for five minutes with a vote each for Arthur, Harold and Sophie and two votes each for Mildred and Angie. Finally, the others said that Gabe could decide.

When Alex pointed to his table, Gabe stood up to speak. "Evidence links all the suspects to the crime, but we vote for Angie as the murderer. She had access to the poison, had the motivation because of being blackmailed by Alex and stood close to the wine when the lights went out."

No other table selected Angie. His tablemates gave Gabe those pathetic smiles that indicated *good try, but we lost.* Finally, Alex made the announcement that Angie had committed the murder. Gabe and the others at his table received wineglasses with the embossed logo of the playhouse.

Gabe received high fives, pats on the back and had his hand practically wrenched off with one vigorous shake. He gave everyone his aw-shucks smile.

If solving real murders were only this easy.

After the show Gabe retrieved the flowers and waited for Angie to appear. When she came out from backstage he handed her the roses and gave her a peck on the cheek. "You're quite an actor."

She twirled around holding the bouquet. "Flowers on my opening night. And only you solved the mystery."

"I've had a little practice."

She gave him a sideways glance. "Maybe you were just lucky, since we change who committed the crime every show."

"Yes. I definitely am lucky — first with my guess and second to have this beautiful actress accompanying me home. And I seem to remember some promise she made in the reception area before the show started."

She snuggled up against him. "Hmm. I don't remember. You'll have to remind me what the promise was."

CHAPTER 33

On Saturday morning Angie slept in, and Gabe fixed French toast and served it to her in bed.

She yawned and sighed. "My, will I get this special treatment every day because I'm now an actor?"

"You get this special treatment because I love you."

"That's a good answer." She winked at him. "Are you trying to start something again, old man?"

"Not at the moment. After last night we might need to wait a day or two."

"Not as young as you once were?"

"I just don't want to distract you from your new profession. You need to conserve all your energy for your new career. I'll give you a rain check."

"Promises, promises."

With some time on his hands, Gabe decided

to try out one of the other items on his retirement to-do list. He went out to the garage and found his golf clubs stashed in a corner, covered with a large black trash bag. After dusting them off and making sure the squirrels hadn't nibbled on anything in the bag, he loaded them into the trunk of his car and drove off to the municipal golf course and driving range.

He purchased a bucket of balls and strolled out to the driving range. Stretching his arms, he selected a seven iron, placed three balls down on the artificial turf pad and whacked the first one. It sailed past the hundred-yard flag, right down the middle of the range.

Not bad, he told himself. He hit the second ball and it flew ten yards farther, still in the center of where he aimed. The third ball sliced a little, but was a respectable shot. He next selected his driver and punched three balls out in the two hundred-yard range. This was easy. He worked his way through the clubs, typically hitting two good shots for one misfire. When he completed the basket of balls, he congratulated himself and decided he had time to play nine holes if he could join a scheduled group. He checked in at the office, and a young man with a ponytail looked through a list. "You're in luck. There's a threesome teeing off in fifteen minutes. The Katzen party. You can join them."

Gabe paid his fee and headed off to practice a few putts. Then he sauntered over to the first tee to find the group. He didn't know a Katzen, but figured he could join anyone. He found three men in their forties waiting. He immediately recognized one of them — defense attorney Neal Welch. *Uh-oh.* Not his idea of someone he'd like to spend part of Saturday morning with. Sucking it up, Gabe approached the group. "Is this the Katzen party?"

Welch spun around and regarded Gabe warily. "It is. And why would it be your concern, Detective?"

Gabe let out a sharp breath. "It seems I've been assigned to fill out the foursome, whether either of us wants it or not."

"Great." Welch spat on the ground. "You send any innocent people to prison lately?"

"No, but have you sent any serial killers back on the streets lately?"

"Yeah, right. I guess we're stuck with you. Meet the others." Welch introduced two other defense lawyers from Denver to Gabe. "This should put a dent in your reputation when your fellow officers find out who you're associating with, Detective."

252

Gabe shrugged. "No skin off my back. I'm retired anyway."

"So you finally gave up the badge?"

"Pretty much. I'm actually working on two cases part time, but I'm essentially retired. That's why I thought I'd give golf a try. I never had the leisure time like you gentlemen to pursue this game."

Welch leered. "Well, if you're going to join our group, you'll have to ante up. Three bucks a hole. Lowest scores on each hole split the twelve dollars."

Gabe looked at his watch. "Okay. I'll only be able to play nine holes." He figured the most he could lose would be twenty-seven dollars.

The other three teed off, sending their balls straight down the fairway. Gabe set his ball on the tee, took two practice swings and lined up his club behind the ball. He took in a deep breath, let the air out, brought his club back and took a swing. Thunk. The ball trickled off the tee to the left, ten yards into a patch of weeds.

Welch whistled. "Man, quite a shot."

Gabe felt warmth spread up his cheeks. "It's been a while since I've played."

Welch chuckled. "This could be a very profitable day for three of us."

Gabe glared at him and strode off to find

his ball. After successfully extricating himself from the weeds and shooting eight on the first hole, the second hole went better, and he only lost to the third place player by two strokes. By the fifth hole he actually tied Welch for lowest score, winning back six dollars. But after that things fell apart again.

On the seventh hole, Gabe sent an errant drive hooking onto the next fairway. It missed a man by inches. The guy shook his fist at Gabe.

"Sorry," Gabe shouted.

"You may need me to defend you against a lawsuit," Welch chortled.

Gabe sent eye daggers at the lawyer. "Too bad the ball didn't hit a defense attorney."

The eighth hole required teeing off over a pond. After sending three balls into the water, Gabe figured he could quit as soon as he lost all his golf balls. Fortunately or unfortunately, the fourth shot ricocheted off the far shore and bounced onto the fairway. After the ninth hole, Gabe opened up his wallet and handed a twenty and one to Welch.

"Much obliged, Detective. Join us again any time."

In your dreams.

Gabe threw his clubs in the trunk of his

car. *Enough of this.* He wouldn't be playing this game again.

Gabe arrived at the Bearcrest Community Center at eleven-fifty to pick up the eight meals he needed to deliver to the east side of town. He loaded the food into his backseat, took the list of names and addresses and headed off. The first person on the list turned out to be a woman in a wheelchair, who greeted him at the door. "Oh, good. Lunch is here. What did you bring me?"

Gabe shrugged. "To be honest, I didn't have time to check, ma'am. Smells like spaghetti though."

"My favorite. Thank you, young man."

He smiled at her. "I haven't been called young man in forty years."

"It's all relative, young man."

His next stop was two blocks away. This woman wore dark glasses and held a cane when she came to the door. He put the bag in her hand. "Here's your lunch."

"Much obliged. I don't recognize your voice."

"No, ma'am. I'm Gabe. This is my first time delivering meals."

She gave a faint smile. "Well, you come back again, you hear?"

■ ■ ■ ■

Walking back to his car after delivering the seventh meal, Gabe spotted an old gray Volvo driven by playhouse actor Arthur Buchanan, who had a furtive grimace on his face.

Gabe's detective's intuition kicked into gear. He made a snap decision, jumped in his car and followed. Arthur drove to the outskirts of town and stopped at a small farmhouse.

Gabe pulled to the side of the road and waited. When Arthur didn't come back out after fifteen minutes, Gabe realized he had to finish his last delivery. Reluctantly, he jotted down the address and drove away. When he reached his destination, he saw an ancient bald man sitting in a rocking chair on the porch of a house with peeling white paint.

As Gabe strode up the cracked walkway to make the delivery, the man squinted at him. "About time you got here. My stomach's been growling. I always eat at twelve-thirty, and it's already one o'clock."

"I'm sorry." Gabe gulped. "I got delayed."

"I hope you aren't going to make a habit of that, sonny." The man took out a fork from his shirt pocket and began shoveling in the spaghetti.

"No, it won't happen again."

The man burped and pointed his fork at Gabe. "You play cribbage?"

"I used to."

"As soon as I finish my vittles, how'd you like to play a game?"

Gabe didn't have any pressing engagements and figured he owed it to the old man to make up for the late delivery. "Sure. I'll give it a shot."

"You any good?" the old man asked.

Gabe shrugged. "It's been a number of years since I played." Gabe remembered that he had put cribbage on his retirement to-do list. No time like the present to test it out.

The man's eyes lit up like the midday sun, and he cackled. "Hah. That sounds interesting."

The guy returned to shoveling in the food and within minutes had decimated every scrap Gabe had brought him. He stood, burped again and waved Gabe into the house.

The place had brown carpet and looked as if it had been recently cleaned. The man flicked on the light switch in the dining room, took a deck of cards out of his pants pocket and sat down at the table, where a cribbage board already rested. "Take a seat, sonny." He shuffled the cards three times, executed a perfect one-handed cut and placed the deck on the table. "Penny a point, sonny. Can you handle it?"

Gabe figured this was his day to be taken to the cleaners by all the locals.

And as expected, Gabe quickly fell behind the card shark. When the old man finally won, he looked up at Gabe. "What do you do for a living, sonny?"

Gabe decided not to play his retirement card given the age of his companion. "I'm a detective with the Bearcrest Police Department."

The man squinted at him. "You on the vice squad?"

"No. I primarily handle crimes against persons. Homicides, assaults, domestic violence, that sort of thing."

"None of that around here." He eyed Gabe warily. "You aren't going to haul me in for gambling, are you?"

"I'll let you off this time."

"Good. You owe me forty-three cents."

CHAPTER 34

Having completed his meal deliveries, Gabe stopped by the police department. The place was practically deserted. Outside of the dispatchers and one weekend duty officer writing a report, he had the place to himself. As he walked down the hallway, his footsteps echoed. He heard no other sounds. He sniffed the aroma of sweat mixed with cheap aftershave.

He logged on to his computer that hadn't yet been reassigned and checked the address of the house where he had seen Arthur Buchanan visiting. It was owned by a Francis Stallwart. After conducting several more searches, Gabe determined that Stallwart was the proprietor of a barbershop in Bearcrest. With nothing else planned, he decided to pay a visit to the Stallwart residence.

When Gabe pulled up in front of the farmhouse, he noticed that Buchanan's Volvo he'd seen earlier was no longer parked there. He headed up the walkway and knocked on the door. A man in his sixties answered. "Yes?"

Gabe held out his identification. "Are you Francis Stallwart?"

The man squinted at Gabe's badge and then stood up straight. "Yeah. What do you want?"

"I'm Detective Tremont. I'm involved in an investigation and understand that Arthur Buchanan recently visited you. May I come in?"

Stallwart opened the door and regarded Gabe wearily. "I suppose." He led Gabe into the living room. "Make yourself at home. Would you like some coffee?"

Gabe held up his hand. "No thanks."

They took seats, Gabe on a wooden chair that had seen better days and Stallwart on a leather couch.

Gabe took out a pad and pen. "First of all, please tell me how you know Arthur Buchanan."

Stallwart let out a deep sigh. "He was engaged to my niece, Kendra Jamison. They planned to get married in six months, but she broke off the engagement. Strangest thing. After singing Arthur's praises for months, she met another man who caught her fancy and decided Arthur wasn't for her."

"Did you meet this other man?"

Stallwart shook his head. "She was very secretive about him. Never even mentioned his name and didn't bring him over."

"And why was Arthur visiting you earlier today?"

Stallwart flinched. "How did you know that? Were you following him? Is he a suspect in some crime?"

"Let's just say he may have some pertinent information regarding an investigation I'm conducting. Can you tell me about his visit today?"

Stallwart nodded. "He came here to see Kendra. He explained that he hoped to talk her into reconsidering her decision. Kendra had been staying here with my wife and me over the last three months."

"Did Mr. Buchanan speak with Kendra today?"

"Nope. Wasn't possible. She packed her bags and left yesterday. I don't know where she went. Craziest thing. That girl used to be so dependable, but lately she kind of went nuts. I can't figure out what happened to her."

Gabe readied his pen. "Does she have a cell phone with her?"

"Yeah. She never gets off the blasted thing."

"I'd appreciate it if you could give me her number."

After Gabe left the Stallwart house, he sat in his car and called Kendra's cell. He got her recorded greeting and left a message for her to call him immediately.

When Gabe got home his neighbor, Al Schilling, accosted him as he parked in the driveway. "Hey, Gabe. It's time you joined me for a bridge game at the Community Center. This is your lucky day."

"As you know, I've been pretty busy with a case, Al."

"I hear Angie's deserted you for the theater. No sense you being home alone pining away. Besides, she specifically told me you needed some new retirement activities. I'm not taking no for an answer. You and I are going to the Community Center in thirty minutes. Go get ready for an afternoon of fun."

Gabe groaned. Al would never let up. Still, Gabe had nothing he had to do right away. "I'll make a deal with you, Al. I'll go this one time. But afterwards if I say I'm not going again, you have to quit bugging me."

"It's a deal."

Gabe went inside to change and crossed golf, volunteering and cribbage off his list of retirement activities. He had quickly pinpointed what he didn't want to do with the rest of his life. Now he only had to discover what he did want to do. Angie had left him a note that she had gone to a pre-show rehearsal at the playhouse.

When Gabe left the house and locked the door, Al was waiting in his white Saab with the engine running. "Jump in, Buddy, our bridge game awaits us."

Al told his absurd jokes all the way to the Community Center, highlighted by the one about a goat walking into a bar with a stalk of celery up its nose. Gabe resisted the urge to jump out of the car at every traffic light and run for his life. It didn't matter what subject Gabe tried to bring up, Al diverted the conversation to one of his ridiculous stories. The guy had more one-liners than the comedy channel, the only difference being that Al's weren't funny. With his memory, why couldn't he have memorized good jokes?

After entering the Community Center, Al steered Gabe into a room with half a dozen bridge tables and a group of people congregated alongside a counter holding platters of finger food and paper cups of juice.

"Grab a snack, and let's get started." Al rubbed his hands together. "We're going to kick some serious heinie this afternoon."

Gabe filled a paper plate with crackers, cheddar cheese and apple slices and helped himself to a cup of lemonade. Surveying the room, he realized he was one of the youngest people here. He only had a chance to eat one apple slice before Al pushed him toward a table with two gray-haired geezers.

After Gabe sat down, he recognized one of his opponents. As their eyes met, the old guy made the same connection, and he pointed a grizzled finger at Gabe. "You're the late delivery boy and not much of a cribbage player."

Gabe winced. "I thought you were homebound and didn't get out."

The old guy gave a dismissive wave of his hand. "I had to give up my wheels. Can't see well enough to drive anymore. But my bridge partner here is younger — he's only ninety-three — and still has his license." He picked up a deck of cards and executed one of his perfect one-handed cuts. "Penny a point, gentlemen?"

Back home, Gabe reconciled himself to supplementing Social Security for two senior citizens through their bridge winnings. Al wasn't much of a partner, and the two old fogies had cleaned their clocks. He took out a black marker and drew a thick line through bridge on his retirement activity list.

He didn't plan to attend Angie's performance that night since the show conflicted with his monthly poker game. So instead of the theater, he headed off to enjoy an evening with some of his colleagues from the police department. The host, Ken Sanchez, led him to the table where four other men had already assembled. "Hey everyone, our semi-retired detective finally arrived. Did you hear that his wife whupped him at Texas Hold'em this week?"

Gabe's cheeks grew warm. "How did you know that?"

"My wife spoke to Angie yesterday and told me the whole story." Ken whistled. "Your wife took you to the cleaners."

Gabe tried to change the subject by mentioning that he and Ken had been working on an interesting case at the Bearcrest Mystery Playhouse, but the damage had been done. He'd be ribbed about this for months.

After Gabe sat down at the table, Ken brought a parakeet over on his finger. "I

265

bought this bird for my daughter last week. It makes a great pet." The bird was passed around, eagerly stepping from one person's finger to the next. When handed to Gabe, the parakeet pecked his hand and flew over to Ken.

"It's never done that before." Ken stroked the ruffled bird.

Gabe looked at his hand. In addition to the red mark caused by the bird's beak, the animal had left another present on his wrist. "I need to use your bathroom to wash this off."

After an evening of getting shellacked at poker, making it a hat trick for the day on card game losses, Gabe put on his windbreaker to leave.

Ken Sanchez grabbed his arm. "This wasn't your night, Gabe, but there's a poker tournament at the County Fairgrounds next weekend. It would give you a chance to redeem yourself. You want to go there with me?"

Gabe vigorously shook his head. "I think I'll pass, Ken. I'm swearing off card games for a while."

When Gabe got home he struck lines through getting a pet and poker on his retirement list. He ran through the remaining items that had not been crossed off. Would he ever find one that suited him?

CHAPTER 35

On Sunday Angie slept in after her late-night performance. Gabe was restless. He had not received a call back from Arthur Buchanan's ex-fiancée, Kendra Jamison, so he punched in her number, and once again it cut over to voicemail. He left another message. With nothing else to do, he took out his retirement list and scanned through it. What to try next? Nothing immediately grabbed him. He looked again.

Maybe he'd do a little fishing. He had a new rod, courtesy of the Chief. Why not give it a shot. He could go up into the foothills and cast into the upper reaches of Bearcrest Creek. And he would be careful not to step on any slippery rocks.

Out in the garage he found the brand-new fishing rod and set it down on the cement floor. Then he reached up on the shelf to open his old tackle box. Inside, he found some tangled line. He pulled it out and a hook jabbed into his finger. "Ouch!" He shook his hand and knocked the tackle box off the shelf. Grabbing for it, he missed as it fell to the floor and crushed the new rod.

After Gabe extracted the hook from his finger, he threw the broken pieces of the fishing rod into the trash. Fishing wasn't going to be his retirement pastime.

Back in the house, he tapped the sheet of paper with the list of potential retirement activities. Why not get on his computer and start a Facebook page? That would be something easy to do, and he'd see what would happen. Al had bragged about the six hundred friends he had on Facebook. If a jerk like Al could accumulate that many friends, this would be easy for Gabe. He might as well join the twenty-first century and become a social network devotee.

He accessed the Facebook website and began following the directions to set up his account. Didn't look that difficult. He flexed his fingers, entered his email address and decided to use a password of "detective63" for his ex-occupation and age — something he would be able to remember. That was the problem with passwords, he had a bunch of them and had to write them down somewhere so he could remember them. How secure was that?

In the section, "About Me," he wrote a brief description of being a retired detective who enjoyed living in the Front Range of the Rocky Mountains. He filled in some basic information about his education and work. He thought about adding some hobbies under "Activities and Interests," but he hadn't found any yet, so he left that section blank.

He uploaded a picture that Angie had taken of him on a vacation to Cabo San Lucas two years earlier, figuring the photograph of him in a T-shirt with the ocean in the background would be better than any of the official shots of him from the police department.

Under "Notification" he selected to have an email directed to him if someone posted a message, added him as a friend or confirmed a friend request. There was something about if someone posted to his wall, but he had no idea what a wall was so didn't check that one. What was all this stuff? He thought he could just sign on and then friends would start appearing. He had been relatively computer-competent in the police department but never an expert. Still, all of this confused him.

After becoming frustrated by trying to figure out security settings, he selected a few options and gave up. At least he had now set up a basic Facebook page. He'd see who befriended him and take it from there.

What if no one found him or wanted to be a friend? He felt like he was back in high school entering a popularity contest.

Thinking of high school, he decided to search for some of his best buddies from that era. Of the gang he used to hang out with, he found three names already on Facebook. He sent friend requests to these. Then he searched for some of his relatives and found his brother, son and two cousins. He requested them as friends.

He went back to check his email and found a message had popped up from his son, Adam. It read, "Hey, Dad. I didn't know you were on Facebook. I've accepted you as a friend. Imagine that."

So Gabe now had his first Facebook friend — his own son. What a weird world social networking was.

Then another email message appeared. It read, "Hector Blandsome wants to be friends with you on Facebook." Who the heck was Hector Blandsome? Gabe opened the message and found a request to respond now to confirm a friend. He positioned the cursor over the little green box and clicked it. He now had two friends. Then he got to thinking. He'd better learn more about this Hector Blandsome. He went to Hector's page and found a description that Hector was out on parole after being incarcerated for two years. It all came back to him. He had arrested Hector for armed robbery.

Great. He was now befriending criminals from his past. Then up popped a message from Hector. It read, "Hey, Detective Tremont. Remember me? You're the one who sent me to Cañon City. I'm out now. Good to see you're retired. I guess you won't be after me anymore. That's good to know. Ha. Ha."

Gabe rolled his eyes. If this was Facebook, he thought he'd had enough of it. He logged off his computer and looked at his retirement activity list. He put a heavy line through Facebook and decided to try photography and painting.

He searched through the drawer of the desk and found his digital camera. He had taken pictures of crime scenes and used to take pictures of Angie and the kids and grandkids on visits but hadn't used his camera recently. Why not go take a few snapshots? In the hall cupboard he located a pad of watercolor paper, a set of watercolor paints and a brush left over from the kids and grabbed a water bottle from the refrigerator.

"I'm going out for a while," he announced to Angie who was now up and rummaging around the kitchen.

"Okay. I'll be here until around four when I head over to the theater. You'll be on your own for dinner."

Would this be his new life as a theater widower? Living on fast food or suffering through microwave meals?

Gabe drove off. He stopped at their neighborhood park and jumped out of the car, strode over to a maple tree and watched two squirrels playing tag. He aimed his camera and took a picture. Yes, maybe photography would suit him. Then he looked up toward the mountains and framed a picture with a pine tree in the foreground and a wisp of clouds over the peaks. He took another shot of two kids playing in the sandbox before returning to his car. Now where did he want to go?

As he rode around town, he found himself heading right to the Bearcrest Mystery Dinner Playhouse. He pulled up in front, stepped out of the car and took a picture of the front of the building. Then he walked around and took photographs of all sides. When he got back in the car, he reviewed the pictures he had taken. The squirrels were a blur, the mountain looked pathetic and one of the two kids in the sandbox was picking his nose. The pictures of the play-house looked accurate but nothing special. He sighed and tossed the camera into the backseat. No, photography wasn't his thing either.

Maybe he'd do better with the painting. He drove to an overlook where he had a nice view of the foothills and parked the car. He assembled his painting supplies and sat on the hood of the car, framing a picture in his mind.

He thrust his thumb out at the scenery, squinted and imagined a gorgeous painting resulting from what he saw. He took the lid off the water bottle, dipped the brush in and dabbed it into the blue paint. He brushed the paper at the top to form sky. Then on to brown mountains and green meadows. This wasn't so bad. He added black for crevices in the rocks, tried mixing blue and green to make some shadows. He worked for half an hour and then stopped to regard what he had created. The water had dripped down, and his sky dribbled over the mountains and the mountains sagged into the hills. It looked like a five-year-old had painted it. He tore it up and got back in the car.

When he got home, Angie had left, and he found a note on the table. "How are things going with your retirement activity list?"

Not so hot.

He pulled out the list, drew lines through photography and painting. What to try next? Why not write stories about some of his police experiences? He took out a sheet of paper and a pen and sat down at the desk. He could start with Hector Blandsome, since that incident was still on his mind. He couldn't use real names, so he would call Hector Fred Jones. He tapped the back end of the pen on the corner of the desk. There wasn't much to the case. He had been called to investigate the robbery and found Hector unconscious in the back alley.

Hector had tripped and hit his head against a wall, knocking himself out. A duffel bag held all the stolen jewelry, and it had been an open and shut case. Hector had plea bargained before duly being incarcerated in prison.

Gabe spent half an hour crossing out the first sentence and trying again. He gave up in disgust. Writing wasn't for him.

Sunday night Gabe stayed home and watched a CSI program. Maybe something from his world would interest him. Immediately the crime scene investigator started taking over the case. *Wait a minute.* The detective should orchestrate the investigation, not the CSI tech. This beautiful female crime scene investigator proceeded to collect DNA from a spider web, shine an ultraviolet light on a fingerprint on a frozen package of peas in the freezer and go back to the lab to process the DNA in thirty minutes. He turned off the program in disgust. Where did they get all this inaccurate information?

As he sat in his easy chair tapping his fingers on the armrest, an earlier event at the Bearcrest playhouse nagged at him. He couldn't piece together Clara's actions and responses to his questions. What did she really intend to do with the poison? And her casual comment that she had misplaced a baggie of potassium cyanide. He needed to put this all together.

When Angie returned home, she dashed in the door. "You'll never guess what happened tonight."

"I hope not another poisoning?"

"No, nothing like that. Mildred had a meltdown. After the show I found her sobbing in her office. I went in and closed the door. She started swearing and calling Peter a loser, while knocking things off her desk and having a general hissy fit. Next she said she missed him. Then she started cussing again, this time at Clara for killing him. Finally, she ranted that Helen was trying to drive her out of business and had worked with Clara."

"Lots of accusations flying around."

"You can't blame her since you carted Clara off to jail. To an outsider that looks as if Clara committed the murder."

"And as I told you before, I'm not convinced that Clara poisoned Peter."

Angie regarded him thoughtfully. "Always the suspicious detective."

Gabe smiled. "You know me so well. Something still doesn't fit. Although I had to take Clara in, I'm searching for new evidence."

"Then who do you think did it?"

"I haven't figured that out yet. But my gut, as my perceptive wife picked up, doesn't accept Clara as the murderer."

"Maybe you're having sympathy feelings since I'm playing that role now. You couldn't see little old me poisoning someone."

Gabe sat up straight in the chair and snapped his fingers. "That's what's been bothering me. I can't see Clara poisoning Peter either. Clara has such bad arthritis that she couldn't get the bottle of cyanide open on Wednesday night. How could she have opened the vial on the previous Sunday night to pour it in Peter's wineglass?"

CHAPTER 36

On Monday Gabe donned his oldest jeans, a ready-for-Goodwill long-sleeved shirt and his work boots. He stopped briefly in the office to check for messages and to see if Camille had any new information for him.

She eyed him up and down. "You going undercover as a homeless guy?"

He laughed. "No, today I'm going through the trash in Peter Ranchard's apartment. Not much different than Dumpster diving."

"Speaking of your investigation into his death, that baggie you gave me contained potassium cyanide. I also found some prints on it."

"Anyone we know?"

"Yeah. Clara Jager's."

Gabe cocked an eyebrow. "Interesting. No other prints?"

She shook her head. "None but yours."

"I thought we might find Helen Lameuse's since it showed up in her pocket."

"Nope."

Then Gabe remembered. "Of course. Helen wore black leather gloves the night Peter died. If she had done anything with the bag of poison, she wouldn't have left fingerprints."

Gabe headed over to Peter's apartment with a surgical mask and a bag full of latex gloves. He had a hunch he might need more than one pair of gloves during the course of sorting through the trash.

When Gabe arrived, Tom Buelson and two husky helpers were already there with a Dumpster in place in the parking lot.

"I'll put a tarp down next to the Dumpster," Tom explained. "We'll put any valuables or documents into white trash bags and leave them there for you to sort through. Any outright trash, we'll put in black bags and toss directly in the Dumpster."

"That works for me," Gabe replied. "You can start in the living room to clear a better path into the apartment. I'll work in the bedroom near the desk since I may be able to find some crucial information there."

Gabe grabbed a handful of black and white trash bags and slogged through the mound of refuse, careful not to land on his butt again.

In the bedroom he positioned himself near the desk and began to drop newspapers, magazines, junk mail and fast-food containers into a black bag. Periodically, he found a bill, which he saved in the white bag. After an hour he had cleared a one foot ring around the desk down to rug level. The carpet showed brown stains and would need to be replaced before anyone could live here again. As Gabe continued to clear away crud, he found an interesting item — a label for OxyContin filled at the Barton Pharmacy a month earlier for Peter Ranchard. He placed this in an evidence bag and continued digging.

As he reached the bottom of the trash heap, he found a metal box. He carefully opened it and found a note that read, "Someone is trying to kill me. If that happens, give this note and the money below to Kendra Jamison. Kendra, please have my remains cremated and conduct a simple ceremony of life in my memory." It was signed "Peter." Underneath, Gabe found a stack of hundred-dollar bills. He counted them. Five thousand dollars.

Gabe whipped out his cell phone and called Kendra again. On the third ring she answered.

"Ms. Jamison, I'm Detective Gabe Tremont, investigating the death of Peter Ran-chard. I understand you were a friend of his."

There was no sound. Gabe wondered if she had disconnected. He tapped the phone. "Are you there?"

He heard a sob. "I was so shocked to hear that Peter died. We were . . . uh . . . seeing each other."

"I've been going through the things in his apartment. Have you ever been there?"

"No. We . . . uh . . . always met elsewhere."

Figures. "He left you a note that I want to show you. Could you meet me at Bearcrest Police Headquarters this afternoon?"

There was a long pause on the line. "I guess I could be there at two."

At noon Gabe trudged out of the bedroom, his head spinning from the stuffiness and overriding aroma that something had died besides Peter. Tom and crew had cleared away a five-foot semicircle around the door-way.

"You really think you can complete this in two days?" Gabe asked.

Tom flicked a piece of paper off his shoul-der. "Yeah, although you'll have a longer task taking a look at the stuff we're saving for you."

"How much have you kept for me?"

"So far three white bags out by the Dumpster."

Gabe whistled. "What did you find?"

"Lots of unopened mail, some computer printouts, coins and even some cash. Anything that isn't outright garbage, we kept for you."

Gabe returned to his sorting project, but after his arms became stiff and he longed for fresh air, he drove home to grab a bite to eat.

Angie blocked his entry at the door. "You're not coming in here looking and smelling like that. I'll get you a bar of soap, and you can wash up with the hose."

"But I'm starving," Gabe protested.

"I'll bring out a roast beef sandwich, and you can eat on the deck." She eyed him up and down. "And tonight when you get home you can leave everything you're wearing outside."

"You want me running around in my skivvies?"

"You come in the back way, and no one will notice."

After eating, Gabe changed into clean clothes and drove to police headquarters to meet Kendra Jamison.

She was a slender blonde with a cute upturned nose and dimples. Gabe could understand why Peter and Arthur Buchanan were both attracted to her. He led her to a meeting room.

"May I get you some coffee, tea or water?"

Her eyes darted around the room. "No, I just had lunch. I'm fine."

Once they both sat down, Gabe asked, "I've been trying to reach you for several days, but you didn't return my calls."

"Things have been really crazy. I saw a number pop up I didn't recognize. I should have called back."

"And you moved out of your uncle and aunt's house?"

Kendra nodded. "I needed to be by myself for a while. I'm staying in a motel on the other side of town."

"I understand that you were at one time engaged to Arthur Buchanan."

She snuffled. "Yes. But I broke things off with Arthur after I got involved with Peter."

"Did you notice any animosity between the two of them?"

"Arthur wasn't happy that I broke our engagement. He shouted at me and said that he was going to get Peter."

"Did he say what he planned to do?"

Kendra shook her head. "Only that he said

Peter wouldn't get away with this. He was very angry."

"Did you have any indication that Peter may have been taking pain pills?"

She bit her lip and looked down at the table between them. "No. He wasn't suffering any condition that would require pain medication."

Gabe put the metal box on the table. "Peter left this for you."

Kendra looked at the box for a moment and then opened it. She pulled out the letter and read it. "Oh, no." She put her hand to her cheek and began sobbing.

Gabe nudged a box of tissue on the table toward her.

She took one and blew her nose.

"What do you make of that letter?" Gabe asked.

Kendra looked as pale as the walls. "If he thought someone was out to kill him, could it have been Arthur?"

"Mr. Buchanan was one of the people on stage with Peter when he died. He's definitely a person of interest."

She shook her head wildly. "No, I can't believe Arthur would do that. He may get angry, but he's not the physically violent type."

"Are you aware of anyone else who might

have had a grudge against Peter?"

"He told me the other actors at the play-house were all out to get him. I took that as Peter being paranoid, but look what happened." She began crying again.

Gabe waited.

Kendra grabbed another tissue and wiped her eyes.

"Are you willing to carry out the requests in his letter?" Gabe asked.

She nodded.

"Since Peter has no relatives, I have a form for you to sign, and then I can give you the money. Once his body is released from the coroner, you can make arrangements for cremation." He handed her a pen and receipt statement.

She read it and signed. Her sad eyes met Gabe's. "I'll do what he requested and set up a ceremony right away."

"Let me know. I'd like to attend." Gabe gave her his business card. It was a good thing he hadn't thrown them all away when he "retired."

Back at Peter's apartment Gabe spent the afternoon increasing the empty space around the desk. He found two more pharmacy labels and a bottle of Vicodin with the label still on the bottle. Peter had been a

very busy man with his black market drug
business.

CHAPTER 37

When Gabe arrived home, Angie had roast chicken with mashed potatoes ready for him. "Go take a long, hot shower and then you can eat."

He welcomed the chance to clean up. After scrubbing thoroughly and watching the black water circle the drain, he hopped out of the shower ready to demolish his dinner.

As he took the first bite of chicken and savored the tangy sauce, Angie's specialty, she announced, "I clipped an article out of the newspaper for you."

Gabe chewed and raised an eyebrow at the same time, proving how versatile he was. "Oh?"

"I know stamp collecting is one of the items on your list of potential retirement activities. There's a meeting tonight of the Bearcrest Philatelist Society at the Community Center. I thought you might want to check it out."

Dismissing the idea of plunking down in front of the tube and vegging out for the evening, Gabe decided he owed it to Angie and himself to keep trying to find what would occupy his interest when he wrapped up his two current cases. Giving a resigned sigh, he said, "Sure. I'll give it a shot."

After finishing every speck on his plate and resisting the urge to lick his fingers, he helped with the dishes. He had just dried his hands when the phone rang.

"Hello, Dad," his daughter greeted him.

Gabe shouted to Angie, "It's Cindy if you want to get on the extension."

In a moment Angie came on the line as well. "It's good to hear from my wayward daughter," she said.

"As I recall, I was the last one to call you. This goes both ways, you know."

"Just kidding," Angie said. "I always enjoy your calls."

"I want to see if you'd like two guests tomorrow night," Cindy said. "I have a meeting in Denver on Wednesday and could drive up tomorrow night. I thought I'd bring Cal along since his Judo camp doesn't start until next week, and he could spend the day with the two of you on Wednesday."

"That would be great," Angie said into

289

the extension in her excited voice. "I can do sticker books with him."

"I'll be able to free up some time Wednesday afternoon to take him to the park," Gabe added.

"Free up time?" Cindy said. "I thought you were only working part time."

"I have two cases. I'm back working more like full time, but I definitely want to spend some time with Cal." Then Gabe remembered something. "But won't Wednesday interfere with your dinner playhouse performance, Angie?"

"No. With losing two actors and everything going on, Mildred cancelled the midweek performance this week."

"What are you talking about?" Cindy asked.

"Your mother has become an actor."

"What?"

"I'm participating in a mystery dinner playhouse, dear. I'll tell you all about it when you get here."

"You're full of surprises," Cindy said. "I look forward to seeing both of you, and Cal always likes spending time with his grandparents."

After hanging up, Gabe changed his shirt as Angie rushed into the bedroom. "I'll get the two guest rooms set for their visit, and I have two new matchbox cars to add to the toy box in Cal's room."

While Angie prepared for the visitors, Gabe headed off to the world of stamp collecting. His thoughts turned to poisoning and robbery and finding the illusive perpetrators for both cases. He parked and turned the switch in his mind to focus on the meeting he'd be attending and leave the investigating until the next day.

As he strode into the Community Center, he checked his watch to confirm he had five minutes before the meeting was scheduled to start. He liked to arrive on time. He passed a group of seniors playing bridge. No, he had crossed that off his list. The old guy who had beat him at both cribbage and bridge wasn't in attendance.

In the corner stood two personal computers, and two women were pounding away on the keyboards. Probably updating their Facebook pages. Again, not for him.

In the meeting room he found a dozen men and two women sitting around tables looking at huge albums. He was the youngest person in the room. On the job he dealt with people of all ages, but somehow the prospective retirement activities he tried always led him into groups of oldsters. Was this the future for him?

One of the men saw him standing there, jumped to his feet and raced over to grab Gabe's hand. "Ah, new blood. Welcome to the Bearcrest Philatelist Society. We always like to see new faces. What do you collect?"

"I'm . . . uh . . . new to this stamp business and just came to check things out."

"Neophytes or experienced philatelists are all welcome here."

"I'm definitely on the beginner side of the equation."

"Great. Great. I'm Sid Ballard, president of the club. We're glad you could join us. I specialize in Germany, Britain and British colonies."

Gabe wondered if he had gone back in time to pre–World War II.

After Gabe took a seat, Sid grabbed a gavel and rapped it on a wooden disc. "All right, people, let's bring the meeting to order. Let's stand for the pledge of allegiance."

Everyone got up, put their hands over their hearts and belted out the words. Gabe couldn't remember the last time he had been in a group of people reciting the pledge of allegiance.

"Now on to old business," Sid announced. "Alice, would you be kind enough to give us a treasurer's report?"

292

A woman in a white sweater stood, adjusted her glasses and said, "We have three hundred dollars and forty-six cents." She removed her glasses and pointed at a man who had his nose in an album. "Chester, you still owe your dues."

Chester flinched and looked up. "What?"

"You still owe twenty-five dollars."

"I'll pay next meeting after my Social Security check comes in."

"You better. You're six months overdue. The only upcoming expense is ordering flowers for Clyde's wife, who is in the hospital."

A man with liver spots all over his bald head waved a shaky hand. "What about paying for the picnic?"

"Bill, you forgot again," Alice said. "We cancelled the picnic. Too many of you didn't want to be out in the sun, and no one volunteered to make potato salad."

"Oh, yeah," Bill replied.

"Any other questions?" Alice looked around the room. No one raised a hand or said anything so she sat down.

"Any other old business?"

"Anything we do is old business." Bill tried to laugh and ended up gagging. The man sitting next to him whacked him on the back.

"Any new business?" Sid asked.

A hand waved.

"Yes, Raymond?"

"I'm going to need a ride to the next meeting. I didn't pass my driving test."

"How'd you get here tonight?" Sid asked.

"I drove."

Gabe pretended he hadn't heard that.

They went through several more items of business, and then Sid said, "In my role as club historian in addition to president, I'll be the guest speaker tonight."

Alice groaned. "Couldn't find an outside speaker?"

"I had one lined up to talk about famous misprints, but his son got the croup, and he had to cancel. Instead, I'll be speaking on the history of watermarks." He cleared his throat and launched into a technical description of types of paper, how watermarks are made and the techniques for highlighting them.

Gabe almost nodded off as Sid described the differences between the dandy roll and the cylinder mould process. Finally, Sid announced, "Okay. That wraps it up. Any questions?"

Chester, who had been snoring, shook himself away. "Whadaya say?"

"Any questions?"

"Yeah. When's the snack?"

Alice uncovered a tray with cheese on crackers and sugar cookies and poured paper cups of grape juice.

Sid came up to Gabe and asked, "Did you enjoy the meeting?"

"Very . . . uh . . . informative."

Sid grinned. "Yup. Every meeting we have a presentation on some aspect of stamp collecting. Come look at my albums."

Gabe followed him and perused a collection of German stamps. His eyes glazed over. "Quite impressive."

Sid tapped a page. "This was a very valuable collection at one time, but in the last ten years the value of stamps has dropped."

"Why's that?" Gabe asked.

"As you can tell from looking at our members, philatelists are growing older, and we're not getting younger people interested. Fewer collectors, less demand, lower prices. Still, I love stamps." Sid's eyes gleamed in the fluorescent light.

When Gabe got home, he crossed one more item off his retirement list. He knew he would never become a philatelist. Besides, he couldn't even pronounce it.

After working a half day on Tuesday with

the cleaning people to continue sorting through Peter's hoarding mess, Gabe headed home early. Since he was already dirty, he decided he would putter around in the garden for a little while, since this was something on his retirement list.

Noticing a root poking up in the one section of the lawn, he grabbed a shovel and dug into the grass. The thing was huge. He worked up a sweat and finally removed dirt from around it. Then he attacked the root with the blade and after hacking for ten minutes dislodged a foot long piece that was two inches in diameter. The darn cottonwood tree had taken over the lawn. He filled in the hole, dusted some grass seed over the exposed dirt and turned on the sprinkler to water the repaired area.

A geyser shot into the air where he had been digging.

It took Gabe three hours to replace a section of sprinkler line that he had punctured. When he went inside, he drew a thick black line through gardening on his list of retirement activities.

Later that afternoon after cleaning up, Gabe sat at his desk at home and reviewed notes he had made on his two cases. Still nothing had turned up regarding the robbery. No one had seen anyone near the hardware store the morning of the robbery. Camille had found no useful clues. Gabe had put her sketch in the Crimestoppers section of the *Bearcrest Gazette.* This had resulted in only two phone calls. One woman had reported seeing a large man leave the Bearcrest Shopping Center the morning of the crime. Upon checking, Gabe had determined it was a city trash collector.

One other call turned out to be a report of seeing a huge man on another day. Gabe labeled this perp, "The Phantom." How could such a large man not be noticed? He had committed his crime and disappeared undetected. Gabe had no idea if the robber had come to the hardware store by car, bike or on foot.

At that moment, Angie let out a piercing scream.

CHAPTER 38

Gabe raced into the living room to find Angie shaking and pointing toward the fireplace. "There!" she shouted.

Gabe looked through the glass and saw two baby raccoons scurrying around inside the glassed-in fireplace, which hadn't been used since March. A cloud of soot rose from the antics of the two raccoons as they threw themselves against the glass and bricks.

"Uh-oh," Gabe said. "They must have come down through the flue."

"Get them out of there!" Angie shrieked.

"Stay calm." Gabe took out his cell phone and called the Schillings.

Al answered on the first ring as if he had been waiting for a call. "You up for another bridge game at the Community Center, old buddy?"

Gabe flinched, always surprised when someone recognized him from caller ID. "Remember our agreement. I played that one time, and you said you wouldn't bug me again. I'm holding you to it."

"Right."

Angie was waving frantically at the raccoons. Gabe put his hand over the receiver and said, "Stay calm." Then into the phone he said, "Al, do you have an animal carrier you use for taking Gracie to the vet?"

"Sure do. I keep it in the garage."

"Would you mind if I borrow it?"

Al chuckled. "You breaking down and getting a dog?"

"No. I need to use it to get rid of some raccoons."

"I'll bring it right over. Reminds me of the joke about the raccoon and the squirrel . . ."

After suffering through a typical Al joke — the price to pay for asking a favor — Gabe snapped his cell closed and retrieved an old picnic blanket from the hall closet.

A few minutes later Al banged on the door.

Gabe yanked it open and grabbed the animal carrier.

"Need any help, buddy?" Al asked.

"I've got it under control. I'll return this in a day or so." Gabe closed the door before Al could launch into any jokes.

Gabe placed the animal carrier near the

fireplace, opened the glass window into the fireplace and quickly wrapped the blanket around the two baby raccoons. They fought and hissed, but he managed to contain them without getting bitten. He threw the blanket containing the two struggling creatures into the animal carrier and slammed the door. They escaped from the blanket and raced around inside the container.

Angie waved her hands in the air. "Get those things out of here."

"Right." Gabe lugged the carrier outside and tucked it away in the back of the garage. He got a flashlight and ladder and climbed up onto the roof. When he leaned into the chimney and flashed the beam of light downward, it reflected off two large eyes. Obviously, the mother raccoon. He chastised himself for never having put a cap on the chimney.

Next, he drove off to the hardware store. He found both Violet Kartagian and Sanford Madison standing behind the counter. He approached Violet and figured he could kill two birds with one visit. She looked even more frazzled than the day of the robbery. "Have you remembered anything further about the robber?"

She twitched. "I . . . uh . . . can't think of

anything else. Have you found the money yet?"

"No. We still haven't been able to locate anyone fitting the description you gave me. Any other details you could come up with may be important."

"Well . . . uh . . . nothing else . . . I guess the guy is difficult to find."

Gabe watched her. She seemed nervous. "Anything at all that you can recall would be helpful."

She shook her head as if trying to rid herself of insects caught in her hair. "No. I can't . . . remember any more."

Gabe wasn't getting anywhere, so he decided to take care of the main part of his mission. "I need to buy a live trap and a chimney cap."

Sanford Madison looked up from his paperwork. "Sounds like you have unwanted visitors in your chimney."

Gabe grimaced. "You can say that again. A mother raccoon and her two babies. Angie is going nuts."

When he returned home, Gabe set up the live trap, a three-foot long wire cage, along the backside of the house. He placed the animal carrier containing the two baby raccoons with the door facing the back of the trap. He covered the carrier with towels. The only way the mother could get close enough to see her babies was to go into the trap.

The babies squeaked and chattered. Gabe admired his makeshift raccoon elimination system before going back into the house.

From the doorway Angie asked, "Are they gone?"

"Not yet. I have to catch the mother first."

Gabe knew this would take some time, so he returned to his den and sat down at his desk to review his notes. He had to figure out some way to catch the phantom hardware store robber. He heard a scurrying sound on the roof. Good. The mother must have heard her babies and come out of the chimney. Then a tapping sound. He figured the mother was climbing down the drainpipe. He looked out the window and saw a raccoon on his patio. He waited fifteen minutes and stuck his head out the back door. He heard loud squawking. He went to check and found the mother raccoon firmly secured in the live trap.

Next, he went up on the roof and attached the chimney cap. He put the live trap and the animal carrier in the back of Angie's SUV. He drove up into the foothills, listening to scratching and squeals the whole way.

He parked off the dirt road where he had taken his aborted hike through the stream and lifted the two containers out of the car. He released the babies first, and they scurried into the underbrush. He carefully opened the live trap, staying out of range of the angry mother. She charged after the babies and disappeared. He dusted his hands. One problem resolved.

If he could only solve his two cases as easily as getting rid of unwanted raccoons.

At eight-thirty that evening, the doorbell rang. Gabe answered to find his daughter, Cindy, with an overnight bag and his grandson, Cal, holding a stuffed bear. "Come on in." He gave Cindy a hug and patted Cal's head. "Who's your friend?"

"This is Jeremy. He goes with me on sleepovers."

"Well, your grandmother and I are glad that you've come to see us. You get to sleep in your regular room."

Cal's eyes lit up. "The one with the toy box?"

"That's the one. Your grandmother may even have added some new toys since your last visit."

"Oh, boy." Cal charged into the house.

"Thanks for putting us up on such short

notice, Dad."

"Hey, this is a treat for your mom and me."

Angie helped Cal and Cindy get settled in their rooms, and the four of them reconvened in the living room.

"So what's the meeting tomorrow?" Gabe asked.

"I'm negotiating a deal with a telecom company. I should be done by four. I'll pick up Cal afterwards, and we'll head back to the Springs."

"Too bad you can't stay longer," Angie said.

"We'll come back for a longer visit, but I thought this would be a good chance for you to spend time with Cal while I worked. Speaking of which, it's bedtime for you, young man."

"Aw, we just got here."

Cindy wagged a finger at her son. "You'll have all day tomorrow to see Grandma and Grandpa. Go get the pjs on. Grandma or Grandpa can read you a story."

Cal looked like he was going to argue, but turned on his heels and headed upstairs to get ready for bed.

Gabe waited five minutes and followed to find the eight-year-old brushing his teeth in the bathroom. "What would you like me to read to you?"

Cal spat in the sink and looked up. "I brought the Harry Potter book I'm reading."

"One of those thick books?" Gabe asked.

"Yup. I like reading about how Harry plays quidditch."

"Tomorrow afternoon we can go to the park and play catch but not quidditch."

"It would be so cool to fly around on a broomstick."

Gabe laughed. "We'll stick to the ground and a tennis ball. Now let's go get that book of yours."

After Gabe read the next chapter of the adventures in the Hogwarts School of Witchcraft and Wizardry, he tucked Cal in and turned out the light. "You and Jeremy have a good night's sleep."

Back downstairs, he spoke to Cindy about her job and his so-called retirement. She still enjoyed her work, and he was still trying to figure out how to retire.

"I remember some wonderful camping trips we used to take as a family," Cindy said. "You should go camping."

"That's a thought," Gabe replied.

"You'll have to go on your own," Angie said. "I've graduated from camping to motels. I like sleeping on a mattress and not on the ground."

"Are you ever going to really retire?" Cindy asked Gabe.

"After I complete these two cases, I'll see."

She gave an eye roll. "That will be the day."

After Cindy and Angie headed up the stairs for the night, Gabe shambled out to the garage to check on his camping equipment. Maybe he would try it again. He found his old tent up in a cupboard, took it out of the package, and shook it out. On close inspection, he discovered there were holes in the fabric and the floor material had black splotches of mildew. He located his sleeping bag and unrolled it. A dozen spiders scrambled away. In another cabinet he found his old cook stove. It was rusted. He pitched all these items into the trash can. Camping wasn't going to happen soon.

On Wednesday morning Gabe got up early and prepared a batch of pancakes. Cindy grabbed a cup of coffee, ate one pancake and dashed off for her meeting. A few minutes later Cal clomped down the stairs and stumbled into the kitchen with Jeremy under one arm as he rubbed his eyes with his other hand. "Something smells good, Grandpa."

"Pancakes especially for you. How many do you want?"

"Three." Cal hopped up on a chair, and Gabe placed a plate in front of him.

After breakfast Angie took over, and Gabe excused himself to get ready for his partial workday.

The cleaning crew finished clearing out Peter's apartment, but Gabe's work had only begun. Ten plastic bags of paperwork had been saved for him to look through. He threw them in the trunk and backseat of his car and headed to the police station. He pulled into the garage area and parked.

At that moment, his cell phone rang. He answered to hear Kendra Jamison on the line.

"I've set up a ceremony and reception at the Bearcrest Community Church for this Friday," Kendra said. "I've invited everyone from the theater and put a notice in the newspaper."

"Thanks for taking care of the arrangements and letting me know." He snapped his phone closed after signing off.

Henry, the maintenance supervisor, strolled out to greet him. "What's up, Gabe?"

"I need floor space to sort some trash."

Henry peered through the back window of Gabe's car and chuckled. "You been Dumpster diving?"

"Something like that."

"Use bay two. Nothing planned there for the next few days. There's a tarp on the back shelf."

As Gabe reached for the first bag, he again realized that Dr. Denton had not called him back about the results of the medical tests. Why was this taking so long? Had some serious problem caused Dr. Denton to double-check the results before calling? This lack of information bothered him. One thing to do. Dive into work.

Gabe dumped the first bag onto the tarp. It took him an hour to sort through mail, slips of paper with phone numbers, last year's tax return and various newsletters from theater groups. Nothing relevant to the investigation.

He returned the innocuous contents to the bag and took it to the Dumpster. Anything with personal information he set aside for shredding. On to bag two.

At lunchtime, Gabe took a break and drove home. As he left the car, Gracie, the cockapoo next door, began yipping at him. He strolled over to the wire mesh fence and held his hand out.

She sniffed a moment and growled at him.

"What's with you, Gracie? You act like we're enemies."

The fluff ball continued to emit low menacing sounds.

"I'd think you disliked the smell from Peter's apartment, but you always bark and growl at me."

Gracie snarled once more, turned her back and trotted away.

After a thorough scrubbing of his hands, Gabe fixed an egg salad sandwich for himself, Cal and Angie.

"Any hot new leads?" she asked.

Gabe shook his head. "I went through a lot of paperwork from Peter's apartment this morning, but nothing's showed up yet."

"What are you looking for?"

"I'm not sure. Peter had his hooks into all the other cast members and Helen Lameuse. He felt threatened and even sent a letter to the police department saying someone was going to kill him. I guess I'm hoping to find something that will link him to one person-of-interest in particular. Someone who had such a compelling reason to see Peter dead that he or she acted on it."

"I like the dog that lives next door," Cal said. "She's really friendly."

"That beast," Gabe said. "She's always barking at me."

"Not me," Cal said. "She came up and licked my hand."

"I hope you washed your hands before eating lunch," Angie said.

"Oops."

Angie's eyes grew wide.

"Just kidding." Cal grinned. "I washed them good."

After lunch Gabe returned to his task of sorting through the bags of papers. Halfway through the tenth and final bag of what he now considered a useless exercise, he removed a spiral notebook. He opened it to find the first page labeled "Peter's Journal." In a distinct script of large looping letters, the first entry described how Peter planned to document the life and times of a soon-to-be-recognized acting talent. The first entry was dated six months ago, described how he had sent his résumé off to acting companies around the country and concluded with the statement, "Now I'll wait to see who wants me first."

Gabe read through and found entries recounting rejections from some of these theater groups. With each rejection, Peter's writing became increasingly angry, as he described the idiots who didn't recognize true talent. Then he came across a rant that said the cast members at the Bearcrest Dinner Playhouse were untalented, but each would serve his purpose.

A detailed account followed describing how he seduced Sophie, including a graphic description of the affair. He bragged about luring Mildred in and rejecting her. His account of the "useless Clara" and her painkiller addiction fit all that Gabe had heard from her. Peter bragged that he had stolen part of Dr. Viceroy's prescription pad on each visit. The diary entry from the last visit concluded with: "The bag of wind never even noticed."

Likewise, he gloated over what he had done to Harold and Arthur, as well as his plans to get back at Helen Lameuse. The entry for the Saturday, the day before his death, began, "Arthur called me this morning. He said he'd had enough of the blackmail and planned to take action if I didn't quit. I laughed at him and said he was a fool. He said I'd regret that statement." Several paragraphs followed, reviling all the people he had been dealing with. It ended with, "Now let's see if any of them have the guts to do anything other than mouth useless threats." The next page in the journal had the date of his death at the top, but a diagonal tear showed where the remainder of the page had been removed.

Thinking over all he had read, Gabe realized Peter had been an angry man, frustrated with his career. He had alienated everyone around him and seemed to be daring someone to kill him.

Who acted on that dare?

Gabe studied the torn page. An egotistical hoarder wouldn't throw away something he had written. The missing partial page had to be stashed somewhere. If only Gabe could find that missing piece of paper.

Gabe tapped the notebook. What had the final entry disclosed, and where would it be?

Looking through this final bag, he found nothing else of use, so he sealed the bag, dropped it in the Dumpster and returned to his desk, where he sat staring at the spiral notebook. What became of the torn-out page? Given the state of Peter's apartment, no one else could have even found this notebook to tear out the page. Peter had removed it himself. But why, and what was on it? He felt increasingly confident that the missing page contained the one last clue to unravel the mystery of Peter's death.

CHAPTER 39

When Gabe returned home, he thoroughly washed his hands to pass muster with Angie, grabbed a tennis ball and took Cal out to the car.

Cal climbed in the backseat and fastened his seatbelt. "I don't need to use a child's seat anymore, but I still have to sit in the backseat. My mom says to be safe in cars."

"Good for you."

"Where we going?"

"There's a park on the other side of town I thought you'd like. It has a large field for playing catch, a stream nearby and a playground with lots of climbing equipment. But no quidditch pitch."

"Darn."

At the park they played catch. Cal had a good arm and winged the ball to Gabe with enough mustard to make his hand hurt. Cal caught the balls in both hands with only a few drops. Then they headed toward the stream and crossed part way over a bridge to where they stopped to look down in the water.

"There's a fish." Cal pointed.

A trout darted out from behind a rock and swam toward a hole.

"You ever go fishing?" Gabe asked.

"Not yet. My dad might take me later in the summer."

Gabe thought of his destroyed fishing rod. No, catching fish wasn't in his future. At the current time he had some criminals to hook.

Next, they strolled over to the playground, and Cal went on every apparatus there, including three slides, a rocket ship, a suspension bridge and a climbing rock. Then he sat down in the sandbox to dig with his hands.

Gabe sat on a bench and watched his grandson mold a two-foot high castle. "Is that Hogwarts?"

"Yup."

A boy larger than Cal came over, stood watching for a minute and kicked at the castle.

"Hey," Cal shouted. "What're you doing? I'm building here."

The boy kicked again.

Gabe started up from his bench to intervene but at the last moment decided to wait to see how Cal handled the situation.

Cal stood up and looked directly at the other boy. "You can build with me if you want, but don't knock over my castle."

The bully shoved Cal. "I'll knock it over if I want to."

Cal held his ground. "Go find someone else to bother."

The kid pulled his arm back and threw a punch at Cal.

Cal stepped aside, grabbed the boy's arm and threw him to the sand.

The boy lay there with his mouth open.

Cal planted a foot on the bully's chest. "You don't listen very well. I said you can play in the sand but not to mess with my castle." He removed his foot.

The boy shook his head, jumped to his feet and ran away with tears in his eyes.

Cal sat back down to rebuild his castle.

Gabe watched in amazement. "How did you learn to do that?"

Cal tilted his head toward Gabe. "My dad signed me up for Judo lessons. I've been taking them for two years. We're taught to never attack anyone but to defend ourselves if attacked."

Gabe thought over the playhouse case. Peter was a bully and had met his demise. Had someone resorted to more than a Judo throw to rid him- or herself of his bullying? Gabe's grandson had given him a good insight. He had his own type of Judo skills — his investigational abilities. It was time for him to use them to solve his two cases.

Later, Gabe took Cal to the downtown mall to get an ice cream cone. As they walked to the ice cream shop, Gabe thought briefly about stopping at the hardware store to check if there was any new information about the robber but dismissed the idea. He wanted to dedicate himself to his grandson.

"My mom would never let me have ice cream this close to dinner," Cal said. "She has this rule. No snacks after five o'clock."

Gabe rubbed Cal's head. "That's the advantage of being a grandpa. I can break all the rules."

"I don't know," Cal said thoughtfully. "You're with the police. You have to follow the rules."

"That's true. But I have a special dispensation to buy ice cream for my grandson whenever I want."

Cal had a cone with one scoop of cookie dough and another of chocolate fudge. Gabe settled for a cup with peanut butter and chocolate. They sat down outside the ice cream shop on a bench to watch people pass by.

"You have even better ice cream here than in Colorado Springs." Cal licked his lips.

"You'll have to come up more often to try it."

"My Judo camp starts next week. I'll be going for six weeks."

"Maybe after that you can come up for another visit."

Cal's eyes lit up. "Yeah. Then we could have ice cream every day."

At that moment a woman screamed. "My purse. He stole my purse."

Gabe looked in the direction of the voice. A man in ragged jeans holding a purse ran toward him. He jumped up, and at the same time Cal stuck out his foot. The man tripped over Cal's leg and stumbled. This gave Gabe enough time to grab the guy by the shoulder and drop him to the ground.

A whistle blew, and Officer Janet Lyon ran toward them.

Gabe held the purse-snatcher down while Janet snapped cuffs on the man.

"Good thing you were nearby," Gabe said to Janet.

"I've been on mall patrol for several hours. Better thing you were here to stop the guy."

Gabe put his arm around Cal. "And my

grandson is a hero. He tripped the bad guy so I could catch him."

Cal had a grin from ear to ear. "That was so cool, Grandpa."

"Stick with me, kid, and you'll have all kinds of adventures."

Gabe helped lift the arrested man to his feet.

"I'll give you half of the money in the purse if you let me go," the purse-snatcher said to Janet.

"It's not your money, and I can tack on a charge of attempting to bribe a police officer. That could get you four to twelve years in prison. That suit you?"

The man closed his mouth, and Janet led him away.

Gabe remembered a time someone tried to bribe him. It was a number of years before when, as a patrol officer, he made a traffic stop of a speeding motorist. When asked to produce his driver's license, registration and proof of insurance, the man handed over the documents with a hundred-dollar bill tucked in.

Gabe had returned the money. The motorist handed it back again. "Just give me a warning, and this is yours."

Gabe arrested him on the spot under Colorado statute 18-8-302 for bribery. The man turned out to be an influential real estate developer who lawyered up and eventually plea-bargained out for a class two misdemeanor.

Gabe had always prided himself on being an honest cop, just as most of his peers were. In the last few years he had dealt with only one bad cop. This particular guy was a bully, like the kid who knocked Cal's sand castle over. Gabe never understood how the man made it through the psychological testing to qualify as a police officer. The officer had finally been fired and arrested for soliciting sexual favors in exchange for dropping charges for a woman he apprehended on a DUI violation.

Gabe shook his head. The stupid things people did.

His thoughts were interrupted by Cal tugging on his arm. "Grandpa, can we find some other criminals to arrest?"

"Not now, Cal. I think that's enough excitement for today."

Gabe headed back to the car with Cal bouncing along as if he were on a pogo stick.

When Cindy returned from her meeting, Cal told her all about the man they had captured in the mall.

Her eyes grew as large as silver dollars. "You put my son in danger?"

"Not at all," Gabe replied. "He was out of the way, but he had the foresight to cause the purse-snatcher to stumble so I could catch him. One of our police officers was on the scene immediately, so everything was contained."

"I don't know." Cindy frowned.

"It was cool, Mom. No sweat."

That evening after Cindy and Cal left, Gabe sat in his easy chair thinking over his daughter and grandson's visit. He had particularly enjoyed his afternoon with Cal. The young tyke had a lot of spunk. His thoughts turned to how he should visit his kids and grandkids more often. Maybe, one of these days, he and Angie could get a motor home and cruise between Bearcrest, Colorado Springs and Tacoma.

He had been very fortunate. He had survived the dangers of police work and was still happily married. So many of his peers from police academy days had burned out or become divorced under the stress and crazy hours. He had somehow navigated the risky rapids and emerged into the still pool of retirement with his family life intact. He chuckled to himself. Not exactly a still pool.

Here he was back investigating again with two cases to solve.

His reverie was interrupted when Angie entered the room and asked, "How is your retirement list progressing?"

"Not well at all. I keep eliminating items but haven't found anything that really interests me."

"We've discussed this before, but why don't you get your old model train set out of the attic. You should either start using it or give it away. No sense letting it collect dust up there."

"Good idea. I think I'll set it up in the unfinished section of the basement." He could envision building a large wooden table with a hole in the middle. He'd construct mountains with tunnels, a village, trestles, a depot. He pictured himself in an engineer's cap with his hand on the controls as engines pulled long lines of cars all around him. His pulse increased. Yes, this just might be the activity for him. He might have found what he really wanted to do.

He retrieved a step ladder from the garage, carried it to the upstairs landing and climbed into the attic. He had to sort through several boxes but finally located his model railroad gear. This was nothing compared to what he had been through in

Peter's apartment. He lugged two boxes down to the basement and opened them. Everything was covered with dust. He got out the vacuum and cleaned things off as best he could. Assembling track on the cement floor, he formed an oval, before connecting the controls and placing an engine, coal car and passenger car on the tracks. He added a railroad crossing signal and two houses. He stepped back to admire what he had put together. Simple, but a start.

Images of trains racing around the tracks surged through his mind. He was itching to get started. And speaking of itching, something was bothering his toes. He removed his shoes and socks, scratched the top of his feet and readied himself for the first test of his train. He plugged the controller into the socket and flipped the switch.

Bam! A spark shot out of the controller, and the lights went out.

"What did you do?" Angie shouted from above.

"I popped the circuit breaker," Gabe called back. It was pitch black. He started to where he thought the stairs were and stepped on something sharp. A shooting pain ran through his foot. He reached down, felt a metal object and removed the railroad crossing signal stuck in his foot.

Angie appeared at the top of the stairs and shone a flashlight beam down the basement stairs.

"Bring that down so I can find the electrical panel," Gabe said.

With the assistance of Angie's flashlight, he reset the circuit, and the lights came back on.

Angie pointed to the cement floor. "What are those bloody footprints?"

Gabe looked down. Red spots from his bleeding foot trailed across the floor.

Once Angie had washed and bandaged his foot, Gabe put all the model train gear back in the boxes. He would call Goodwill the next day to make a donation.

Gabe woke up at five in the morning, images of Peter's spiral notebooks swirling in his head. He had to find that missing page. The day before when he had sorted through all the bags saved by the cleanup crew, it hadn't shown up.

Where could Peter have put it? He had written it on the fateful Sunday and then torn it out. He wouldn't merely toss it into the hoarding mess.

Gabe put on his sweatsuit and decided to take a walk. As he left the house, Gracie came up to the fence and yapped at him.

"Here we go again. Why do you have it in for me?"

Gracie barked one more time, then trotted over to a hole in the flower garden and began digging. Moments later she dropped a bone in it, covered the hole, regarded Gabe as if to say, "Stay away from my hiding place," growled once at him and headed back to her house.

"That's it," Gabe shouted. "Thank you, Gracie." He now had an idea what Peter had done with the missing page on the Sunday before he died.

After an hour walk and a shower, he spent the morning reviewing all his notes on the case and rereading Peter's diary. He became more convinced than ever that finding the torn page would be the key to his investigation. Knowing that Mildred wasn't a morning person, he waited until eleven to call her. Still, she complained of being awakened at an ungodly hour. Gabe told her that he needed to meet her as soon as possible at the playhouse, so she reluctantly agreed to be there at one.

After a corned beef sandwich, Gabe drove over and found Mildred in her office. "I have an important question to ask you."

"You've had nothing but questions these

last two weeks."

"Did Peter have a favorite place in the theater? Maybe a spot where he would unwind or go to be by himself."

She thought for a moment. "There's an old stuffed chair backstage. He would sometimes go off by himself and sit there."

"Mind if I go have a look?"

"Help yourself. You may even find some money in that old chair."

"Is that a bribe?" Gabe smiled.

"Yeah, right. No one around here has much money to misplace. You can donate anything you find to the Police Widow's Fund or something."

Gabe thanked Mildred and followed her directions to find a greasy, gray easy chair against the wall near the dressing area. He snapped on rubber gloves, lifted up the seat cushion and ran his hand around the edge where the cushion had rested. True to Mildred's prediction, he found two pennies and a nickel plus a Snickers wrapper, a paper clip and the cap from a pen. He reached farther down and felt a piece of paper. Hoping that this might be the missing page from the spiral notebook, Gabe pulled it out but immediately saw an unlined sheet, not torn at the top. The typed message read, "You stay away from Kendra or you're a dead man."

CHAPTER 40

That afternoon when the cast arrived for rehearsal, Gabe pulled Arthur Buchanan aside. "Please come with me to Mildred's office."

"What's going on?"

"I have something to show you. We should look at it in privacy."

Arthur gave an exasperated sigh. "I certainly would like to focus on my acting and not be distracted all the time. When will this all be over with?"

Gabe thought how he'd like to have this case wrapped up as well. "Soon I hope. Please follow me."

They entered Mildred's office, cluttered with papers as always, and Gabe closed the door. "Take a seat and look at this note, but don't touch it."

Arthur dropped into a chair.

Gabe stood next to him, cleared one corner of the desk and placed the letter on that one uncluttered spot.

Arthur visibly paled. "What the heck is this?"

"That's what I'd like to ask you, Mr. Buchanan."

"It has the name of my ex-fiancée, but I didn't write it."

"Did you ever threaten Peter Ranchard?"

Arthur rubbed his cheek. "I was pissed at him but never said I'd kill him."

"Think this through very carefully. How do you account for this note being found here at the playhouse?"

Buchanan paused for a moment and then shrugged. "You got me. Looks like someone tried to set me up. Why are you here anyway? I thought Clara killed Peter."

"I'm not convinced she did. This note sheds a whole new light on the case. Anything else you'd like to tell me, Mr. Buchanan?"

"No. Now I need to get back to rehearsal."

Gabe followed him back to the stage and tapped Harold Coats on the shoulder. "I'd like a moment with you."

Harold gave an exaggerated sigh. "Here we go again."

"Let's step into Mildred's office for privacy."

As they walked downstairs, Gabe wondered if he was wearing out the rug with all the trips back and forth between the stage area and the office. He wouldn't need to bother hiking for exercise. He was staying in good shape by doing the stairs at the playhouse.

Once they settled in Mildred's office, Gabe reviewed in his mind what he had read in Peter's journal and said, "I understand you called Peter the day before he died and threatened him."

Harold harrumphed. "I did no such thing."

"You informed me about the blackmail scheme. Did you reach the breaking point and decide to take action?"

"I've told you everything already. I didn't do anything to him."

"It will be very easy for me to check phone records to see if you called Peter that morning."

Harold leaned over and put his head on the desk. Sobs began to wrack his body.

Gabe waited until Harold stopped crying and straightened himself up. "Yes, I told the bloke to get stuffed." Red eyes pleaded with Gabe. "But I didn't kill him."

"Very suspicious timing. You threaten him one day, and the next day he's poisoned." Gabe's gaze bored in on Harold.

Harold twitched. "I hated the guy, but I wouldn't resort to murder. Besides, I thought Clara did it."

"The case is still open." Gabe realized he really had no legitimate grounds to hold Clara any longer now that he had the recent information pointing to other suspects.

Gabe accompanied Harold back to the rehearsal.

Harold stopped, turned and looked Gabe in the eyes. "By the way, your wife's a brilliant actor."

Gabe leveled a stare back at Harold. "Yes, there seems to be a number of good actors around here."

Gabe waved to Angie before leaving the theater to drive back to his office, where he gave the sheet of paper to Camille to have it processed for fingerprints. "Can you dust this right now and check any prints against the people on stage the night Peter Ranchard died?"

Camille smiled. "I have a report to complete this afternoon, but for you, Gabe, give me half an hour."

Gabe sat in his office thinking over everything that had happened with the case. Peter had stolen prescription slips from Dr. Viceroy, forged his signature and obtained pain pills, which he sold to Clara Jager.

Clara had dropped a vial of potassium cyanide on the floor the previous Wednesday night and then given a halfhearted confession. Helen Lameuse had potassium cyanide in the pocket of the vest she had worn the night of Peter's death. Mildred had initially lied about her relationship with Peter, and her fingerprints were on the bottle that contained the poison given to Peter. Sophie was still upset over her breakup with Peter and the way he had abused her. A threatening email had been sent from her computer to Peter. Harold Coats had been blackmailed by Peter and had reluctantly admitted to threatening Peter the day before he died. Arthur Buchanan had been angry because Peter lured away his fiancée, and now this menacing letter referring to Kendra had turned up.

Gabe twiddled his pen as he tried to put all these pieces together. There had to be one thread he could unravel from this tangled ball. He had no new insights by the time Camille reappeared.

"Two fingerprint matches," she announced. "You'll find this very interesting. Arthur Buchanan and Peter Ranchard."

"I'll be. Most likely Peter put the letter in the cushion, but Arthur claims not to have written it."

331

"Somewhere along the line Buchanan handled that sheet of paper."

Gabe nodded his head. He was dealing with actors who knew how to play parts. Not much difference between pretending to be someone else and lying. Although Angie had acting talent, she didn't resort to lying. An interesting line that some crossed and others didn't. Which one out of this cast of characters had crossed that line?

Gabe returned to the playhouse and waited for a break to confront Arthur Buchanan again. He motioned him to the side, away from the rest of the cast.

"I need to speak with you again."

Arthur threw his hands in the air. "When will this police harassment end?"

"When you're upfront with me, Mr. Buchanan."

"What's that supposed to mean?"

"One simple fact to explain. We found your fingerprints on that threatening note I showed you earlier."

"I told you before. I didn't write it."

"But at some point in time, you held that sheet of paper in your hand. I want to know when."

"I must have touched it as a blank sheet of paper, because I've never seen that note before." He stood bolt upright. "Wait a minute. Several weeks ago Peter handed me a revised script that was held with a paperclip. I leafed through it, and the last page was blank. I pulled off that blank page and handed it back to him." Arthur smacked his forehead with the palm of his hand. "That must be it."

"Unfortunately, Peter isn't around to verify your statement."

Buchanan slumped. "Yeah. You're right."

CHAPTER 41

On his way home, Gabe stopped at the supermarket. He had agreed to fix dinner that night and had a shopping list he had prepared for this special meal. After grabbing a shopping cart, he took in a deep breath, smelling the aroma of popcorn that was being given away to customers. He grabbed a bag and started nibbling on it as he headed to the meat section to pick out two large chicken breasts.

Then he sauntered through the produce area until he found mushrooms. Next to the deli section. Rather than making mashed potatoes from scratch, he grabbed an already prepared package. No sense rushing too fast into this cooking item on his list of retirement activities. He'd work into it gradually, one step at a time.

Finally, he selected a bag of frozen peas. After a final stop at the liquor store to purchase bottles of Marsala wine and sherry, he drove home.

"I'm ready to fix you a feast," Gabe announced to Angie as he set the shopping bags on the kitchen counter.

"Do you know where to find what you need in the kitchen?"

"I think so. Oregano and pepper are in the cabinet above the stove. And flour is in the cabinet next to the sink."

"Pretty good memory for a guy your age."

"I've cooked a few things in my day, so I know my way around the kitchen . . . a little bit."

She put her arms around him. "You make an excellent omelet and, of course, plied your grandson with pancakes while he was here."

"Yeah, but it's time for me to expand into dinners." Gabe rubbed his hands together.

Retrieving the skillet from the cupboard next to the sink, he set it on the counter and took the recipe he had clipped out of the newspaper to check the measurements. He filled a measuring cup with the required amount of Marsala wine and sherry, poured flour into a bowl, sprinkled in oregano and pepper and rolled the chicken breasts in the mixture. He put oil in the skillet, set it on medium and dropped the chicken breasts in to start sizzling. Then he washed and chopped the mushrooms. Remembering he needed to prepare the mashed potatoes and peas, he got these out and put them in bowls.

For a moment, thoughts of the mystery playhouse case surged through his brain. If only he could find a recipe there.

His thoughts were interrupted by the sound of grease splattering. He had forgotten to turn over the chicken. Thrusting the spatula under the first chicken breast and flipping it over revealed charcoal black. The second one was equally burned. He watched the skillet this time to make sure the other side of the two pieces of chicken browned rather than burned. He lowered the heat and tossed in the mushrooms and wine.

He started the potatoes in the microwave and kept his eyes focused on the chicken. After the potatoes finished, he put the peas in the microwave and turned the chicken over. He groaned when he saw the black side again. He hadn't wanted this to look like a Cajun dish.

The chicken didn't look like it was cooking, so he turned the heat up. He went to put two glasses of water on the table and add the silverware. Upon returning, the wine had boiled away to black goo with little islands of coagulated mushrooms. Turning off the skillet, he put the chicken, black side down on plates, scooped some goo and mushrooms on top, added the potatoes and peas and served the meal.

Angie looked at what he had prepared. "No salad or anything else?"

"Give me a break. I had enough trouble with the chicken."

Gabe sat down and took a bite of chicken. It tasted like charcoal and was raw inside. After he deposited it in the trash and ordered pizza, he crossed out cooking on his retirement list and spent the next half hour cleaning up the grease that had splattered on the stovetop and kitchen floor.

After they ate pizza in silence, Angie said, "You had home repairs as an item on your retirement list, and you promised to put that shelf up in the bathroom."

"With everything going on with the dinner playhouse case I forgot."

"No time like the present."

Folding the pizza box, Gabe threw it into the trash. "I have a mystery novel I was about to start reading."

"You've had that book on your nightstand for over a week. Why don't you install the shelf and then you can start your book? That will give you two more things on your retirement list to try."

Realizing he wasn't going to win the argument, Gabe ambled into the garage to retrieve his toolkit and the shelf.

In the bathroom he measured where to make four holes in the wall to mount the decorative shelf. He smiled to himself. He was going to make the place look better and accomplish something useful.

Gabe envisioned all sorts of home improvement projects he could complete. That would keep him gainfully occupied for years. Maybe he'd even redo all the cabinets in the kitchen. And add new backsplash tile. And while he was at it, he could put in an upgraded shower in the master bathroom. He drilled three holes. Yup, home improvement guy in action. He drilled the fourth hole. There was a flash, something went pop, and the light in the bathroom went out.

"Uh-oh."

Angie came running. "What now?"

Gabe hung his head. "I think I drilled through the electrical wire to the bathroom light."

When Gabe went to bed, he picked up the mystery novel he hadn't started yet. He read the blurb on the back cover. Looked like a good police procedural story about a cop in

New Jersey.

Now knowing that home improvement was off his list, there was no time like the present to start his reading project. He looked at his bookshelf across the bedroom. There must be a dozen good books lined up there he hadn't read yet. That would keep him occupied for a healthy period of time.

He opened the book, read the first two pages and fell fast asleep.

On Friday Gabe went into police headquarters and learned that Clara Jager had been released on bail. She would be able to return to the playhouse for that evening's performance. Then it struck him. That meant Angie's acting career would be on hiatus.

When he next answered his phone, he heard a resonating voice say, "This is Doctor Denton."

Gabe's heart skipped a beat. "Do you have my test results back?"

"That's why I'm calling."

If it's taken this long for a call back, here comes the bad news.

"I'm sorry I didn't get back to you sooner. I've had several critical cases, and my assistant has been away on a family emergency. After examining the lab reports, I have two recommendations for you."

Uh-oh. I hope this doesn't include surgery. "And those are?"

"Keep exercising and stay away from fatty foods. Your cholesterol levels test slightly high for your age group but not in the danger zone. With proper diet and regular activity you should be fine."

Gabe felt like he had escaped a death sentence. "So nothing else is wrong?"

"Nope. Your PSA remains low, so no prostate problems. No indications of heart disease or diabetes. But I want to emphasize, diet and exercise are the most important preventive steps you can take in the future. Walking for thirty minutes every other day will do you a world of good."

Gabe would do that. He'd have to reconsider any thoughts of the sedentary life when he fully retired. In fact, with all the investigation work he'd done in the last week, he'd been walking more than an hour a day. He'd find some way to stay active. It would be worth it not to have to worry about his health.

"Thanks, Doc. Message received loud and clear."

After hanging up, Gabe pondered his life, now that he had received a medical pardon.

Life was good, he had a wonderful wife and he was semi-retired. Right. He had two cases to solve. Still a lot to track down concerning the mystery playhouse case, and then the robbery at the hardware store — no clues and no suspects — was almost like the perfect crime.

He thought back over the incident with the raccoons and how he had fooled the mother raccoon. Then it struck him. Someone had gamed him as well. Of course. That had to be it. He considered for a moment how he wanted to work this.

First, he had Shirley reserve an interrogation room for him. With that completed, he gathered a set of photographs. Then he called the Bearcrest Hardware Store.

Sanford Madison answered the phone.

"Mr. Madison, this is Detective Tremont. I have some photographs of possible suspects that I want Violet to look at. Is she in today?"

"Yes, sir. Working at the register."

"Would you be able to cover the store and have her come to police headquarters to take a look at the pictures?"

"Sure. I'll insist on it. She'll be there in fifteen minutes."

Gabe hung up, satisfied that he had a viable game plan.

In twenty minutes the receptionist rang him. "Gabe, there's a woman here named Violet Kartagian to meet with you."

Gabe grabbed his collection of photos, checked that the room he wanted to use was still unoccupied and headed out to the lobby to fetch Violet.

He did a double take when he saw her standing there. Her hair looked like a rat's nest, and she had deep circles under her eyes.

"Ms. Kartagian, if you'll come with me, we can find a place to talk." He led her to the interrogation room, a small cubby hole with a wooden desk in the middle and institutional metal chairs on both sides. He pointed toward the chair farthest from the door, and she sank into it with a groan. He studied her again. It was as if she had aged twenty years in the last week.

"I've been meaning to speak with you again about the robbery," Gabe said. "Thank you for agreeing to meet with me."

"Well, yeah. Mr. Madison said I had to come here."

Gabe thought again about what had bothered him with his case. He never had one with such a complete lack of leads. *Nada.* Nothing. He regarded Violet again. The soft young woman he had seen a week ago had changed into a hardened older woman. This fit in with his suspicions.

"Have you figured out who took the money?" she asked.

"I'm afraid not. We couldn't find any useful evidence. Is there anything else you remember that might help our investigation?"

She shook her head. "Could I have a glass of water?"

"Sure." Gabe left the room, went to the lunchroom and filled a paper cup with water. He watched Janet Lyon pass by, a confident woman and an outstanding police officer. Just the opposite of Violet Kartagian. Violet had recently changed in a suspicious manner. He would get to the bottom of it.

He returned to the room and handed the cup of water to Violet.

"Thanks." She drank it down like someone who had been in the desert for a week and put the empty cup down on the table. Her fingers twitched as if she had Parkinson's.

"Ms. Kartagian, I'd like to start by showing you some photographs." He spread six pictures in front of her. "These are men who meet the physical description of the man you saw robbing your store. Go through these and see if any resemble the man you saw."

Violet bit her lip and stared at the pictures. After a moment she tapped one of them. "This could be the man." She nodded her head. "Yeah, I think that might be him."

"That's interesting. That happens to be a picture of our police chief, and I know he was sitting in his office in this building the morning of the robbery."

Violet gulped. Her eyes turned down and away from Gabe's stare.

"All right," Gabe said. "I need to read something to you." He proceeded to go over her Miranda rights. "Do you understand what I've reviewed with you?"

She swallowed. "Yeah."

Gabe watched her carefully. "Let's get to the real facts. Tell me how you staged the robbery and who you worked with."

Tears pooled in her eyes. "Is it that obvious?"

"I couldn't figure out why it was such a clean robbery until this morning. Go over with me exactly what happened."

She let out a deep sigh. "I didn't think the police would find anything. It would have worked."

Gabe tapped the table. "The details, please."

Violet put her head down in her hands for a moment, and then her bloodshot eyes met Gabe's. "It's a long story."

"I have all the time in the world, so go ahead and tell me."

She let out a deep sigh. "I met a guy named Rick Wyle two months ago. We hit it off pretty good. We started going together, and it got serious." She gulped again. "Could I have another glass of water?"

"Sure." Gabe took the cup, refilled it and returned.

Violet guzzled it as if she was in a chugging contest. She wiped her mouth with the back of her hand and let out a non-ladylike burp. "Excuse me."

"You were saying."

"Right. So Rick and I got involved, and I thought I was in love with him. He's a handsome guy with long wavy black hair, and he seemed to be in love with me. He was short on money and came up with this scheme to support both of us." Violet paused and picked at the wood on the table with a long nail.

Gabe sat back and waited.

Finally, Violet looked up again. "I told him that the hardware store always had a lot of cash in the safe on Fridays. He said we should find a way to get our hands on it. So he convinced me to help him. He came with me when I unlocked the store last Friday. I opened the safe and gave him all the money. Then he hit me on the head, not too hard, but enough to leave a bump. He snuck out the back door, I sat down, waited ten minutes and then called nine-one-one on my cell."

"And I bet he isn't six-foot-five with a build like a weightlifter."

She shook her head. "No. He's five-nine and thin."

"Why are you confessing all of this now?" Gabe asked.

Anger shot through Violet's eyes, and she clenched her fists. "That money was for Rick and me. Instead, he took all of it and ran off with his bimbo ex-girlfriend to Las Vegas. I want you to nail him."

CHAPTER 42

After turning Violet over to be booked, Gabe checked his watch and realized he needed to scramble to get to the Bearcrest Community Church in time for Peter Ranchard's ceremony. Angie, who didn't like funeral services, had begged off joining him, so he drove over and found a place in the back of the church just as the minister stepped up to the lectern.

Gabe surveyed the small audience. He quickly picked out each of his suspects, noted Kendra sitting in the front row in a black dress. There were half a dozen other people he didn't recognize.

"We gather today to celebrate the life of Peter Ranchard," the minister's deep voice resonated. The man had on a white surplice adorned with a black preaching scarf. His nearly bald head shone in the light from a chandelier hanging overhead. On either side of him stood baskets of bright yellow flowers — Asiatic lilies, snapdragons, daisies and gladioli. In the background, organ music sounded the chords of *Amazing Grace*. The minister closed his eyes and waited until the music finished.

"I want to thank all of you for coming to pay tribute to Peter's life and untimely death. We are all saddened by this loss. He will be remembered by those he loved as a man of creativity and inspiration."

Arthur Buchanan coughed.

Mildred Hanson, who sat next to Arthur, elbowed him.

Arthur scooted as far away from Mildred as he could.

The minister continued, "Peter was an actor who put his whole being into his performances. He left no biological family to mourn his passing, only members of his theater family."

This time Harold Coats gagged.

Undeterred, the minister pressed on. "I'd like you all to pick up the hymnals and turn to page two-forty-five. Please stand."

The organist struck a chord, and the attendees rose to their feet and began a timid rendition of *Faith of Our Fathers*.

When it was completed, the minister waved his hand. "Please be seated." He launched into a short sermon, punctuated with a statement indicating he had never met Peter but knew he would be missed.

Helen Lameuse made a choking sound.

Finally, the minister asked if anyone wanted to come forward to say something about Peter.

No one budged. Finally, Kendra turned around, stared at the people behind her and stood, wiping a strand of hair from her forehead. She shuffled up the stairs to the microphone. "I . . . uh . . . knew Peter for only a few months. He was kind to me. I miss him." She sniffled, wiped away a tear and returned to her seat.

No one else volunteered to speak. The minister wrapped up the ceremony with one last round of platitudes and then said, "Please join us downstairs in the community room for refreshments."

The organist pounded out a loud verse of *A Mighty Fortress Is Our God,* and people filed out.

Gabe watched everyone pass him. No one smiled. Then he followed the small group to the reception.

Kendra had arranged a good spread of crackers, cheese, cookies, wraps, iced tea, coffee and soft drinks.

Gabe stepped over to where Sophie Elmira was speaking with the minister. Gabe introduced himself, and Sophie said, "Detective Tremont is investigating Peter's murder."

The minister wrinkled his forehead. "It's sad when something like this happens. Any suspects yet, Detective?"

"Actually the room is full of them."

The minister winced, and Sophie glowered at Gabe, before turning her back and striding away.

"The people he worked with?" the minister whispered.

"The very same." Gabe exchanged a little chitchat with the minister and then excused himself to watch other people in the room.

In one corner of the room, Mildred Hanson and Helen Lameuse stood toe-to-toe. Mildred pushed Helen, and Helen shoved back.

"Get your hands off me, you bitch!" Helen shouted.

"Who are you calling a bitch, you useless worm," Mildred shot back.

Gabe stepped over. "Ladies, remember this is a memorial service."

"Yeah, but I don't know why she showed up." Mildred thrust a finger at Helen. "She's probably the one who killed Peter."

"Don't give me that," Helen said. "You poisoned him. I know you did."

"Ladies, it's up to me to find out who

350

poisoned Peter. Your accusations don't help. Please stay calm."

The two women glared at each other and then stomped off to different parts of the room, like prizefighters heading back to their corners between rounds.

Gabe realized he needed to solve this case before any further deaths occurred.

When Gabe returned home, he told Angie about the memorial ceremony and that he had solved the robbery case.

"Good detective work?"

"No. A suspicion, and then a jilted woman turned in her boyfriend."

She smiled. "That will do it every time."

"One other piece of news. I received a call from Dr. Denton."

"So what's his prognostication?"

Gabe smiled broadly. "It's good news. I ain't dead yet."

"I could have told you that. I also received a call from Mildred saying that Clara would be returning for the show tonight."

"Yeah. I got the word at work that she had been released on bail. Are you sad that you have to turn the part back to Clara?"

"I had a great time, but I don't want to do that on a regular basis. Besides, one of those people might be a murderer."

"In working with them, did you ever pick up any suspicions of who could have killed Peter?"

Angie shook her head. "I tried imagining each one in turn putting the poison in the glass but couldn't pinpoint anyone in the group."

"You have a good intuitive sense. I'd think someone would pique your interest."

Angie arched an eyebrow. "Well, you pique my interest but not in that way."

"You're trying to tempt me because you know I have to get back to work."

She winked at him. "Maybe another time. Truth be told, in spite of all their reasons to get back at Peter, I can't see any of them committing murder."

"I wish I could find the breakthrough on this case. I thought I had something yesterday when I found a note in the chair where Peter sat at the playhouse."

"That old gray armchair?" Angie laughed. "Mildred made lots of references to Peter and his favorite chair. Did you know that Peter replaced the foam pad inside the cushion? Said the old one wasn't soft enough."

"When did he do that?"

"Mildred made a comment that Peter had been fiddling with the chair on the Sunday he died."

Gabe jumped up. Just like with the staged robbery, things weren't as they seemed. "That must be it."

CHAPTER 43

Gabe drove to the Bearcrest Dinner Playhouse so fast, he could have been the first detective on the force arrested for exceeding the speed limit by thirty miles an hour. He rushed inside to find Mildred sitting at her desk.

"I need your permission to look at the gray chair backstage again," he gasped.

She looked up from her paperwork and flicked her wrist. "Go for it."

"Thanks."

Gabe dashed upstairs, clambered on the stage, raced through the curtains and skidded to a stop in front of the ugly gray chair, sitting there tempting him to find anything useful. Gabe grabbed the seat cushion and spun it around. He tugged at the zipper. Stuck. He took a deep breath and tried again. This time it budged an inch. He coaxed it along the track and finally opened it all the way. Removing the foam inside,

Gabe squeezed it and felt something crinkly. He bent the pad and found a slit. He stopped and slipped on his rubber gloves before thrusting his hand into the opening in the pad. His fingers touched a piece of paper, and he extracted it. Holding it up to the ambient light, he saw the serrated edges from a spiral notebook. The top had a diagonal tear.

Gabe read the handwriting, satisfied that he had found what he sought. He thought over the best way to deal with the information. One way to wrap this all up. He returned downstairs to Mildred's office.

"When will your cast be here?"

She looked at her watch. "In thirty minutes."

"I need you, Sophie, Clara, Arthur and Harold to meet me in the dining area."

"Do you need Alex?" Mildred asked.

"No, I only want the people who witnessed Peter's death."

"I hope this doesn't take too long. We have a quick run-through planned."

"This has priority." He stepped out of her office, took out his cell phone and called Helen Lameuse. She answered on the third ring.

"This is Gabe Tremont. I need you to

come immediately to the Bearcrest Play-house."

"I'm not sure I'm welcome there."

"I'll be here to protect you. I need you to join us ASAP."

"Okay. Okay. I'll be right over."

Gabe headed up to the dining area and set up six chairs facing the stage. Then he sat on the edge of the stage and thought how he wanted to handle this meeting. It was time to get everything out on the table.

Clara arrived first. She shuffled in rubbing her hand and wrinkled her nose. "What's going on?"

Gabe pointed to the semicircle of chairs. "Take a seat, and I'll explain when everyone gets here."

Arthur Buchanan stormed in. "I don't like this. What kind of game are you playing, Detective?"

"Relax and take a seat."

Buchanan huffed but dropped into a chair.

Sophie Elmira strolled in. Gabe motioned toward the chairs. She shrugged and sat down.

Moments later, Harold Coats arrived, followed on his heels by Mildred Hanson.

"Please have a seat," Gabe told them.

Harold whispered in Sophie's ear, and she

nodded. He crossed his arms and stared at Gabe.

Footsteps echoed on the stairs, and Helen Lameuse stuck her head through the doorway.

"What's she doing here?" Mildred shouted.

Gabe held up his hand. "Stay calm, Ms. Hanson. I asked her to join us. Ms. Lameuse, please take a seat with the others."

Helen entered the room, glared at Mildred and plunked down on the end of the semicircle in the one remaining chair, which she moved as far away from the others as possible.

Mildred wrinkled her nose as if she smelled a dead rodent and glared at Helen. Gabe could feel the heat passing between the two women.

Once everyone settled down, Gabe announced, "I've asked you all to come here because of the death of Peter Ranchard."

Harold sighed. "Are you going to interrogate us again?"

"No. I already have all the information I need. I think it's time to bring this investigation to a close. All of you have been implicated in Peter's death. I will now take a moment to review all the evidence with you."

"Then you're going to nail one of us," Mildred said, rubbing her hands together. "Helen is behind all of this. I just know it."

"Why don't you mind your own business, Mildred?" Helen spat out the words. "Let's just listen to the man."

Gabe nodded. "Good advice. There's no need to be accusing each other."

"But I thought Clara had confessed to killing Peter," Sophie said.

Gabe held up his hand. "We'll get to that in a moment. I'd like to start by going back to the Sunday night before last. The lights went out. Then someone poured potassium cyanide dissolved in water into a wineglass and dropped the vial and a tissue underneath the table on stage. Peter drank the poison. Then he staggered backstage and died."

"And you're going to inform us who put the poison in Peter's glass?" Harold asked.

"In a moment."

Everyone looked around the semicircle at each other.

"I still think Helen is the one," Mildred said.

"She did it and tried to set me up," Helen responded.

Gabe held up his hand again. "Please, ladies. Let me continue. All of you were on stage at the time. Any one of you could have put poison in the wineglass. And each of you had a reason to want Peter out of the way."

"So?" Sophie replied. "I was pissed off at the jerk, but that doesn't mean I killed him."

Gabe smiled. "Well stated. Let's take a moment to review the reasons all of you disliked Peter. Ms. Elmira, would you like to share why you just made that statement about Peter?"

"Sure. No sense keeping it a secret any longer. We had an affair, Peter abused me and I broke it off."

Mildred jumped up. "Darn it, Sophie. Why were you boinking him? That's why he dumped me. It was because of you."

Sophie's lips twitched. "Considering how he treated women, I did you a favor, but, Mildred, I can assure you I didn't know you had something going with Peter."

Mildred slumped down in her chair. "Yeah, well, now everyone knows."

"One other piece of evidence links Sophie to Peter's death," Gabe said. "I found an email message sent from Sophie's computer to Peter's computer saying, 'Die.' "

"You were out to get even with him," Mildred said, stifling a sob.

Gabe held up his hand. "No, it turns out

359

that Sophie didn't really send that message. Someone else sent the message from her computer, and she didn't kill Peter, either."

Arthur Buchanan cleared his throat. "It seems Peter had an overactive libido. He was also messing around with my ex-fiancée. That's why I hated him."

"Well, as long as we're confessing, I might as well participate." Harold Coats tweaked his mustache. "Peter was blackmailing me. The detective figured it out and confronted me. I wanted the extortion to stop, but I didn't kill Peter. Besides, I thought Clara had confessed."

"Clara presents a very interesting link in this whole sequence of motives," Gabe said. "She's out on bail right now. Clara, would you like to say something?"

She rubbed her hands together. "I guess so. Peter sold me illegal painkillers. My arthritis had been acting up pretty bad. Peter threatened to tell Mildred about my drug habit and wanted more money from me."

"So you killed him and tried to kill another one of us with another vial of poison," Mildred shouted.

"Actually not," Gabe interjected. "I also thought that at first. That's why I arrested Clara. But I finally realized an interesting

360

thing. Clara wasn't able to open the second bottle because of her arthritic fingers. If she couldn't open the second bottle, how did she open the first vial to poison Peter?"

"Yeah, I can't pull a stopper out of a bottle," Clara said.

"So it must be Helen." Mildred pointed an accusing finger. "She came around here snooping and must have poisoned Peter to disrupt the play. She hasn't said anything yet."

Helen took a deep breath. "It's true I came here to spy on your show. I had even arranged with Peter to help me do it."

"That double-crossing insect," Mildred sputtered. "But why'd you kill him, Helen?"

Helen straightened up in her chair. "I didn't."

"Other evidence links Helen to the crime," Gabe said. "I found a baggie of potassium cyanide in the pocket of the vest she wore that Sunday night."

Mildred thrust out her chin. "I knew Helen was behind all of this."

"Actually not," Gabe said. "Someone planted that bag in Helen's clothes."

Helen recoiled. "I get it now. Mildred's the murderer. She tried to frame me. All this palaver accusing me of being the killer. She was a spurned lover of Peter's and tried to set me up for a fall when she poisoned him."

Mildred jumped up. "Why you lying —"

Gabe stepped forward to separate Mildred and Helen. "Both of you, please sit down. Neither of you killed Peter. I have more to say regarding the bag of potassium cyanide found in Ms. Lameuse's vest pocket. It had Peter and Clara's fingerprints on it."

"Ah, ha," Harold said. "So we're back to Clara."

"There is a link to Clara for sure," Gabe said. "She discovered the potassium cyanide in the basement and filled two baggies with it."

"And used one to poison Peter," Arthur added.

Gabe shook his head. "No, we've been over how Clara couldn't have opened the vial to poison Peter. She reported 'misplacing' one of the bags of potassium cyanide."

Mildred dropped back in her chair. "If it isn't Helen or Clara or Sophie, then which of the men did it?" She stared at Harold and Arthur in turn.

Gabe waited for a moment and then continued. "There were a number of threats made on Peter's life. We found a note in his cubbyhole with the same message as from

Sophie's computer, 'Die.' No fingerprints on it, and the letters had been cut out of newspapers here at the playhouse. Then I found a typed note that threatened Peter if he didn't stay away from Arthur's fiancée. That note had both Peter and Arthur's fingerprints on it."

"But I didn't write it," Arthur protested.

"I know," Gabe replied. "But someone typed a message on a piece of blank paper that you previously held. Made it appear that Arthur had threatened to kill Peter. But no, Arthur didn't murder Peter."

Arthur gave a relieved sigh and looked at Harold. "So you're the culprit."

Harold flinched.

"Harold had reason to want Peter dead," Gabe said. "He even called Peter and threatened him over the phone the day before Peter's death."

"Yeah, but I didn't kill him."

"A true statement," Gabe replied.

Everyone looked around the room. Finally, Mildred said, "So you've said none of the six of us killed Peter. Then who did?"

Gabe smiled. "An intriguing dilemma, isn't it? Now, something interesting regarding Peter Ranchard. He stole a necklace from Ms. Lameuse when he formerly worked for her and then gave it to Ms.

Elmira."

"Some present," Sophie muttered. "Stolen goods."

Gabe nodded. "Peter had a number of problems. He even sought help from a psychiatrist in Denver who treats sleeping disorders."

"No wonder the guy couldn't sleep, with all the sleazy things he was doing," Arthur said.

"I'm not convinced that Peter really had trouble sleeping," Gabe continued. "He did suffer from a hoarding disorder. That's why none of you ever saw the inside of his apartment. But he used the sleeping disorder as a ruse. He met with the psychiatrist, so he could steal prescription slips and forge the doctor's signature to obtain pain pills, which he then sold to Clara."

Clara rubbed her hand. "So that's how he always had medication for me."

"Exactly. The psychiatrist did say one revealing thing about Peter. In addition to his hoarding disorder, Peter was narcissistic and very enamored with his own acting ability."

"He was good but not great," Mildred said.

"But he felt underappreciated," Gabe replied. "He thought he should be on a larger stage and be achieving more in the acting field. He wanted to be as revered as Alec Guinness and Sir John Gielgud. He alluded to wanting to put on a performance never before accomplished."

"Well, he never made it," Helen said. "For once I agree with Mildred. Peter exhibited good acting skills but would never be considered world-class. With all his dreams, he ended up dead backstage."

"Which gets to the main problem I had with this investigation," Gabe said. "All of you are on stage, the lights go out, someone puts poison in a glass, Peter drinks it, staggers backstage and dies. In the dark how did someone know exactly which glass to put the poison in?"

CHAPTER 44

Mildred gasped. "I get it. Whoever put the poison in the wineglass may not have been meaning to kill Peter but rather trying to kill another one of us, and Peter drank the deadly concoction intended for someone else."

Harold jumped to his feet. "Was one of you trying to kill me?"

Arthur looked wildly around. "Was I to be the victim?"

"Did someone want me out of the way?" Sophie asked. "I always thought I got along well with all of you."

"Shoot," Clara said. "Did I make one of you so mad you wanted to kill me? I never intended to do that."

"No, I don't think it had anything to do with you, Clara." Helen turned and shook her fist at Mildred. "You tried to poison me and got it in the wrong glass. I understand now."

Mildred gasped. "Aha! Helen admitted she came to my theater to spy. She worked with Peter to be called up on stage. She intended to kill me so she would eliminate a competitor. You dumb bitch. You put the poison in the wrong glass."

"You're trying to divert the detective's attention away from you!" Helen shouted. "Arrest her, Detective."

Gabe stomped his foot. "All of you sit down and quit the accusations. As I was saying, one possible explanation is that the poison got in the wrong glass. As I indicated earlier, none of you here intended to kill Peter. It could have been an accident and meant for someone else."

Gabe paused a moment. All eyes glued on him. "But too many clues had been put together setting up motives for each of you to kill Peter. Someone spent a lot of time with very elaborate preparations, including computer messages, notes and other threats. No, Peter was the intended victim."

"I don't understand," Harold said.

"This doesn't make any sense," Sophie added.

"Bear with me for a few more moments," Gabe said. "I started to get an inkling when Clara dropped the second vial. She gave a very halfhearted confession of trying to poison someone. Clara had reached the end of her rope, with suffering from arthritis pain. She planned to kill herself on stage that night. Is that right, Clara?"

Clara hung her head. "Yeah. I'd had enough. With Peter gone, I had no way to get more pain medication. I thought I'd shoot myself, but that was too messy. Then I figured I'd end it all on stage, but I couldn't get the darn bottle open."

"This gets back to my nagging concern about getting the poison in the right glass," Gabe said. "When Clara intended to kill herself, she planned to pour the poison in a wineglass, which she would then pick up and drink. Right, Clara?"

"Yeah. That was the plan."

Gabe nodded and continued, "Inadvertently, this was a copycat attempt. Peter Ranchard had done exactly what Clara intended. He put the poison in a wineglass that only he knew was poisoned. He set up clues ahead of time to implicate each one of you. He sent a threatening message to himself from Sophie's computer, typed a menacing note from Arthur on a blank piece of paper that Arthur had held in his hand, left a death threat in his own cubbyhole, hid a bag of potassium cyanide stolen from Clara's apartment in Helen's pocket, used a vial with Mildred's fingerprints on it, goaded Harold into making threatening phone calls, then committed suicide during a play so he could achieve the performance of a lifetime."

Chapter 45

Pandemonium broke out as all six suspects jumped to their feet. Chairs clattered to the floor. People gasped, groaned and sputtered.

Mildred and Helen banged into each other and raised their fists, each ready to pound the other into smithereens. Harold tried to separate them, and both women popped him in the jaw at the same time, knocking him to the floor. He sat there, stunned.

Mildred and Helen realized what they had done and began apologizing profusely. Arthur reached over to help Harold to his feet. Harold rubbed both sides of his face. "You women pack a jolly good wallop."

"I can't believe it," Sophie said, shaking her head. "Peter killed himself. Of all the things the bastard did, that tops it all."

"What a way to go." Harold continued to rub his jaw.

"He causes all these problems and then ducks out." Arthur kicked a fallen chair.

"And all the time I thought Helen killed Peter," Mildred said.

"Whereas I thought you were the villain," Helen replied.

"Will you two please forgive each other and try to make peace," Harold said. "My jaw can't take any more of your conflict."

"I suppose." Mildred regarded Helen warily.

Helen stood with her arms crossed, but finally her glare softened, and she reached out a hand. "I guess we can do better."

Mildred shook her hand. "This town is big enough to support two mystery dinner theaters." Her eyes lit up. "Besides, if we hook more customers at one of our theaters, they're apt to try the other's playhouse as well. We could cross promote and build both of our businesses."

Arthur cleared his throat. "I'm glad there's finally peace and love between the two of you ladies, but I still don't understand something. If Peter poisoned himself, why didn't his fingerprints show up on the vial of poison found under the table?"

"Good question," Gabe replied. "If you think back to the Sunday performance, Peter wore gloves."

Arthur smacked his forehead with the flat of his hand. "Good point."

"Hold your water," Mildred shouted. "Everyone shut up for a minute." She eyed Gabe. "We're all relieved to no longer be under suspicion. You've shared a theory with us, but how can you prove it?"

"Another good question. I found written confirmation."

"Written confirmation?" Mildred arched an eyebrow.

"Yes," Gabe replied. "I came across a diary that Peter kept. The entry for the Sunday he died had been torn out. I found that page this afternoon hidden in the foam insert of the gray chair's cushion backstage." He held up the sheet.

Mildred made a grab for the paper, but Gabe pulled it away. "Patience please."

"I just wanted to get a peek." Mildred stepped back.

Gabe made sure everyone had settled down. "Let me read this to you. It's titled 'Grand Finale' and I quote, 'If no one finds this, then one or more of the six people I hate most will be accused of killing me. If this is found, everyone will know how I demonstrated the most spectacular grand finale accomplished by any actor of all time — going out in style during a performance.' "

All six remained motionless. Gabe waited. Finally, Mildred said, "I'll be darned. What a way to end it. Too bad he was such a jerk."

CHAPTER 46

"Quite a case you solved," Angie said to Gabe over a steak dinner at Rulon's, the best restaurant in Bearcrest, after she had heard his account of meeting with all the suspects. "I never would have suspected that Peter killed himself."

Gabe watched the waiters scurry to fill glasses of water, add more bread, and deliver salads and entrees to people at other tables. No one was neglected at Rulon's. "I owed you a nice dinner after you helped me solve the mystery of Peter Ranchard's death. You mentioned to me that Peter had replaced the foam in the cushion of the chair he used at the playhouse. That helped me find the crucial page of his diary." He held a full glass of pinot noir up in a toast. "To the beautiful woman who has put up with me all these years and is the best actor in the family."

"I'll take that last part as a compliment."

She clinked her glass against his. "I now understand how you pieced all the clues together, but why did you go through that little performance with the cast and Helen Lameuse?"

Gabe laughed. "I guess you inspired me. After seeing your acting ability, I decided to take my crack at putting on a show. Once I understood what had happened, I figured it was a good way to wrap things up."

"Now I have a very important question for you, and I want a straight answer. Will you retire again?"

Gabe looked thoughtfully at Angie. "I've tried retirement and, as you so eloquently pointed out, it didn't stick."

As the waiter cleared the plates away, Gabe said, "Please put the steak bone in a box."

"Yes, sir."

Angie squinted at him. "That's not like you. I've never seen you ask to take leftovers home. Have you changed your eating habits? Do you plan to nibble on a steak bone tomorrow?"

"No, it's not for me. I'm going to drop it off tonight for Gracie next door. When I saw her burying a bone, it gave me the idea to hunt at the playhouse for clues that Peter hid. You and Gracie are the best assistants any detective could ask for."

"Which reminds me, I've invited Henrietta and Al Schilling over for bridge tomorrow night. Maybe you can join Al for his senior bridge games again at the Community Center or start playing in duplicate bridge tournaments."

Gabe stuck his finger into the back of his mouth. "That's all I need. The combination of Al's bad jokes and extended bridge games. No thank you. After Dr. Denton's lecture to stay active, I think I'll postpone a bridge career or lying around in a hammock." He brought a sheet of paper out of his pocket and handed it to Angie. "Take a look at this and tell me what you notice on my list."

Angie took the paper and perused it as her eyes grew large. "It's your list of prospective retirement activities. Every item is crossed out."

"Exactly." He took it back, folded it twice and returned it to his pocket. "I tried everything, and there's nothing on that list that I want to do."

"You must have found something that interests you."

Gabe waggled his eyebrows at Angie.

She swatted his hand. "Besides that."

"I have learned something from this whole

process. I retired without doing any planning. In hindsight, I should have been working through my list well ahead of time, so when I retired I'd have known what I really wanted to do. This isn't the time in my life to be sitting around with nothing to do. It's an opportunity to pursue something I enjoy."

"And that would be?"

"Chief Lewis says I can come back to my job at the department without returning the fishing rod I received as a retirement gift."

"Good thing, since you broke it."

"Don't confuse me with facts." Gabe reached over and gave his wife's hand a squeeze. "I could continue as a detective, which I love doing, for a while longer while I do some serious planning. Or there's one other possibility. I might start my own private investigation service. What do you think?"

"Oh, yes. I think you need something more than puttering around the house and watching television. And I figure you'll decide between the police or your own business without my swaying you one way or the other."

"You know me so well."

"Well, I should hope so after all the years we've been married."

He shook his head in mock disgust. "Where has all the mystery gone?"

"That's why you'll keep investigating, either with the police or on your own. You need a little mystery in your life."

"What about you? You seemed to enjoy the acting. Do you want to give theater a shot again?"

"I just might. Maybe I'll see if I can get a bidding war going between Mildred and Helen. See which one will pay me the most to be in their theater company."

After a pleasant drive home, they parked in the driveway and strolled over to the Schillings' house. Al answered the door.

"Hey, Gabe and Angie. What brings you here?"

"I have a present for Gracie." Gabe bent over as the cockapoo approached, baring her teeth. He held the steak bone out.

She snapped, as if intending to bite Gabe's hand, but latched onto the bone instead. Then she turned and trotted away.

"Maybe that will be my first step in improving relations with the animal kingdom," Gabe said.

"Hey, Gabe, I meant to thank you," Al said, whacking him on the shoulder.

"What for?"

"I made a new friend — the guy you met at the dinner playhouse. He called me, and we went to play bridge at the Community Center. We made quite a bridge team, and he has a great sense of humor."

"Does that mean you'll stop bugging me to play bridge?" Gabe asked.

"Yup. I no longer need your services."

Relieved, Gabe took Angie's hand. As they walked back to their house, she snuggled up against him. "My hero. Solving the mystery of the dinner playhouse, bringing Al and his new friend together, and bribing Gracie into liking you."

"I try."

"And I consider it quite an accomplishment that I even talked you into going to a mystery playhouse in the first place. We would have missed out on this whole adventure, and you might not have had a chance to resume your detective career."

Gabe kissed Angie's cheek. "That you did. And I was right."

Angie came to a halt. "Right about what?"

"When we first went to the Bearcrest Mystery Dinner Playhouse, I told you the butler did it."

ABOUT THE AUTHOR

Mike Befeler is author of six novels in the Paul Jacobson Geezer-lit Mystery Series: *Retirement Homes Are Murder, Living with Your Kids Is Murder* (a finalist for The Lefty Award for best humorous mystery of 2009), *Senior Moments Are Murder, Cruising in Your Eighties Is Murder* (a finalist for The Lefty Award for best humorous mystery of 2012), *Care Homes Are Murder* and *Nursing Homes Are Murder,* as well as two paranormal mysteries: *The V V Agency* and *The Back Wing.* Mike is past-president of the Rocky Mountain Chapter of Mystery Writers of America. He grew up in Honolulu, Hawaii, and now lives in Boulder, Colorado, with his wife, Wendy. If you are interested in having the author speak to your book club, contact Mike Befeler at mikebef@aol.com. His website is http://www.mikebefeler.com.

The employees of Thorndike Press hope you have enjoyed this Large Print book. All our Thorndike, Wheeler, and Kennebec Large Print titles are designed for easy reading, and all our books are made to last. Other Thorndike Press Large Print books are available at your library, through selected bookstores, or directly from us.

For information about titles, please call:
  (800) 223-1244

or visit our Web site at:
  http://gale.cengage.com/thorndike

To share your comments, please write:
  Publisher
  Thorndike Press
  10 Water St., Suite 310
  Waterville, ME 04901

CPSIA information can be obtained
at www.ICGtesting.com
Printed in the USA
FFOW01n0132300415
13083FF